IN THE ARMS OF DANGER

A sudden surge toward the ballroom threw Olivia off balance. She stumbled backward to be caught fast against a solid masculine chest. No man had ever held her thus. Hands, their warmth intimately compelling through the fine silk of her gown, rested with easy familiarity just beneath the curve of her bosom, and against their imprisoning clasp she could feel the wild uneven thudding of her breast.

"Sir, you are importunate!" She pulled free and spun around to face the most devastatingly handsome gentleman she had ever seen.

"Undoubtedly," he confessed without a hint of repentance. "But what, pray, is a man to do when the most enchanting woman in the room throws herself into his arms?"

This, then, was the notorious Damian St. Clair, who had every reason to seek vengeance on Olivia's family—and so many means to use Olivia to do so. . . .

SHEILA WALSH lives with her husband in Southport, Lancashire, England, and is the mother of two daughters. She began to think seriously about writing when a local writers' club was formed. After experimenting with short stories and plays, she completed her first Regency novel, *The Golden Songbird*, which subsequently won her an award presented by the Romantic Novelists' Association in 1974.

FLAMING PASSION

- ☐ **LADY OF FIRE by Anita Mills.** Their love was forbidden ... their passion undeniable. Beautiful, young Lea was the most passionately pursued prize in Normandy. Three handsome and eligible men wanted her, but she gave Roger FitzGilbert, the most forbidden, her heart ... until they surrendered to the floodtide of feeling that swept away all barriers to love. (400445—$3.95)

- ☐ **FIRE AND STEEL by Anita Mills.** Proud, beautiful Catherine de Broine vowed never to give her heart to the handsome, daring Guy de Rivaux whom she was forced to wed. She was sure she loved another man, who had captivated her since girlhood. But against a backdrop of turmoil and intrigue in 11th Century Normandy, Catherine found it hard to resist the fiery kisses of the man she had wed.... (400917—$3.95)

- ☐ **HEARTS OF FIRE by Anita Mills.** Their flaming passion lit their perilous path of love. Fiery-haired Gilliane de Lacey's love for Richard of Rivaux ignited in her a burning need, but Richard was honor-bound to wed another. Yet nothing—not royal wrath or dangerous conflict—could stop Gilliane and Richard from risking all for love, giving all to desire. (400135—$4.50)

- ☐ **FOREVER MY LOVE by Lisa Kleypas.** Their fiery embrace sparked love's eternal flame ... Beautiful Mira Germain was only eighteen when she made her bargain with the wealthy, powerful, elderly Lord Sackville, and she tried to keep her word, even when she met the handsome Duke, Alec Faulkner. But in Alec's arms, desire was more powerful than any promise or pledge....
(401263—$4.50)

- ☐ **WHERE PASSION LEADS by Lisa Kleypas.** Only the flames of love could melt the barrier between them. Beautiful Rosalie Belleau was swept up in the aristocratic world of luxury when handsome Lord Randall Berkely abducted her. Now, she was awakening into womanhood, as Sir Randall lit the flames of passion and sent her to dizzying heights of ecstasy.... (400496—$3.95)

- ☐ **LOVE, COME TO ME by Lisa Kleypas.** When strong and handsome Heath Rayne rescued lovely Lucinda Caldwell from an icy death, she little dreamed what a torrid torrent of passion was about to claim her. This dashing, sensuous Southerner was unlike any man she had ever known. He came to Massachusetts a stranger and conquered all the odds—not to mention her heart.... (400933—$3.95)

THE NOTORIOUS NABOB

by

Sheila Walsh

A SIGNET BOOK

NEW AMERICAN LIBRARY

A DIVISION OF PENGUIN BOOKS USA INC.

One

THE SPLENDIDLY SPRUNG traveling coach swept down Piccadilly, creating a variety of sensations among those who turned to watch it pass, not the least of which was envy, for even if one discounted the three attendant coaches laden with baggage and four outriders clad in black livery frogged with silver, the leading equipage itself, drawn by a team of superb black horses, must have excited the interest of all but the undiscerning.

Miss Imelda Durant just happened to be correcting a slight disarrangement in one of the muslin curtains adorning the windows of her sister's drawing room as the impressive entourage entered Berkeley Square and drew up outside Egan House, until recently, the town residence of the Dukes of Meriton. "Oh my!" she breathed, tentatively moving the soft drapery aside, the better to observe the gleaming black coach so tastefully embellished with silver and the similarly embellished lackeys perched up behind like two bedecked crows. "Oh my!" she said again with something approaching awe.

"Imelda! I wish you will not be constantly peering out of the window like a common servant girl." Lady Crockforth's tone was waspish, but for once it failed to achieve its customary effect upon her sister, who was clearly in the grip of some strange and powerful emotion. Her ladyship's voice sharpened. "Imelda—do you hear me? Come away this instant!"

"But Gertrude, *he* has arrived at last. And in *such* a fashion! Do pray come and see for yourself. Ah!" This final sigh was so filled with wonder that, albeit reluctantly, Lady Crockforth found herself approaching the window, quite dwarfing her sister, who stood clutching her shawl about her thin shoulders with one frail hand while the other trembled as it retained its grasp upon the curtain.

Below, the lackeys had sprung into life and were engaged in letting down the steps, opening the door to allow the gentleman within to descend. This he did with the careless assurance of one for whom such niceties are commonplace. It was impossible to discern any hint of the features beneath the brim of his high-crowned beaver hat, but there was a decided "man of the world" air of authority about him, while a glimpse of gleaming Hessians beneath a coat with a great many capes confirmed him as a gentleman of indisputable elegance. And if all that were not enough, hardly had the skirts of his coat settled around his long legs when the second coach also disgorged a passenger, and such a passenger as to draw from the romantically inclined Miss Imelda that last blissful sigh.

He also was tall—and so imposing, so magnificent a figure as to take and hold one's whole attention. His face, several shades darker than olive, stood out against the brilliant white of his turban and of the full Turkish trousers and tunic that rippled as he moved without apparent haste to reach the portico of Egan House ahead of his master, who had turned back to lift down a tiny, dainty creature swathed in the most extraordinary diaphonous draperies that shimmered in the light as she glided at his side.

"Is it not the most prodigiously romantical thing ever? Better by far than anything one might hope to see at the Opera!" Miss Imelda sighed.

"Pretentious mummery!" declared her ladyship unequivocally. "Much worse than I had feared." Even as she spoke, the gentleman turned, and looked straight up at the window, for all the world as though aware that he was being observed. Her ladyship drew in a sharp breath and reached for her lorgnette. The features had grown leaner, harsher with the years, but even so, it could surely be no other. . . .

Word reached Mount Street with almost indecent haste, brought first by Mr. Gilbey. "Had it not an hour ago from Pinchmold at the club, m'dear," he told his wife. "Said he was on the point of leaving home this morning when who should turn up at Egan House with a highly colorful retinue in train but that young scapegrace, St. Clair—you remember, the one who got under Meriton's skin so damnably years ago. Older now, of course, but every bit as cocksure, and looking mighty prosperous and full of himself. Sporting a bang-up rig—the finest cattle you could wish for, regular prime 'uns, black and perfectly matched, according to Pinchmold. Ain't seen him so impressed in ages."

It took Mrs. Gilbey some time to wrest her husband's mind from its preoccupation with horses and fix it instead upon the new occupant of Egan House, whose very name had instantly called up unpleasant memories from the past which were like to set all her present plans on end. When she presently entered her drawing room, she was relieved to find her niece alone. Olivia, unlike her mother, could be relied upon not to throw a tantrum. Mrs. Gilbey had not been blessed with children, but this second daughter of her sister, Honoria, the Dowager Duchess of Meriton, had always been as dear to her as any of her own would have been.

Lady Olivia Egan looked up, amusement warming her dark eyes as she held out a page of *The Mirror of Fashion* for her aunt's inspection. "Is that not the most hideous half-robe you have ever seen, dear aunt? I vow it would contrive to make even an angel look like an antidote!"

"Quite hideous," Mrs. Gilbey agreed absently as she wondered how best to broach the news to her niece.

It was perhaps as well that Olivia was now more mature, though she occasionally caught glimpses of that merry, high-spirited girl who had come to London all of four years ago for her sister's wedding and already looking forward with lively anticipation to her own come-out the following spring; half child, still, with the awkward gangling grace of a young colt, but showing even then the beginnings of that classic look which almost always characterized the Egan women—the rich abundance of dark hair glowing with golden lights, the delicately pointed features and creamy skin, the winged brows above deep-set eyes, thick-lashed and as black as sloes, and a tall slender figure which looked as if it might break in two at a touch. Except that Egan women never broke. Throughout history they had been the strong ones, and Olivia was no exception.

Who could have foreseen, on that happy day four years ago, the cruel circumstance that would twice deprive Olivia of her much anticipated debut. In 1811, her beloved elder brother, Charles, had been tragically killed at one of those dreadful Peninsular battles, and less than a twelvemonth later, when they had scarcely come to terms with this blow, an even worse one befell the family with the untimely demise of the duke.

Mrs. Gilbey, while mindful that it did not behoove one to think ill of the dead, could not in all conscience bring herself to forgive the gambling-mad eighth Duke of Meriton, a man well beyond the age of kicking up larks, for having taken one chance too many in attempting to put a young, untried horse at a notoriously difficult fence while riding with the Quorn. It was so like him—never an ounce of consideration for anyone but himself!

The full measure of his irresponsible behavior had only come to light, however, when it fell to his man of business to break the unpalatable news to his relict that she was virtually penniless. The duchess had still not wholly recovered from the loss of her dearest firstborn, and upon learning that not only was she widowed, but her fourteen-year-old son, Justin, now the ninth duke, had inherited nothing but a pile of debts and an estate encumbered to the hilt, she uttered a shriek of despair and collapsed. For weeks she had lain behind closed curtains, while Sir Geoffrey Frome, husband of her eldest daughter, Charlotte, did what had to be done. He had disposed of four houses, including Kimberley, lovely, sprawling Kimberley in the heart of Surrey where her sister and the children lived for the best part of each year—Kimberley, which had been the country seat of the Dukes of Meriton since the sixteenth century. The speed at which the sale had been accomplished surprised everyone, the entire estate going to an anonymous buyer through an intermediary. When every debt had been paid, there remained a modest villa close to Bath just large enough to provide a home for the duchess and her still considerable family together with a respectable competence for herself and sufficient money in trust to enable the ninth duke to complete his education and live modestly thereafter.

But for poor Olivia no such provision had been made. And worse, her mama, unable, or unwilling, to come to terms with their reduced state, had clung to her with all the tenacity of a mother petrified of losing yet another of her offspring, which in turn reflected on the younger children, who were unsettled by the change and looked to Olivia for stability. This she had given generously, and as time went on, all thoughts of her own future were indefinitely laid aside.

It was Charlotte, on a recent visit to Bath with her three offspring (and increasing yet again), who had eventually pointed out with brutal clarity that Olivia was now turned one and twenty, and that if she was to have any hope of contracting a halfway decent marriage, one which would benefit all, there was no time to be lost. The effect upon Honoria had been dramatic; forever outrunning the budget, and by now tired of scrimping and scraping, she roused herself sufficiently to write with some urgency to her sister, Constance, who had married well and moved in first circles, and who had ever been fond of Olivia, begging her to have the dear girl for the Season, and *take her about a little,* "for I am certain that a gentleman of wealth and position might easily be found, willing to forgo a dowry and think himself fortunate to take a duke's daughter to wife."

"Aye, but will the duke's daughter think herself equally fortunate?" Mr. Gilbey had commented in his forthright way when apprised of his sister-in-law's aspirations. "Anyone but a looby must know that with a whole string of prime fillies on the Mart—*and* most of 'em with papas plump enough in the pocket to be choosy—the only interested parties are like to be in their dotage or mushrooms of the worst kind. Not a happy prospect."

His wife had said reproachfully that she found his observations quite odious and not a little coarse, and that she had no doubt but that her niece knew what was expected of her. Yet there was a degree of truth in what he said which depressed her. So that it was with mixed feelings that she awaited Olivia's arrival—feelings which swiftly turned to horror when the carriage arrived from Bath bearing not only her niece, but also Honoria.

"A brief visit only," the dowager had proclaimed in failing tones as she was helped from the coach. "The very least I could do . . . to see my darling child safely delivered and established . . ."

Olivia's "Yes, Mama's" and "No, Mama's" as she helped Honoria to a hastily prepared room where she might lie down to recover from the journey, indicated a subjugation to duty that brought Mrs. Gilbey almost to the point of despair.

But later, alone with her aunt, a very different Olivia had emerged as, with a rueful twinkle, she had apologized for saddling her with an extra burden. "I did try all I could to dissuade Mama, but you know how she can be when she has taken the bit!" Her aunt had struggled for words, but before she could frame any politeness that was halfway honest, Olivia was continuing, "I know you are much too amiable to admit of any difficulty, dear Aunt Constance, but it would be idle to pretend that Mama will not cause a decided upheaval during her visit, which I trust may be mercifully short as the young ones are left in the sole care of their governess, Miss Ridge."

This frankness was so close to the bone that it almost found Mrs. Gilbey at a loss. "I am sure my sister is very welcome to stay as long as it suits her," she insisted with rather too much enthusiasm. "Though I confess I was looking forward to having you to myself. Still, we shall have lots of time for that, I daresay, before the Season really gets underway. The town is still very thin of people, though more are arriving every day."

Olivia had cast off the shabby pelisse and bonnet in which she had arrived, but her aunt could not help noticing that the simple high-waisted gown she wore was a practical rather than pretty shade of gray. Clearly, there was much to be done. Mrs. Gilbey's spirits lifted as she began to devise plans for turning her niece out in prime style. And then Olivia's frankness surprised her again.

"I cannot tell you how much I appreciate your having me to stay, Aunt Constance, but you must not think I am expecting miracles." And when her aunt demurred, she added quizzingly, "Come, I am much more than five, you know, and have none of Mama's illusions about my expectations. I should think it the height of absurdity to suppose that any gentleman with means enough to suit Mama, and agreeable enough to suit me, could not do better for himself than take a dowerless wife whose overriding consideration must be to ensure the future well-being of her improvident family. However, such a paragon may exist, so I mean to keep an open mind."

"Oh, my dear!" exclaimed her aunt, clasping this

most favorite of nieces to her ample bosom, and secretly appalled by the irony amounting almost to cynicism which accompanied her words, and which seemed ominously to reflect Mr. Gilbey's opinion. "You were such a carefree child! I cannot bear to see you grown so . . ."

"Sensible?" Olivia laughed then, showing a glimpse of that other, earlier Olivia. "Dear ma'am, I am not really so much changed. It is simply that I have grown up. The green girl who once dreamed of finding her handsome prince and marrying for love has learned that fairy tales have no place in real life." Impulsively, she kissed the older woman's cheek. "Pray, do not look so wretched, Aunt Constance. I have not abandoned quite *all* my dreams, nor do I mean to grow dull, which is why I am very happy to be here with you, and I give you fair warning that I mean to make the most of every moment!"

In the three weeks that followed, Olivia had been as good as her word and they dealt extremely well together. The closest they came to disagreeing was over the shocking extravagance displayed by Mrs. Gilbey in buying her niece so many pretty clothes and gew-gaws, and it took much persuasion on the older woman's part before her niece could be convinced that she was enjoying herself more than she had done for years, and would be mortally offended if deprived of her pleasure. The one small cloud on their horizon was the continuing presence of Honoria, who spoke frequently of returning home but evinced little actual evidence of doing so. Mrs. Gilbey suspected that Honoria wished to ascertain for herself who among the current prizes on the Marriage Mart might be induced to solicit for her daughter's hand so that she could urge Olivia to make a push to engage their interest. How little she understood her own daughter! Or, indeed, the exigencies of Olivia's position.

"Are you all right, Aunt Constance?"

Mrs. Gilbey started at the sound of her niece's voice.

"Yes. Yes, of course, child. I was simply lost in thought. Where is your mama?"

"She had the headache and has gone to lie down."

"Would that she had returned to Bath last weekend as she had declared her intention of doing." Her aunt's voice betrayed more agitation than she knew.

Olivia rose at once and came to take her arm. "Dearest of aunts, has Mama done something to upset you? If so, pray tell me and I will contrive to make matters right. I know she can be trying at times . . ."

But Mrs. Gilbey had already recovered herself. She patted Olivia's hand and said she was more than used to her mama's odd quirks, and that in any case, this time Honoria was not at fault. Which was not to say that her naturally amiable disposition had not been surely tried by her sister's continuing presence.

"It is simply," Mrs. Gilbey continued, settling her ample form comfortably on the sofa and selecting one of the sugar comfits which were her particular weakness from the bonbon dish which Olivia had so kindly fetched from the side table and was holding out to her, "that I fear your mama will not take kindly to the news that the *person* who bought up your papa's estate has at last arrived with much pomp and ado to take up residence in Egan House."

If she had been less flustered, she might have noticed a lack of surprise on the part of her niece, together with a slight flush which suffused the girl's face. In fact, Olivia had, unbeknown to her aunt, formed the habit of taking an early morning walk. Country habits die hard, and she had been used to being up with the light. It was pure chance that first led her steps down Mount Street in the direction of Berkeley Square. But once there, she had been drawn to Egan House—and drawn back again on successive days as she saw that servants were beginning to be busy about the place, cleaning and polishing in readiness for its occupation. Only yesterday morning, finding the front door open, she had approached the steps. Beyond the hall, the staircase rose in a graceful curve, and just for an instant time fell away—she saw Charlotte coming down the stair in her wedding gown to where their brother Charles waited in the hall below, bursting with pride in his Hussar uniform, while she herself hung on his arm clad in soft folds of cream muslin. It was the last time she could remember being truly happy. Tears had stung her eyes, and as she brushed them away, the picture splintered. A servant coming to brush the step looked at her oddly, and feeling foolish, she had muttered some excuse and hurried on her way.

Mrs. Gilbey, preoccupied with present exigencies, was continuing her narrative. "I am bound to say that in this instance I would not blame your mama for throwing a crotchet, since it does seem monstrously insensitive in him to make so much noise about his coming. I suppose that such *people* cannot in the general way be expected to feel quite as we do about these things."

The note of disparagement in Mrs. Gilbey's voice did not escape Olivia. The identity of the mysterious buyer, and his continuing absence, had been the subject of much conjecture over recent months, and she herself, once over the first shock, had occasionally allowed her lively imagination free rein—anyone from a nabob to some mysterious eastern prince. But if she interpreted her aunt's reactions correctly, it would seem that he was nothing more than some encroaching cit with more money than sense. Ah well!

"I will own that it is a trifle disagreeable to think of a complete mushroom making free of all that one once held dear," she said with a wry smile, "but I was never in the London house a great deal, you know, so I don't feel its loss as keenly as that of Kimberley. That was my true home and I still begrudge him every stick and stone of it, especially as he obviously cares so little about it that he has been content to leave it lying empty! Such very odd behavior—to have purchased the whole estate in that scrambling way and then make no attempt to take up residence in any of the properties. However, now he is come at last, I suppose we must make the best of it. One can hardly expect him to spare our feelings at the expense of his own."

Sparing did not come into it, thought her aunt with unaccustomed wrath as she pondered the curiously twisted motives that must have driven Mr. Damian St. Clair to acquire the Meriton estates in such a hole-and-corner fashion. When Gilbey had revealed his name a few moments since, the whole sordid affair had come back to her with unwelcome clarity. Her first coherent thought had been how grossly unfair it was that old scores should be played off against the innocent, and in particular against this favorite of all her nieces. Her second and more immediate concern was that it must now be her painful duty to tell Olivia the whole before someone else blurted it out.

She patted the sofa. "Come and sit beside me, my love. There is something I believe you should know. I would be as lief keep it from your mama . . ." she sighed, "though I doubt that can be managed, for it is like to become one of the choicest *on-dits* about town before the day is out!"

"Aunt Constance, you alarm me!" Olivia could usually rely upon a little gentle raillery to bring her aunt back into humor, for she would be the first to acknowledge her particular penchant for anticipating a scandal broth where none existed. But this time Mrs. Gilbey's face remained grave. So, it must be serious. A small flutter of apprehension was swiftly quashed as Olivia told herself firmly that, however bad the news, nothing could be worse than what had gone before.

"I see that my levity is misplaced," she said. "Forgive me, and tell me at once what it is that troubles you so. I promise *I* won't throw a crotchet, or anything of that nature."

"As if you would, my love. But it is not easy for me to speak of events, which, not to put too fine a point on it, concern a departed and much lamented loved one."

"If you mean Papa," Olivia said with that incurable

honesty that occasionally made Mrs. Gilbey wince, "you need not concern yourself about my sensibilities, for I am very sure *he* never did."

"Olivia!"

"I'm sorry, Aunt Constance, but it's true. Papa never made the least push to engage the affections of his children when he was alive, and while his death was a shock, I, for my part, find it well nigh impossible to lament the passing of someone who seemed to care little for anything that did not hang upon a wager, someone who was so selfish, so uncaring of his family—especially Mama and Justin—as to gamble everything away without so much as a thought for their future!" Try as she might, she could not quite keep the bitterness from her voice at the last.

Her aunt scarcely knew how to answer. To hear her own feelings expressed with so much truth, so much clarity of reasoning shocked her immeasurably. She could not bring herself to refute it. And yet, for Olivia to be speaking of her late parent in such a way—as a mere *someone*—could surely not be condoned?

If Olivia had a failing—though Mrs. Gilbey was loath to admit any such possibility—it was that she had almost too much frankness, too much resolution for a girl. "Resolution, be damned!" Mr. Gilbey had observed robustly, when she had ventured this opinion to her espoused. "Mark my words, Connie! Olivia may not care to admit it, but she's got a deal of her father's pride in her."

"Oh no, George!" she had protested. "How can you possibly even think such a thing? Olivia is such a darling . . . not the least like Meriton!"

"I never said she was. Very fond of the girl! All I'm saying is, she occasionally has a way of looking down that Egan nose of hers in the very same *damn-you* way he had, so don't expect her to suit easy. Like any high-bred filly, she'll need gentling. Find her a man she can respect, and she'll lay her hands under his feet, sweet as you please, but God help any fool who thinks he can coerce her!''

The thought occasionally kept Mrs. Gilbey awake at night, for there was just enough truth in his observation to trouble her. An advantageous marriage on Olivia's part would solve so many of the family's problems. But, loath as she was to admit the truth of her husband's argument, she grew more certain with every day that passed that it would take a very special gentleman to satisfy her niece.

Olivia, aware that she had confused and upset her, leaned forward impulsively. ''I have scandalized you, dear aunt. I had not meant to do so. Most of the time, I try not to think of it, but when I see Mama brought so low . . .'' She shook her head. ''Come, let us forget my lapse and tell me what it is you thought I should know.''

But before Mrs. Gilbey could collect her thoughts, Blore, her butler, came to announce Lady Crockforth. She stifled her annoyance and rose with considerable reluctance to greet her visitor.

Two

LADY CROCKFORTH, both physically and from sheer force of personality, could be guaranteed to dominate almost any room she entered, and this afternoon proved no exception. She swept in, arrayed in a vividly striped spencer over an outmoded gown of black bombazine, her strong, rather masculine features not best served by a high poke bonnet with much ruching beneath the brim; that it appeared ludicrous seemed to concern her not at all.

"Good. I hoped to find you at home, Constance," she said, brushing aside Mrs. Gilbey's attempt to observe the social niceties, and scorning the comfortable chair indicated by her hostess in favor of one of the plain, straight-backed variety. "Upbringing," she said obliquely. "Mama never allowed us the least opportunity to slouch. Two hours every day in the schoolroom with boards strapped to our shoulders proved a certain cure for any lack of resolve."

"Really?" murmured Mrs. Gilbey, acutely aware that her niece, standing out of sight of their guest, was attempting to stifle a laugh. It did not seem to be the time to make her presence known.

"Still, that is neither here nor there. I ain't, as you will know, given to minding other people's business, Constance. I leave all that sort of nonsense to Imelda—

spends half her life at the window straightening the curtains, she calls it, and thinks I don't twig!'' Lady Crockforth uttered something remarkably like a snort. "Well, this time, though it pains me to say it, her prying has been to some purpose, and as a consequence, I came straightaway to put you on y'r guard. Egan House is occupied at last—''

"I know!" Mrs. Gilbey cut in out of sheer desperation.

"You *know*?''

"Yes. Gilbey told me, but a half-hour since. I was just speaking of it to my niece." In a desperate bid to silence Lady Crockforth, she beckoned Olivia forward. "My love, I think you have not yet met Lady Crockforth. Do, pray, come and make her your curtsy.''

Olivia, stifling her curiosity, dipped in obeisance, and straightened up to find herself being raked from head to foot by critical eyes.

"Just like y'r grandmother,'' came the abrupt verdict. "Always used to say the first decent puff of wind would carry her away, but it never did. Outlasted y'r grandfather by twenty years! You should feed her up, Constance. You don't slouch, gel, I'll say that for you.''

"Thank you, ma'am,'' Olivia said demurely. "I am really very healthy, you know.''

"Are you, indeed?'' There was something approaching a glint of dry humor in her ladyship's eyes. "I am happy to hear it, though I've no doubt your mama will have advised you to keep that piece of information to y'rself. It seems gentlemen in general prefer their womenfolk to err on the fragile side. Blest if I know why! Crockford never affected any such nonsense, I'm happy to say.'' The trend of the conversation put her in mind of the exquisite barque of frailty she had seen earlier with St. Clair. She cocked an eye at her hostess. "Honoria is still here, I suppose. Does she know yet—about the new owner of Egan House?''

Mrs. Gilbey, her nerves already stretched to the limit,

was abnormally snappish. "No, Gertrude, she does not!"

One quirkish eyebrow lifted. "Still badly hipped, is she? Well, I don't envy you the task of breaking the news."

Olivia felt that she could bear the suspense no longer. "Aunt Constance, if Mama is going to be upset, you had much better explain the whole to me at once. I shall then be prepared."

"Sensible child," said Lady Crockforth approvingly. "Much wiser to get it over with now, before the gabble-grinders get to work. Tell her m'self, if you haven't the stomach for it."

But this was going too far for Mrs. Gilbey. "I hope I may never be accused of shirking my duty, Gertrude, however unpleasant! And as for your presuming to take so much upon yourself . . . !"

"No need to fly up into the boughs," said her ladyship, unperturbed. "I only thought—since the affair more or less came to a head at one of Crockforth's card parties . . ."

"But, of course! Do you know, that had quite slipped my mind! It must be all of twelve years ago."

"Sixteen," declared the other. "Crockforth's been gone fourteen years this July, and it happened some time before his demise."

Olivia, fearful that they would descend into tedious reminiscence, sat beside her aunt and took hold of her hands. "Dear Aunt Constance, I can bear the suspense no longer! *Please*, please, tell me at once!"

Both ladies seemed a trifle taken aback by her insistence, but the moment could no longer be delayed.

"Damian St. Clair," began Mrs. Gilbey, "was —still is, I collect, unless Sir Patrick St. Clair is deceased, which could well be the case for he long since retired to his Irish estates and has not been heard of since, to my knowledge. Though that is neither here nor there, of course."

"Do get to the point, Constance . . . never heard

anyone make such a mull of a simple tale! The boy was Sir Patrick's by-blow!''

"Gertrude!" Mrs. Gilbey threw her a reproachful glance, but forbore to take issue, being all too aware that delicacy of feeling was not high among Gertrude Crockforth's good points, and she might, if encouraged, become even more outspoken. "Damian St. Clair was, as I was saying, the only child of an impoverished Irish baronet. There was, I believe, some slight mystery concerning his mother, but nothing of a definite nature was ever known." She looked defiantly at Lady Crockforth. "At the time we are speaking of he was a youth of about eighteen summers, but in many ways mature beyond his years, a quite distractingly handsome young man." Her voice grew a trifle dreamy.

Lady Crockforth uttered a "tch" of disapproval. "A thoroughly amoral young man!"

"Oh yes, that too, of course. Though he had charm enough to insinuate himself into some of the highest homes in the land, and get himself admitted to White's *and* Boodle's! Always looked well . . . that I do remember, his linen was faultless and his manners above reproach, which, allowing that his father was in no position to support him, led one to assume that he lived very successfully by his wits.''

"You mean he gambled?" Olivia put in, beginning to see at last where her aunt's peroration was leading.

"That, and . . . other things." The two older ladies exchanged glances, each recalling the lovely women of influence who had been only too happy to frank Damian St. Clair in return for favors most willingly rendered. "There can be no doubt that he had an amazing degree of luck in games of chance.''

"There were some who inferred that luck wasn't the name for't," murmured her ladyship dryly.

"Are you saying he cheated?"

Her aunt grew flustered. "Oh . . . well, as to that, nothing was ever proved!"

"Your father wasn't in any doubt of it," declared

Lady Crockforth unequivocally. "Called him an arrogant, misbegotten young upstart, among other, less flattering appellations!"

"Yes, but to be fair, Gertrude, that was largely because St. Clair was one of the few people capable of beating him—and Meriton hated losing, especially to a much younger man."

"Whatever the reason, there was a decided atmosphere at Crockforth's card party from the moment St. Clair arrived," her ladyship continued a touch irascibly. "He wasn't invited, but someone—and after all this time I'm blest if I can remember who—brought him along. It was quite late on, when a few too many bottles had been broached, that y'r father challenged the young man to a hand of picquet, a game at which he was wellnigh supreme. It was his intention to teach the upstart a lesson. Only, d'ye see, St. Clair achieved the impossible . . ."

"Ah, yes—I see," Olivia said, not needing to be told the outcome. She knew her sympathies ought to be wholly with her father, but she was that oddest of creatures, an incurable romantic with a strong practical streak, and she could not but feel a curious little spurt of admiration for the foolhardy young man who had dared so much—and won.

"Quite so," said her ladyship dryly. "That was when y'r father all but accused the young man of cheating. How Crockforth kept them from each other's throats, I don't know, but he did. But at the last it was Meriton who triumphed, for he made very sure that the name of St. Clair was vilified on all sides, and that he was blackballed from both White's and Boodle's. As a result, his so-called friends began to cut him, until only a few stalwarts remained."

"Really, Gertrude, I hardly think . . ." began Mrs. Gilbey with a swift glance at her niece's shocked face.

"I ain't telling the gel anything she won't hear elsewhere. Better she have the truth from me than fall prey to some of the less charitable fictions that will even now be gathering momentum.''

Olivia had little difficulty believing in the vindictiveness of her papa's revenge. ''What did Mr. St. Clair do?'' she asked.

Lady Crockforth shrugged. ''Only one thing he could do. Turned his back on us all and took ship for India, or somesuch outlandish place.'' She chuckled with unexpected glee. ''And has had the last laugh, it seems, for he has returned a veritable nabob, parading a dark-skinned servant who looks like a god—and probably with more money than any man can spend in a lifetime!''

So he *was* a nabob. Olivia felt a stirring of interest, which was cut short by her aunt.

''Enough and more, in fact, to enable him to take his revenge upon the duke's family by buying up almost every stick and stone of Meriton land,'' Mrs. Gilbey reminded her stiffly.

There was a sound at the door, a gasp presaging a series of breathless, high-pitched little cries. All three ladies turned as one to see Honoria, Dowager Duchess of Meriton, one white hand pressed convulsively to her mouth, standing rigidly unmoving amid a cloud of black draperies.

Three

A BALL GIVEN by Lady Bryony could be guaranteed to draw the cream of London Society to Grosvenor Square, for her late husband, Sir Joshua Bryony, a gentleman of many parts, had been intimate with Prinny himself, as also—if malicious tongues were to be believed—had the late gentleman's wife. But Arabella Bryony could afford to ignore the tabbies. She was, after all, beautiful, immensely wealthy, and could count among her friends many persons of influence as well as those who liked her for herself alone. She was also, though no longer in the first flush of womanhood, still young enough and clever enough to exploit her situation to the full.

So it was no surprise to find upward of five hundred guests thronging her elegant reception rooms on this fine evening in early June, and spilling over into the ballroom where an energetic country dance was in progress. The sound of mingled laughter and music drifted down the curving staircase to the cool deserted hall where several footmen stood motionless amid banks of flowers under the eagle eye of Lambert, Lady Bryony's butler. The outer doors opened with a gentle *whoosh*, and for an instant the balmy softness of the night invaded the fragrant bower. The footmen came to attention as a tall gentleman of unquestionable presence was admitted, followed by a servant in flowing white robes, who at a murmured word from his master, bowed his head and took up an impervious stance to one side of the door. The gentleman advanced.

Lambert had an excellent memory for faces: this one was rather older than he remembered, an experienced face, darkened by sun and wind, making the clear deep-set gray eyes seem brighter, if a good deal more cynical than of old. But, notwithstanding the letter her ladyship had dispatched to Egan House earlier in the day, he was convinced he would have had little difficulty recognizing in the gentleman who stood before him, the carefree, scapegrace youth who had been a frequent visitor in happier days. But this was a much-altered Mr. St. Clair, for he had undoubtedly grown in stature and authority with the years.

Rumors concerning his activities and whereabouts had circulated from time to time, of course, as was their wont—some being so fanciful as to defy belief. But if the single pear-shaped stone adorning Mr. St. Clair's waistcoat was what he thought it was, they had maybe not been so far from the truth, after all, for the gentleman who now stood before him did indeed display all the trappings of prosperity. Lambert could not immediately place the origins of the plain black swallow-tailed coat that lay in unwrinkled perfection across Mr. St. Clair's fine shoulders; it was not Weston, that much he knew, but the cut must surely rival Weston at the very peak of his craft.

"Good evening, sir," he purred, snapping his fingers to summon a footman to receive the latecomer's high-crowned hat, his light gold-crutch walking cane, and his gloves. "May I be permitted to say how very pleasant it is to welcome you back to London?"

"Thank you, Lambert." The gauntly handsome features twisted wryly, echoing the expression in St. Clair's eyes. "I doubt your view will be widely shared." And, cutting impatiently across the butler's embarrassed disclaimer, "Her ladyship is expecting me, I think?"

Relieved, Lambert bowed. "Yes indeed, sir. If you will follow me?"

But St. Clair was already on the stairs. "Don't trouble to announce me. I still remember the way."

Lambert stifled his disappointment. He would have given much to witness the reaction among her ladyship's more top-lofty guests upon seeing Mr. St. Clair.

Arabella Bryony saw him almost at once, standing in the doorway with an ease bordering on insolence. A ripple of pleasurable anticipation ran through her as she hurried forward with hands outstretched.

"Damian! I had almost given you up! Lud—I declare, I am almost in awe of you, so formidable have you grown with the years!"

He raised each of her hands in turn to his lips. "That's doing it a bit too brown, my dear. There was a time, not so long ago in Florence, when you weren't in the least in awe of me."

"Hush! Abominable man! If anyone hears you I shan't have a shred of reputation left!"

A lazy smile filled his eyes as they roved familiarly over the gown of gold tissue, several shades deeper than her hair, that skimmed the curve of her breast and clung to her shapely form in a manner calculated, deliberately, he suspected, to mock propriety. "If it is now become your custom to dress like a houri, and invite reprobates to your balls, I can only assume that your reputation is well nigh inviolable."

She chuckled appreciatively. "*Are* you a reprobate? What fun!"

"From which I infer that Joshua has left you so plump in the pocket that even the stiffest neck is prepared to bend a little to your whims or risk being cast into the social wilderness."

"Something like that." Momentarily, Arabella remembered the Egan girl, and rather wished she had not been so impetuous on this particular occasion. But what was done, was done, and surely in such a crush it should be possible to keep them apart. And if not? Well they had to meet sometime.

Her conscience thus assuaged, her fingers moved irresistibly to touch the jewel at his waist. "My dear! Is it . . . can it possibly be a diamond!" He admitted somewhat quizzically that it was. "Lud! I would sell my soul for such a prize!" She chuckled and tucked a hand possessively under his arm. "Come. I can't wait to show you off."

"What you really mean, my dear Arabella," he drawled, offering no resistance as she propelled him toward his fate, "is that you cannot wait to see how many people will dare to brave your displeasure by cutting me. But, be warned, my beautiful one, the mantle of sacrificial lamb don't sit well on me, and, should I choose to retaliate in kind, the blame will be wholly yours."

The chuckle became a laugh which pealed out.

It was a sound so joyous, so totally uninhibited, that Olivia, emerging breathless from the ballroom, was at once eager to discover its source, for it seemed to echo the sensation of sheer exhilaration induced in her by—oh, everything! There was an unashamed extravagance in everything around her—the glittering chandeliers, the flowers in all their profusion, and, not least, the gowns and the jewels of the guests, which ought to have shocked one who, duke's daughter or no, had grown used to making over dresses and being obliged to mend holes in even her third-best pair of stockings.

Now, thanks entirely to the generosity of her aunt and uncle, who had, she suspected, spared no pains or cost to make her debut as memorable as possible, she was attending her first formal ball, wearing the prettiest gown she had ever owned. It was of amber crepe over a white satin slip, with little puff sleeves, the bodice very brief and caught under the bosom with a cluster of flowers from which floated long satin ribbons. If that were not enough, she was also on the arm of a most amiable exquisite; that she had known him forever took nothing away from her pleasure, for he was but one of a gratifying number of gentlemen who had already solicited for the honor of dancing with her.

Olivia located the source of the laughter as, through a gap in the crowd, she glimpsed her hostess engaged in playful repartee with a gentleman whose complexion was positively swarthy by comparison with his pale and painted fellow guests. It was perhaps this, and the fact that his black hair grew lush and longer than the distinctive swirl dictated by fashion, with a tendency to curl about his ears, which conveyed the illusion that, in spite of the elegance of his dress, he possessed all the natural arrogance of a gypsy. This likeness was further enhanced by the way in which he was presently looking down at Lady Bryony—a way which, even at a distance, caused Olivia's pulse to quicken.

"How beautiful Lady Bryony is, Pom," she said a trifle breathlessly. "And so generous. There is a delightful informality in her manner which instantly removes one's qualms and sets one at ease."

The Honorable Edwin Pommeroy put up his glass to watch her ladyship, her face uplifted as she imparted some gem of wit to her latest conquest. Generous—well, yes, one might in charity say generous, though it was not precisely how he would have described Arabella's more accommodating qualities. But he could not off-hand define them in a way that would not give Olivia quite the wrong impression, so he murmured in his droll way, "Oh, Arabella is a splendid creature, m'dear—not an ounce of harm in her, though she's too confoundedly restless for my taste!"

"For shame, Pom!" Olivia exclaimed, eyeing with considerable amusement the excessively high shirt points that curtailed the movement of his head. She rapped his arm lightly with the little enameled fan of chicken feathers he had earlier presented to her in his deceptively off-hand way as a small token of her social debut. "You may affect to be a Pink of the *ton*, but I still remember that tow-headed little shag-rag who was forever getting poor Charles into scrapes."

"Hush, Livvy!" he implored her, his voice an agonized mumur. "Do have a care, I beg of you! It needs but a hint and my reputation is ruined!"

She laughed. "Poseur! But, as you will. I won't spoil sport."

"Good girl."

"Who is the gentleman with Lady Bryony?" she asked casually. "Do you know? He looks rather splendid, too."

"Do you think so?" Mr. Pommeroy obligingly put up his glass once more. "Don't recognize the fellow, but I'd give a monkey to learn the direction of his tailor! Daresay he's one of Arabella's—" he was about to say flirts, but with great presence of mind substituted "—many acquaintances. Would you care for a glass of cordial, m'dear?"

"Oh, Pom, thank you. I would love one."

"Right. I'll just restore you to Mrs. Gilbey."

Olivia wrinkled her nose. "Must I return to Aunt Constance? I'd as lief not while Lady Crockford is with her."

Mr. Pommeroy groaned. "The Gorgon! Say no more. I take your point."

"Oh, I don't dislike her ladyship. In fact, I find her highly entertaining. But she will doubtless wish to speak about Mama, and although it may seem dreadfully selfish in me, I don't want to talk about Mama just now."

Olivia briefly related the events of the afternoon to Pom, without mentioning St. Clair's name. Poor Mama! So distressing to have the past thrown up at her just when she was beginning to grow stronger. And poor Aunt Constance, for now she would most likely have Mama upon her hands for considerably longer than she had expected. Not but what the affair had not had its comical side, for although the family had long been

familiar with what Uncle George in his forthright way
referred to as "Honoria's distempered freaks," Lady
Crockforth had not until that moment been privileged
to witness the phenomenon, and in the time it had taken
Olivia to find Mama's vinaigrette, she had risen
majestically from her chair and, seizing the small jug of
water kept permanently on a side table with a small
phial of sal volatile, had dashed the entire contents in
the dowager's face. The ensuing pandemonium had
taken some time to resolve, with Mama furiously
spluttering and crying at the same time, and Lady
Crockforth declaring with some satisfaction, "Always
does the trick with Imelda!"

A gleam of appreciation warmed Mr. Pommeroy's
sleepy eyes. "I wish I had been privileged to witness it.
But I understand perfectly why you don't wish to be
plagued by her ladyship. If you are content to stay here,
I shouldn't be gone above a moment."

Olivia was more than content to remain where she
was, watching the constant movement of people. But in
spite of her determination not to let the thought of her
mother spoil her evening, guilt still riddled Olivia as she
remembered that her first thoughts upon seeing Mama
working up to one of her turns had been whether or not
she would be obliged to forgo Lady Bryony's ball, and
indeed, by the time order was eventually restored, with
the dowager carried to her bed and ruffled feathers
soothed all around, except for Mama's vowing never to
speak to Gertrude Crockforth again, the likelihood had
grown slim. But it had been Mama herself, one limp
white hand blindly extended in a dramatic gesture which
the most talented tragedienne of the day must have
envied, could she have been privileged to witness it, who
had whispered from amid the myriad pillows of a bed
just visible in the gloom of her close-curtained bedchamber, "I will not for anything have my dear child
deprived of this most important moment in her life
because of my stupid weakness! I beg you will not
consider me!" From which everyone inferred that

Olivia must on no account lose this or any other opportunity of becoming noticed.

However, Olivia mused, the fact had to be faced that Mr. St. Clair's arrival in London might well complicate matters. There was bound to be talk, if nothing else. She cared not a fig for herself; in fact, were it not for the onerous charge laid upon her by the family to contract an advantageous marriage, she rather thought she might have liked to travel the world as Lady Hester Stanhope had done with great success, not caring if she was considered an oddity. But Lady Hester had had no cause to heed the expense. The thought of travel brought Olivia's mind back to St. Clair. If only half the rumors were true, *he* had certainly traveled to some purpose. She still saw him as a rather romantic and ill-used figure rather than the villain of the piece, in spite of her mama's view that anyone who was capable of deriving satisfaction from ruining the lives of innocent people by buying almost every stick and stone from over their heads, must of a certainty be wholly devoid of sensitivity, let alone compassion.

Olivia began to take an interest once more in the scene about her. From somewhere close by a female voice filled with ennui, and not a little spite, caught her attention.

"One sometimes despairs of dear Arabella! If she chooses to ape a demi-rep when she must be all of four and thirty, I'm sure that is her business, but in truth, I do think it less than discreet in her to flaunt that St. Clair man under our noses not five minutes after his arrival in London, when everyone knows that Sally Jersey saw them in Florence together while Arabella was still in black gloves for Sir Joshua!"

Olivia stood riveted to the spot, hardly daring to so much as breathe for fear of missing anything.

"Disgraceful!" came timid agreement. "Except that . . . well, he is quite the most wickedly handsome man one could ever hope to see, don't you think? And so wealthy! He has everything, but *everything* . . . An

Indian servant quite eight feet tall, so one hears, and even—'' the voice sank to a confidential whisper so that Olivia was obliged to take a step nearer—''a ravishing concubine! But then, he was ever a shameless rake. And although it is dreadfully vulgar to make such a parade of one's fortune, I doubt any truly dedicated match-making mama will be deterred by such trifling consider-ations.''

There was a murmur of agreement. ''I believe the Meriton girl is here tonight. I'm sure I feel for her. They say she is almost at her last prayers! One wonders whether she is hoping that, having bought up practically every stick of the late duke's property, St. Clair might be persuaded to take her, too, thus completing his conquest of the Meriton dynasty!''

The pair moved away to the accompaniment of soft laughter, leaving Olivia with burning cheeks and so full of anger that she scarcely knew how to contain it. She forgot Pom—forgot her aunt. Her one consideration at that moment was to get out of the crush and into a quiet anteroom, or better still, to the retiring room, if she could but find it—anywhere so long as she might be free of people. How naive! she berated herself as she pushed unceremoniously through the crowds with many a stifled ''excuse me'' and ''I do beg your pardon.'' How impossibly puffed up she had been in her innocence, to imagine that people would accept her on her own merits!

She had almost gained the doorway when a sudden surge toward the ballroom threw her off balance; in-voluntarily, she stepped back onto a large and rather solid foot which further unsteadied her, and in a moment she was caught fast against an equally solid masculine chest. No man had ever held her thus, not even her brother; hands, their warmth intimately com-pelling through the fine silk of her gown, rested with easy familiarity just beneath the curve of her bosom, and against their imprisoning clasp she could feel the wild uneven thudding of her heart. It was beyond everything that was seemly! Acutely embarrassed, and almost wholly deprived of breath, she demanded to be released.

"Must I?" His voice against her ear was softly resonant, and as her protest was reiterated, he sighed, "Very well, but only with the greatest reluctance, fair divinity!" As his arms slid away, she felt his fingers trail lingeringly and quite deliberately across the softness of her breast. Raw color stained her cheeks; with every sensibility already outraged, this was one indignity too many.

"Sir, you are importunate!" She pulled free and spun around to find Lady Bryony's admirer regarding her with a glint of appreciation which only the greatest sapskull could have failed to interpret.

"Undoubtedly," he confessed without a hint of repentance. "But what, pray, is a man to do when quite the most enchanting woman in the room throws herself willy-nilly into his arms?"

"Oh, what a whisker! I'm not—and in any case, I didn't!" Confused, Olivia blurted the words out before thinking. She was a stranger to the delicate art of flirtation and had no idea how to cope with it. Pom's notion of flattery was to tell her that she looked *as fine as a fivepence*, and his eyes certainly didn't convey the kind of message she was presently receiving—a message that held her in a momentary suspension of time. They were quite beautiful eyes, she concluded languidly, of a light, almost luminous gray, the iris darkly ringed—and so compelling was their brightness against his sunburned skin that she felt a curious sensation of being drawn irresistibly into another dimension full of the most dangerous, yet pleasurable sensations. And then a sardonic smile lifted one corner of his mouth and the illusion was gone.

In a belated attempt to reassert herself, she straightened, lifted her chin, and gave him the Egan look. "He might," she suggested, achieving a passable measure of cool composure, "try to behave like a gentleman!"

"Ah, well, there you have me," he said. "I have been so long away from England that I am sadly ignorant of the current trend in manners. But I am very willing to learn, given the right teacher!"

He was laughing at her, but not kindly, and in truth she couldn't blame him. It was a terrible thing to say—downright presumptuous of her, in fact, to imply that he was not a gentleman, even if . . . In spite of herself, her own lips began to twitch. "Oh, pray let us forget the whole thing!"

"Must we?" He sounded genuinely disappointed. "That would be a pity. I really feel we should discuss it further."

The resonance of his voice seduced her and she almost succumbed, although they had not been introduced and she was not so green as to be heedless of the fact that to be found speaking to him at all in such circumstances would put her quite beyond the pale, the more so as the exodus to the ballroom had left them almost alone. And then a plump and rather elderly exquisite came sauntering past, and paused to look more closely at her companion. "Good God!" he exclaimed, and with a smile that was almost a leer, made a clumsy attempt at ribaldry. "Well now, what have we here, St. Clair? Not back on the town above five minutes, and already at pains to show us you ain't lost y'r touch with the ladies, what?"

St. Clair! The name seemed to echo and re-echo in Olivia's head. Shock, followed by a sense of outrage, filled her to the exclusion of all other emotions as the man sauntered on, unaware of the magnitude of his faux pas. But her fury was as nothing compared with St. Clair's. As she rounded on him accusingly, the words dried in her throat; his eyes, so gently teasing a moment earlier, now looked after the departing figure with an expression that eclipsed her own anger to such a degree that she shivered and involuntarily followed the restrained ferocity of his gaze, for it seemed impossible that anyone could endure such a look—and live!

To Olivia, it seemed that the moment went on forever before, with exquisite formality, Mr. St. Clair said in a voice devoid of expression, "Forgive me for exposing you to that and allow me to make amends by returning you to your friends."

His voice broke the spell and she whirled away from him, her own anger returning in full measure. "No! Don't touch me!"

He shrugged, his mouth twisting in a humorless smile, while his narrowed eyes still glittered in that frightening way. "As you will, fair divinity."

"And don't call me by that horrible name!"

"You do not care for it? How odd. Young women who throw themselves at me are not usually so averse to flattery. But since I do not know what else I may call you . . . ?"

"Nor do I mean to tell you!" The sudden panic in her voice did little to assuage his temper.

"I see. In the light of your all-too apparent revulsion, I must deduce that my reputation has gone before me with a vengeance. A pity, but you need have no fear—should I be on hand the next time you stumble, I shall strive to smother my more chivalrous instincts and allow you to drop where you will."

The correctness of his bow contained a supreme irony all of its own. Olivia watched him go, contemptuous pride bristling in every line of his back. And she could have wept. His behavior had been unpardonable, and yet he had somehow managed to put her in the wrong. No, to be fair, she had put herself in the wrong. She had meant—if, or rather when she met Mr. Damian St. Clair—to treat him with cool politeness, to show him and the world at large that she cared nothing that he was now master of Kimberley. Instead of which, just for a moment, she ahd actually come close to . . . she closed her mind to the shocking nature of her thoughts and attempted instead to defend her behavior. After all, how could she possibly have guessed his identity when in her mind she had visualized him as a youthful scapegrace Irishman with laughing eyes, and not at all this man who appeared so . . . dangerously different!

"Lady Olivia?" A tentative hand on her arm made her tense for fear that he had returned. The hand was hastily removed as she turned an unnecessarily fierce look upon the pleasant, rather shy young man who stood regarding her with some anxiety. "Forgive me . . . I am not mistaken? The sets are about to form and I believe the cotillion is promised to me?"

Oh heavens! "Of course. You are Pom's friend." Olivia smiled. "Mr. Peveral, is it not? I'm so sorry. I was overcome . . . the crowd, the heat . . ."

"Quite so." He looked crestfallen. "It is very warm. If you are feeling faint, we could sit in one of the anterooms instead?"

"Certainly not," she said. "I wouldn't dream of doing anything so poor-spirited. Besides which, I am now quite recovered."

Mr. Pommeroy encountered them as they were about to enter the ballroom. He was carrying a glass of cordial in a slightly bewildered fashion, as though he didn't quite know how he had come by it. "Livvy, I have looked for you in vain . . ." There was gentle reproach in his voice as his glance traveled from the glass to each of them in turn and then back again. "And to no purpose, it would seem."

Olivia chuckled, her spirits for the moment fully restored. "Oh, my poor Pom! I had quite forgotten. Never mind, you can drink it instead."

"That's the ticket. You'll enjoy it," said Mr. Peveral, beaming at his friend, whose look became even more pained. "Forgive us now, dear old fellow, but we must go if we are not to be left out."

The cotillion proved every bit as enjoyable as the country dance. Mr. Peveral acquitted himself well, and once over his shyness, proved to be an agreeable partner. Olivia was a natural dancer, and had learned all the steps along with her sister in the days prior to Charlotte's marriage, in readiness, so Mama had said, for her own come-out. She had acquitted herself wonderfully well, far better than Charlotte, though until now her opportunities to prove it had been few. There had been a few sedate assemblies in Bath, once she was out of black gloves, but the company was almost invariably thin and lacking in young people, and she gained the distinct impression that to be seen actually enjoying oneself would be considered bad *ton*. But here in Lady Bryony's ballroom, with its atmosphere of lightness and gaiety, she responded to the lilting music as a thirsty flower responds to rain.

"That niece of yours displays well, Constance," observed Lady Crockforth. "A true Egan. Takes me back, just watching her."

"Quite beautiful!" murmured Miss Imelda, seated beside her on the dais where proud mamas and dowagers mingled.

Mrs. Gilbey had been quite cool with Gertrude Crockforth when she first came to sit beside her, in order to signify her displeasure at the chaos she had caused by her summary treatment of Honoria. But her ladyship, impervious as ever, seemed not to notice any lack of warmth in Mrs. Gilbey's manner, and it was not in the latter's nature to hold a grudge for long. Now, all else forgotten, her eyes followed the dipping, swaying figure with misty-eyed partiality. "She *is* a delight, is she not? If only life were not so unfair!"

"Hm. Have you anyone in mind for her?"

Her companion sighed. "Mr. Gilbey has suggested several possibles—all of them ineligible, to my mind. But I am trying not to think of it at present. The poor child has endured such a wretched life of late that I want her to enjoy her freedom for as long as she can."

"Good God!" Lady Crockforth exclaimed suddenly, putting up her lorgnette. "If that don't beat everything! Well, I'll say this for him—he ain't lost an ounce of his audacity with the years!"

Mrs. Gilbey, mystified, urged her to explain.

"Well, you won't like it above half, Constance, but

you must surely see him . . . in the doorway there, just moving in front of the mirror. I always said Arabella Bryony's thoughtlessness would be her undoing one day, though I'd vouchsafe your niece is like to suffer more from this piece of work!''

Mrs. Gilbey turned pale. "You don't—you surely cannot mean . . .'' At first she did not recognize the gentleman in black, but when she did, her placid nature for once deserted her. "Oh, my poor Olivia! Where is she, Gertrude? Can you see her? Mr. Gilbey must be fetched from the card room and we must leave at once! Oh, why is he never there when he is needed?''

Lady Crockford exhorted her to be calm. "Carrying on in that hubble-bubble way won't help the girl! Whatever you do must be accomplished with discretion.''

Damian St. Clair, on his way to the card room, had paused for a moment at the entrance to the ballroom. The violent feelings unleashed by the distasteful conclusion to his earlier enlivening encounter still soured his thoughts, coloring his opinion of the whole scene. His mouth twisted into something approaching a sneer. Such a very English scene, with all its pomp and glitter and triviality. Odd now to remember how desperately he had once longed to be a part of it. Indeed, it had been his parting vow that he would not set foot on English soil again until he could be revenged on them all for their mealy-mouthed snobbery and make them accept him on his own terms. And when, last year, on one of his infrequent visits to Ireland, he had learned from his agent, Freeman, that the Meriton estates were coming on the market, it had seemed that Nemesis was presenting him with a peculiarly apt opportunity to redeem that vow.

Now, looking around him, he felt cheated, for he was experiencing none of the exhilaration which ought surely to arise from the vindication of all those past wrongs. There was only a sensation of anticlimax—of passion wasted. What need, after all, had he to prove himself to these people? He had achieved more, witnessed more, accumulated more riches in sixteen years than they would know in a lifetime. In that instant, he was on the brink of a decision—to seize the earliest opportunity to return to India, the land which had captured his heart. He had enemies there, too, of course, dangerously determined enemies, but he also had powerful friends.

And then his eye was caught by the girl in the amber gown who carried her head like a queen. She stood out from her overdressed, bejeweled companions by her very simplicity, her graceful, wandlike figure moving as though it had no bones—an illusion not as fanciful as it seemed, for although he had held her only briefly, he was able to recall every sensation in vivid detail; the way her heart fluttered like an imprisoned bird beneath his touch, the oddest notion that if he were not very careful she might break under his hands. But there was an invincible spirit beneath her apparent fragility, and a humor and intelligence which belied all that righteous indignation—he was sure of it—and but for that interfering fool whose name escaped him, he would have worn down her resistance. The memory of her angry reaction to his name puzzled him almost as much as her rejection of his overtures piqued him, which of itself constituted a challenge, for he was unused to being repulsed by any woman with such damning finality. His senses began to stir; by God, he had a mind to complete what he had begun. His blood began to race at the prospect. Perhaps, after all, the next few weeks might not be wholly tedious. He would find Arabella and persuade her to introduce him, a tiresome but necessary deference to protocol if the challenge was to be met and overcome.

But Arabella proved surprisingly reluctant to oblige him. She was by now regretting the mischievous impulse which had prompted her to invite Damian to her ball. Not that she was not overjoyed to see him, and to know that he had been accepted by most of her guests with perfect propriety, if not enthusiasm. But it had been unthinking folly on her part to expose the charming Meriton girl to unwelcome speculation, as she tried belatedly to explain to Damian.

"My dear, *don't*, I beseech you, ask this of me! Can you not see how the poor child will suffer with everyone looking on?"

The identity of his quarry had momentarily shaken him, and certainly explained her instant aversion to his name, but that, he determined harshly, only added a certain piquancy to the situation. "We have to meet sooner or later, so why not get it over and done with? Any daughter of Meriton's should be equal to anything."

Arabella knew him well enough to recognize the futility of further argument. The cotillion was almost at an end and she prepared to thread her way between the dancers in order to intercept Lady Olivia before she was returned to her aunt.

The music died away, and the couples began to disperse. A gap opened up and through it St. Clair's eyes met Olivia's, surprising in them again that look of sheer panic and, as Arabella began to move, of unconscious pleading. He had long thought himself proof against any such look, yet he suddenly found himself saying abruptly, "No matter, Bella. I have changed my mind."

Four

THE FLOWERS ARRIVED on the following day, at a time when Mrs. Gilbey's drawing room was more than usually busy with callers. Some were genuine friends and some, like Lady Jersey, harbored a somewhat malicious eagerness to discover how the return of Damian St. Clair had been received in Mount Street. As things had fallen out, she had not been privileged to witness Mrs. Gilbey's reaction on the previous evening when his presence at the ball had been made known to her—for which circumstance that good lady had given profound thanks. It was, she freely admitted, quite the worst moment in her largely uneventful life, and one she would as lief forget. Even thinking about it now brought on a severe attack of palpitations.

Gertrude had been right, of course. In the end, she had pleaded a severe headache—a circumstance so rare as to make Mr. Gilbey stare—and they had managed to take their leave without incident, and without, thank God, encountering Damian St. Clair.

But as Mrs. Gilbey looked around her drawing room, she could not but be aware that the matter would not go away. The presence of Olivia had so far constrained anyone from making outright reference to Lady Bryony's unexpected guest, but the whole atmosphere positively bristled with lively speculation being aired *sotto voce*, and with people like Sally Jersey, who was not dubbed Silence for nothing and positively thrived on gossip, ready to make the most of the situation, it seemed inevitable that Olivia must sooner or later become the object of the most singular attention, if not outright pity.

It was at this point in Mrs. Gilbey's morose reflections that the butler entered, followed by Edward, the new young footman, who was staggering under the weight of an enormous basket of pink and cream roses.

"For Lady Olivia, ma'am," the butler murmured.

There were exclamations of interest, and much pleasurable conjecture as Olivia rose uncertainly from her chair, turned a trifle pink, and said, "For me, Blore? Are you sure there is not some mistake?"

"Oh no, m'lady," the butler replied, pleased to be able to reassure this young lady of whom he thoroughly approved, there being, as he had told Cook on more than one occasion, nothing in the least top-lofty in her manner. "Lady Olivia Egan, the note says, plain as day." He directed Edward to set the basket down over by the window and indicated the missive nestling among a cluster of pink roses.

"My dear, how delightful," exclaimed her aunt, preening a little that this small coup by her niece on her very first appearance in public should be witnessed by her visitors, several of whom could be guaranteed to spread the word. "Who they can be from, I wonder?"

Olivia was wondering much the same thing as she crossed the room, very conscious of all eyes on her, bewilderment vying with little bubbles of excitement inside her. No one had ever sent her flowers—and so many! She touched the velvety petals with something approaching awe and bent her head to inhale their perfume.

"Come on, old thing," said Mr. Pommeroy, who had followed her. "Let's be knowing who your beau is."

"Hush, Pom, not so loud!" she pleaded, reaching

with a curious reluctance into the bouquet to lift out the note and break open the wafer.

Mr. Pommeroy obligingly lowered his voice. "I'll wager it's Harry Peveral. He was properly cast in the suds after you left last evening. Thought then it wouldn't be long before he was dangling after you. Bashful fellow, as you'll have gathered, or he'd be here this morning. Must be well and truly smitten to be lashing out on baskets of flowers."

But Olivia wasn't listening. She was staring down at the paper on which was scrawled with admirable brevity, *To propitiate a Fair Divinity.* It was signed, *Your Importunate Gentleman.* Oh, how could he! Her fingers were trembling slightly as she hastily folded the wafer, aware suddenly that although conversation did not cease, all eyes were upon her.

"Well?" said Pom. "Am I right?"

She pushed the note into her reticule, despising herself for the blush that suffused her face and spread, could they but know it, right down to her toes. "I . . . it doesn't say."

The faint sigh of sound that echoed around the room found voice in Miss Imelda Durant's, "An anonymous admirer. How romantic!"

"Well, if that don't beat all!" Mr. Pommeroy exclaimed. "Just wait till I see Harry!"

"Oh no!" Olivia besought him, panic trembling in her voice. "Pray don't say anything to him! If you are wrong, I should be quite mortified!"

Lady Crockforth, assessing the situation, saved the day by collecting up her reticule and gloves and saying briskly, "Come, Imelda. It is time we were leaving. I promised Mrs. Arbuthnot most particularly that we would call on her."

"Yes, of course, Gertrude." Miss Imelda's glance still lingered mistily on the flowers as she was led away.

Lady Jersey also rose to leave. She graciously acknowledged Olivia's curtsy, bestowed upon her an enigmatic smile, and said ambiguously, "Quite charming." She then turned to Mrs. Gilbey. "Your vouchers for Almack's, Constance—Lady Sefton has already mentioned them to me. You may expect them in a day or so."

"So kind," murmured Mrs. Gilbey. She was longing to quiz her niece about the flowers, but for the next hour or so people were continuously coming and going, and no opportunity presented itself. When the door closed behind the last visitor, she sank into a chair. "I declare, I am worn to a thread! I hardly know whether to feel gratified by our apparent popularity, or not. Or maybe I am just growing cynical in my old age!"

This drew a faint smile. "You could never become cynical, Aunt Constance. It simply isn't your nature. Besides, you know as well as I do what brought so many people flocking to your door."

"Oh, my dear child, it is not how I would have wished things to be. That wretched man! He has been gone for so many years . . . why could he not have stayed away for a few more months?"

When no immediate reply was forthcoming, she glanced across and saw that Olivia was standing beside her flowers in a state of abstraction. "My dear?"

Olivia came abruptly out of her reverie. "Oh, I'm sorry, Aunt Constance. I was not attending."

"No," agreed her aunt dryly. "Your mind was clearly elsewhere. Pondering the possible identity of your anonymous admirer, perhaps?" The question evoked such a curious reaction that for a moment she was troubled. "You *do* know his identity, I think?" she pressed with rather more urgency.

"I . . ." Olivia began—and stopped. It was not in her nature to dissemble, and yet to admit that she knew would be impossible without at the same time revealing how she and St. Clair had met—the substance of their encounter—she could not do it. If it had been anyone else . . . "I do know," she began again in a stifled voice. "But please, please, dear Aunt Constance, will you try to understand that I have reasons—pressing reasons—why I wish to keep the knowledge to myself for the present? I promise you that I am not cherishing a foolish tendresse, or anything of that nature."

"My dear child! You are not obliged to tell me if you do not wish to do so." Mrs. Gilbey's concern was now very real as she sought to reassure her niece. "I hope I know you well enough to trust to your good common sense. But have you considered that your mama is not like to be quite so understanding—and will, I fear, insist upon a full explanation?"

"Then I must endure her displeasure," Olivia said with quiet desperation, adding bitterly, "If I were not so sure that she would hear of it from the servants, I would have the wretched flowers taken out and burned!"

"That would be a pity, for they are very beautiful."

Olivia turned away from the roses, whose perfume was evoking strange, irrational thoughts. "Perhaps, but I wish they had never been sent. As for Mr. St. Clair—he may do as he pleases, but he shan't spoil things for me."

Her vehemence surprised Mrs. Gilbey. Really, Olivia was behaving very oddly—not in the least her normal sunny self. "Well, I am delighted that you feel that way, and indeed, there is no earthly reason why he should once the first awkwardness of meeting him is overcome. I have been giving the matter much thought, and I do not see how *that* can be avoided. His friendship with Lady Bryony is such that, if he means to remain in London, our paths must inevitably cross. The prospect will afford some brief amusement for the tattlemongers, but their attention is notoriously fickle and some new scandal will quickly come along to displace it." There was no telling from her niece's expression whether her words had proved reassuring or not. She paused and then added tentatively, "If there is—that is, if you should ever wish for someone in whom to confide, I beg you will come to me. I can be excessively discreet upon occasion."

To her surprise, Olivia rushed across the room and enveloped her in an affectionate hug. "Dearest and most understanding of aunts! How fortunate I am to have you!"

"Well!" said that good lady, emerging breathless and somewhat disheveled. "I'm glad we have *that* settled. You see, I thought it entirely possible that, being unused to London ways as yet, you might occasionally find yourself at a loss . . ."

"Yes, yes, and I will not forget your offer, I promise you."

Mrs. Gilbey had not exaggerated the extent of the duchess's wrath when her daughter steadfastly refused to disclose the identity of the sender of the roses, or the nature of her involvement with him. Worse, when ordered to produce the accompanying note, Olivia declared that she had destroyed it. For some days, the pall of her grace's displeasure hung over the house and everyone in it. Mr. Gilbey took refuge in his club, departing before Honoria was likely to quit her room and not returning until he was certain she must have retired for the night.

But Olivia remained adamant, and when a week had elapsed without any further communication from the mysterious admirer, things gradually returned to normal. Happily, in the light of her mother's aspirations, a number of invitations had begun to arrive, and Olivia's life seemed destined to become one long whirl of pleasure. She had very quickly recovered her spirits and resolved to meet trouble if and when it came with equanimity.

The one thing she missed more than any other was the freedom to walk and ride at will as she had been used to do in the country. Here, Pom proved to be her savior. He procured the loan of a very prettily behaved bay mare and, with the reluctant consent of her mama, who insisted upon a groom's accompanying them, it was arranged that they should ride together most mornings at an hour he assured her at the outset was too unfashionably early to arouse comment. "Wouldn't be abroad m'self in the ordinary way of things. Still, for you, m'dear, no sacrifice is too great."

"Shame on you!" Olivia had teased him. "Why, at home I am out soon after dawn on fine mornings."

Mr. Pommeroy shuddered and turned pale. "Don't! Not even in jest, I beg of you!"

They had left the house with the sound of Olivia's laughter echoing up the stair.

"Oh, Honoria, how good it is to hear the dear child so happy," said Mrs. Gilbey.

The dowager clutched her morning robe about her and frowned. "I do hope Olivia is not developing a fondness for that frippery young man, Constance. I will allow that he is an amiable enough creature, if one disregards his odd quirks of dress. And his background is naturally irreproachable—Meriton and Lord Pommeroy were on excellent terms—but a younger son will never suffice."

"I am sure Olivia's attachment to Mr. Pommeroy is quite harmless, Honoria. I doubt he has marriage on his mind, and as for her—she sees him quite simply as a friend and one-time comrade of Charles's. And, you know," Mrs. Gilbey added persuasively, "it is no bad thing that she should have Mr. Pommeroy for escort. It gives her a certain degree of consequence and protection."

Olivia had never troubled to analyze her friendship with Pom. It was sufficient for her that he was someone with whom she could feel completely at ease, so that they were able to ride together in perfect harmony. On this particular morning, as he had promised her, the Park was gloriously free of people, with no one in sight but for a horseman or two, an occasional carriage, and a sprinkling of nursemaids exercising their charges. A coin tossed to the groom proved ample to persuade him to wait for them at the Stanhope Gate, thus leaving them to make the most of the long deserted expanses of tan.

The temptation was too much for Olivia, who longed to try the paces of the mare. With a sideways grin at Pom she cried, "Race you to that line of trees!" and gave the horse its head. In a moment they were enjoying an exhilarating gallop which left her glowing with healthy color.

"By Jupiter! I wouldn't have thought the little mare had it in her, even if you did cheat, setting off without warning like that!" Pom exclaimed, reining in at last. She jeered at him and he grinned sheepishly. "Well, I'll allow you set a punishing pace, but don't let the doyens of fashion catch you at it. Anything beyond the most genteel of canters puts 'em in a regular pucker!"

She laughed. "I'll remember. But it was fun, wasn't it?"

Olivia looked about her with shining eyes at the newly burgeoning trees, the wide expanses of green. Later in the day the Park would be filled with all the color and pageantry of what Pom irreverently called "the Grand Strut," but for now one might almost imagine oneself at home in the country. And then she remembered that the home that sprang immediately to mind was no longer hers to imagine. But for once the thought failed to depress her.

Presently they heard a carriage approaching and moved over onto the grass verge to allow it to pass. It was an elegant town carriage driven by a liveried coachman, with a dark-visaged, immobile figure in white robes sitting up behind. Even before it drew level, Olivia had guessed the identity of the occupant. She ran a soothing hand along the mare's neck as it skittered playfully, resolving to ignore the carriage, but as it came level her glance was drawn to the interior. Mr. St. Clair, head slightly inclined, was listening with obvious pleasure to his companion who was not, as Olivia had expected, Lady Bryony, but a strangely beautiful young woman, so slight as to appear almost childlike, and with her head draped in some kind of veil that glittered in the sunlight. The concubine, perhaps?

As if aware of her gaze, St. Clair looked up and she immediately became conscious of the shabbiness of her old brown cloth habit, which had not yet been replaced, and of her hair, which had suffered in the gallop and was fast escaping the confines of her hat to tumble around her flushed face. Mortified that he should see her looking for all the world like a hoyden, her chin instinctively lifted. She saw his mouth quirk, and as the carriage passed, he touched his hat in mock salute.

"Well, I'll be damned!" exclaimed Mr. Pommeroy. "You'll never guess who that was, Livvy." And then, suddenly aware of the delicacy of the subject, he paused, uncertain how to proceed without distressing her.

"It's all right, Pom, I do know," she cut in swiftly. "Aunt Constance told me."

"Ah, that's all right, then," he said, his relief all too apparent. "Odd that you should have been wondering who he was the other night. Deuced pretty little thing with him—brought her with him from India, y'know. I wonder what Arabella Bryony will make of her?" Olivia's chin rose another notch, and he grinned. "Sorry. Tasteless remark." She told him not to be silly. "Come on," he said. "Time we went home, or we'll have your esteemed mama reaching for the sal volatile."

In the days that followed, Olivia's life was so full of incident that the event quickly faded from her mind.

"It really is most gratifying," said her aunt, adding an invitation from Lady Sefton to the growing pile, which already contained the much-prized vouchers for Almack's. "We shall not be a single night at home at this rate, to say nothing of attending Mrs. Arbuthnot's musical soireé on Tuesday afternoon, and Lady Troon's breakfast on the following Friday."

In view of all these grand expectations, one might

have expected the duchess to return to Bath, secure in
the knowledge that her daughter was well on her way to
being launched into the very cream of fashionable
society. Instead, to the dismay of both Olivia and her
aunt, she had become imbued with new energy, and
announced her intention of driving to Hyde Park with
them one afternoon, and perhaps attending the odd
function before taking her leave.

It was perhaps fortunate that she did not immediately
put her plan into effect, for that very afternoon as aunt
and niece drove into the Park at the hour of the Grand
Strut, almost the first person they encountered was
Lady Bryony, walking with two friends. She saw them
at once, and with a word to her companions, left them
and came across. Mrs. Gilbey had little alternative but
to instruct her coachman to stop the barouche.

"Dear ma'am—Lady Olivia, forgive me, but I have
had you so much on my mind." A bonnet lined with
peach-bloom silk framed her lovely face to perfection,
and the concern in her eyes was quite genuine. "I beg
you will accept my apology and believe me when I say
that I acted quite without thought the other evening."

The apology was so charmingly delivered that Olivia
leaned forward impulsively, extending her hand.
"Please, there is no need to say more. We understand
perfectly, do we not, Aunt Constance?"

"Perfectly," agreed her aunt dryly, and Lady Bryony
had the grace to blush.

"Well, that's all right, then." Her relief was so patent
as to be almost comical. "However, I hope you will
allow me to make amends, Lady Olivia. Your aunt will
tell you, I'm sure, that I am not without influence in
Society."

"Truly, there is no need," Olivia began, and then
found her glance distracted by an approaching curricle,
its spanking new coachwork catching the sun's rays, and
with four beautifully matched high-bred grays between
the shafts. Even if she had not recognized the driver, she
must have guessed his identity by reason of the figure
who sat up behind in place of a groom. Remembering

her aunt's words, an idea, breathtaking in its conception, suddenly took hold of her. There were any number of people strolling across the grass, or in carriages pulled up to the verge while their owners conversed with friends. Many she recognized from the ball or as visitors to Mount Street. Where better than the informality of the Park to achieve what must, sooner or later, come to pass?

"Lady Bryony," she said, stepping nimbly down before her courage could fail her, "there is something you could do for me, if you will be so kind." The lovely face brightened in anticipation. "I would like to meet Mr. St. Clair, who is, if I am not mistaken, coming toward us at this very moment."

St. Clair had already noticed Arabella among the group gathered at the verge, and was altering course in order to take her up before he realized the identity of her companions. He had little option but to complete the maneuver with Arabella already waving and beckoning to him, but he was cursing beneath his breath as he drew in to the side and summoned Hassan to go to the horses' heads.

Arabella, surprised and secretly a little dismayed by Lady Olivia's request, was unsure what to expect, and she endeavored to convey the nature of her predicament as she greeted him overeagerly. "Damian—only fancy? Lady Olivia Egan had but a moment ago expressed a most particular desire to meet you, and here you are! Is that not an extraordinary coincidence?"

"Extraordinary," he murmured, and, looking Olivia full in the eyes, he doffed his hat and bowed. Arabella hastily completed the formalities, sensing his annoyance and not quite knowing what to expect in view of the delicacy of the situation. She hated not being in full control. True, Damian had never been the easiest person to handle; she still recalled with a shudder how he had so very nearly forced her into a similar situation at the ball. So why should he balk now? However, to her relief, he was graciousness itself to Mrs. Gilbey, who was clearly surprised and pleased by his manner. It was the niece who was the puzzle. Arabella had expected her to turn tail at the very thought of meeting Damian, yet here she was, as cool as you please, greeting him with enviable composure. Even so, there was a very odd atmosphere between them—a baffling contradiction between Damian's smoldering anger and the way he said smoothly, "I am honored by Lady Olivia's interest. In the circumstances, it is more than I could have hoped for."

Olivia remembered how they had parted. Her gaze dropped for a moment to the glittering fob at his waist, which only served to heighten those memories. She summoned all her resources and looked at him, striving for what she hoped was a convincing smile. "We are both in a difficult position, sir, which is why I thought it best to get our meeting over with as soon as possible. And where better than here, in full view of the scandal-mongers and intriguers who hope for nothing so much as to see us at one another's throats?"

He ought to have been duly grateful. It was, after all, the introduction he had been seeking. But he was accustomed to manipulating events to suit his own purpose, and did not care to be robbed of the initiative by this high-bred but blatantly inexperienced slip of a girl, who looked so vulnerable and demure in her high-necked cream walking dress. But perhaps she had some of her father's steel. To test it, he said, "An admirable solution, ma'am. In fact, we might contrive to put the question beyond doubt if you would honor me further by driving a short distance around the Park with me?"

His sheer audacity made Olivia catch her breath. She looked to her aunt for salvation. Lady Bryony was already intrigued by the possibilities. Such tactics would undoubtedly cause comment, not all of it un-favorable—in fact, if the girl carried the thing off well, it might even work to her advantage in the long run. "Damian! What a daring contrivance! And yet unexceptionable, don't you think, ma'am, for they will be in full view all the time? Oh, do go, Lady Olivia, and I will engage to remain with Mrs. Gilbey until you return.''

''I'm not sure . . .'' Mrs. Gilbey began weakly, trying to gauge her niece's mood. There could be no real objection in the ordinary way, and it would certainly give the lie to any hint of a feud, though what Honoria would say if she came to hear of it . . . ''Olivia may not wish to take things quite that far,'' she concluded weakly.

Olivia looked into Mr. St. Clair's clear, faintly mocking eyes and knew that he thought so, too. He was, in fact, calling her bluff and expected her to decline. ''Thank you,'' she found herself saying, ''I think it an excellent suggestion. I am at your disposal, sir.''

She had the satisfaction of seeing him disconcerted, but the glimpse was but momentary, and then he was offering his arm, and she laid the tips of her fingers on it with a confidence she was far from feeling. ''You may be quite easy, Mrs. Gilbey,'' he said. ''I intend to take the utmost care of your niece.''

In silence, and with a hollow feeling in the pit of her stomach, Olivia permitted him to lead her to the waiting curricle where Hassan stood motionless, proud—his splendid head level with the still-fresh leaders, his calmness seeming to communicate itself to them. It was the first time she had really seen Hassan in all his magnificence and as he acknowledged her gaze with a formal gesture of obeisance, she knew exactly how Miss Imelda must have felt upon beholding him for the first time. Her reaction must have been apparent, for St. Clair's low, derisive chuckle echoed in her ear. ''It never fails! The ladies love him!'' he murmured, and lifted her into the curricle with a familiarity of touch that made her gasp. A moment later the springs dipped and swayed as he sprang up beside her and took up the ribbons. With a glint in his eyes, he asked, ''Are you quite comfortable, my lady?'' and when she affirmed that she was, he said ''Right, Hassan, let them go.''

As they moved off, Hassan waited and at the last moment swung himself effortlessly into place. St. Clair

handled the high-couraged team with great dexterity as
he threaded his way between the many other carriages
parading along the tan. He had a fine light touch and
Olivia, not entirely ignorant of the skill involved, could
not but admire the sensitivity of his long, brown fingers
as they controlled the ribbons. She was vaguely aware of
a blur of faces turning curiously to watch them pass, but
the thrill of being once more in a fine well-sprung
curricle whose seats were made of the softest cream
leather far outweighed any momentary embarrassment.
Charles had once owned such a vehicle, not quite so
grand, of course, though to an impressionable fifteen-
year-old it had seemed so—especially as he had taught
her with such patience to drive his pair to an inch.

"You are silent, Lady Olivia." Mr. St. Clair's voice
intruded upon her precious memories. "A haughty
profile won't suffice, you know, enchanting though it
may be. We must be seen to be pleasantly engaged in
conversation if our venture is to achieve conviction.
Shall we begin with the weather? Always a safe subject
with the English, I find. If you were Irish, now, it might
be a different matter altogether."

She turned toward him, ignoring his facetiousness.
"Why are you doing this?"

"Talking about the weather?"

She moved irritably. "You know what I mean."

His glance lingered quizzically on the delicate oval of
her face, so imperiously raised to him. "Why do you
think I am doing it?"

"To embarrass me," she suggested. "As you did in
the matter of the roses."

"Did they cause you embarrassment? I'm sorry. That
was not my intention. They were meant as a gesture of
expiation."

He didn't sound particuarly sorry, and his answer was
a shade too smooth, but Olivia thought it prudent not to
start an argument. "And today?" she persisted.

"Is this an interrogation? If so, I should warn you

that I don't take kindly to being cross-questioned." The quizzical profile creased into a less predictable pattern. "It was a spontaneous gesture aimed to please you—to extend the scope of your initial idea in order that the greatest number of people might see us together. That *was* your intention, was it not?"

"Yes. But I don't believe you care a fig for anyone's opinion, and as for pleasing me—I cannot understand why you should wish to do any such thing. I should rather expect you to be rejoicing in my discomforture. Heaven knows, you have little enough cause to love my family!"

He heard passion in her voice but, strangely enough, no obvious hint of recrimination. "And have already taken my revenge," he countered harshly. "Or had you forgotten?"

"No, but you must have found that a somewhat empty victory," she said in a tight little voice. "After all, if you hadn't bought Kimberley and all the other properties, someone else would."

What an infuriating girl she was! In one short sentence she had pinpointed the nub of his own dissatisfaction and reduced his grand gesture to its true worth. Furthermore, in spite of her exculpation of his actions, the faint tremor in her voice as she spoke of her old home managed to touch a chord of guilt in him that did not sit well. The conversation wasn't going at all as he had intended. In his irritation he tightened his hands momentarily on the reins and the horses jibbed. In the act of correcting his error, he said through his teeth, "You are more kind than I deserve, ma'am, but I have no wish to be absolved of blame."

His sudden venom startled Olivia and she looked away, straight into the eyes of Lady Sefton, who was approaching them in a barouche, and whose astonishment was almost comical to behold. Olivia smiled nervously and bowed, suddenly pondering the wisdom of what she was doing. Her agitation communicated

itself as she said, "I didn't mean . . . I'm s-sorry if my
words appeared patronizing. Of course, any blame must
be my father's, not yours."

St. Clair shot her a sideways glance. "That is a very
unfilial remark."

"I know, and I can't think why I made it, especially
to you."

His mouth quirked wryly. "You were much attached
to your home?"

"Yes, but the family is together, which is the most
important thing. And at least the estate workers will
benefit. Papa neglected the whole estate shamefully.
Their houses were falling down for want of attention,
and they could scarcely scrape together enough to feed
their families."

"All of which you expect me to remedy?" His voice
was dry.

"Of course. In the interests of efficiency, if nothing
else. I'm sure that with all your experience, you must
know that people work better if they are not continually
falling sick.

"I do, however, grieve for my brother, Justin, who
must grow to manhood a peer with an empty title."

"How old is your brother?"

"Fifteen. Almost sixteen. He says he doesn't mind in
the least, but that is the schoolboy talking, and I fear
that when he grows up, he may feel differently."

"If he has the necessary bottom, he'll survive. I did,
though our cases are somewhat different. If you have
any problems, send him to me and I'll talk sense to
him."

"No," she said abruptly.

"I see. Just when we were getting on so well, too."

His clipped voice brought them back to where they
had begun. Olivia could see her aunt and Lady Bryony
up ahead, and knew she had but a moment left to make
him understand that she had no wish to pursue his
acquaintance—that she must not do so. Those unknown

gossips at the ball had voiced what many would echo if one meeting became many.

"I'm sorry. It was kind of you to suggest it . . ."

"My dear young lady, I am never kind, and I seldom do anything without a reason."

St. Clair's eyes sought and held hers. It was but a momentary glance, yet it robbed her of coherent thought and left her feeling decidedly odd.

"Nevertheless," she concluded valiantly, "a public acknowledgment that there is no lingering hostility between us is one thing, but you must see how impossible anything more would be in the circumstances—even if Mama could be brought to understand. . . ." What a mull she was making of it! But, to her surprise, he did not appear to take offense. In fact, he was smiling faintly as he drew up behind her aunt's carriage and handed her down.

Mrs. Gibley looked anxiously from one to the other, and seemed reassured. Certainly one could not quarrel with Mr. St. Clair's manners, she decided, as he thanked Olivia for the pleasure of her company before handing Arabella up into his curricle in her place. That, of itself, should lend the encounter its true perspective. Of course, he had ever a way with women, but although her niece's expression was not easy to read, she did not seem to have been unduly affected.

"Well, my love?" she inquired when they had driven off. "That was not so bad, I daresay?"

Olivia watched the curricle disappearing into the distance. Arabella's head was very close to St. Clair's shoulder. Were they already discussing her, she wondered—perhaps, laughing at her gaucheness?

"No," she agreed. "I only hope that it has served its purpose."

Five

THE ARRIVAL IN town of Mrs. Gilbey's dear friend Sybil Thornton, together with her daughters, Jane and Elizabeth, could not have been more opportune. Elizabeth, the younger of the two, was to make her come-out.

"And Jane?" Olivia asked.

"Oh, my dear, such a tragedy! It must be all of two years ago that Jane was betrothed to Fenniston's heir—an excellent match. And then no more than a month before their wedding day the poor young man took the measles from one of his sisters, and within a week he was dead!"

"How dreadful."

"Quite so. Such a charming girl, too. I do hope the two of you will become friends, for it will not be an easy situation for her—so many memories."

Olivia's spirits sank. She had known heartbreak enough herself, so that all her natural sympathies went out to Jane Thornton. But the thought of being cast in the role of confidante to the bereaved girl was vaguely depressing. Five minutes in her company, however, banished all such thoughts.

Jane was a young woman whose generous proportions matched a disposition that was gently humorous. She was not precisely pretty, but a ready twinkle in her fine blue eyes more than made up for any more distinguishing features.

Elizabeth was destined to be the beauty of the family from the first, Jane told Olivia without a trace of envy, "so I never felt the least obligation to compete. I was used to say that the good Lord practiced on me and then, having corrected all his mistakes, created Elizabeth."

That her sister was lovely could not be denied: where Jane's hair was a soft light brown, Elizabeth's was bright guinea gold framing a perfect heart-shaped face; and while Jane's figure tended toward the statuesque, her sister's was slim and graceful. Both girls had pleasing natures, but the liveliness of Jane's mind was much more to Olivia's taste. She had never had anyone of her own age in whom to confide, her own sisters being so much younger.

"That must have made your situation doubly hard," Jane said sympathetically as they walked together in the park during the afternoon promenade.

"In some ways, I suppose, although when Charles was alive that never seemed to matter, the bond between us was so close. Even after four years, I still miss him dreadfully." Olivia spoke without self-pity. "Charlotte is much older, and the others—well, Emily is only seventeen, Justin is at school, and Sarah, Martin, and Alice are still in the schoolroom. Oh, I love them all dearly," she added hastily, "but with Mama the way she is, I sometimes feel I stand more in the way of a parent. That is why I do so hope to be in a position to bring Emily out next year. One cannot expect poor Uncle George and Aunt Constance to repeat their generosity."

Jane had met Olivia's mama and, with a wisdom beyond her years, had very quickly summed up the dowager duchess's character. She truly felt for her new friend, and hoped that dear Mrs. Gilbey would be able to find her a husband worthy of her. It was bad enough to be obliged to, as it were, sell oneself to the highest bidder for the sake of one's family—something she was certain she could never bring herself to contemplate. And for someone as high-born as Olivia it must be doubly abhorrent.

"I suppose," she asked with some diffidence, "you have not yet had time to meet many . . . suitable gentlemen?"

Olivia smiled wryly. "No one. If one discounts Mr. Antrobus, that is."

"My dear Olivia, you can't! Not even for the sake of your family!"

"He is exceedingly wealthy."

Jane was horrified and did not scruple to show it. "But he is fat and quite revolting, as well as being older than Papa and having absolutely no conversation—"

"No, no, you are quite mistaken! He is remarkably well-informed on the subject of lizards. After listening to him for an hour or more at Lady Sefton's reception last evening, I feel I am become quite an authority myself. Did you know that the slow worm is a legless lizard and is seldom to be found in Ireland or the Scottish Isles?"

The two girls dissolved into peals of laughter, and were still far from serious when Mr. Pommeroy and Mr. Peveral strolled up. The gentlemen had already made the acquaintance of the Thorntons, and after the initial greetings, fell into step beside the two girls.

"Everything all right?" Pom asked, noting Olivia's flushed cheeks and overbright eyes.

"Fine." She glanced at Jane, and her voice was a trifle unsteady. "I've been telling Miss Thornton about slow worms . . ."

Mr. Pommeroy did not wish to seem impolite in the presence of Miss Thornton. "Not familiar with worms, myself. Are you, Harry? Seems a deuced odd topic for conversation."

"Oh, they aren't really worms, Mr. Pommeroy,"

Jane explained, her eyes brimming with suppressed mirth. "They are lizards."

Mr. Pommeroy looked severely at Olivia. "Tell you what, Livvy. Go boring on at people about worms and lizards and they'll begin to think you are queer in the attic!"

This brought a fresh splutter of laughter, swiftly controlled. "Dear Pom, you never spoke a truer word," she said, and passed on to more general topics. She was amused to note that although Mr. Peveral said everything that was proper, his attention strayed from time to time. At last he said haltingly that he hoped Miss Elizabeth was not indisposed.

"Why, no, sir," Jane reassured him, keeping her countenance with difficulty. "My sister decided to stay in the carriage with Mama. I believe you will find them somewhere near the Long Water."

He was patently torn between wishing to go immediately, which must appear rude, or remaining to make polite conversation. She took pity on him. "We were about to make our way back, if you would care to escort us?"

The eagerness with which Mr. Peveral seized upon this plan caused his step to quicken. Jane obligingly kept pace with him while Olivia followed on with Mr. Pommeroy. "Amazing, the power that golden curls and a cupid's bow mouth can exert," she remarked. "Are you smitten, too, Pom?"

"Lord, no. Tell the truth, blondes ain't much to my liking." They stood waiting for several carriages to pass and he turned to look down at her over his amazingly complex cravat. "Thought Harry was sweet on you."

"Ah, but that was before he laid eyes on Elizabeth."

"Silly clunch!"

Olivia smiled at him with particular warmth. "Thank you, my dear Pom. You are very good for my morale." She was still smiling as Mr. St. Clair passed them in his curricle, an animated Lady Bryony at her most

ravishing in pale blue trimmed with swansdown, up
beside him, punctuating her conversation every now and
then with the graceful gesture of a hand. She saw Olivia
and waved, laying a hand on St. Clair's sleeve to draw
his attention to her. He raised his hat, but made no
attempt to stop.

Not that she wished him to, she assured herself. Their
drive, which had occasioned a brief moment of
notoriety, had at least enabled them to meet socially
without obvious embarrassment, the more so as Mrs.
Gilbey had gone to great lengths to let it be known that
the drive had been arranged with her consent as a conciliating gesture. And once the tattlemongers had
tried—and failed—to discover any word or gesture in
either of them to titillate the imagination, the topic was
swiftly abandoned in favor of more fertile scandals.
Only the duchess refused to let the matter rest by continuing to reproach her daughter for having dragged the
family's pride in the dust by speaking to "that man."

"That man," meanwhile, had quickly overcome the
objections of all but a few hardened old dowagers with
long memories, from whom could be heard occasional
mutterings about baronet's by-blows and past wicked-
ness and cries of "poseur" when he passed with Hassan
as his continuing shadow. This, had they but realized it,
merely made St. Clair more attractive to the majority of
hostesses, who were more interested in the present than
the past. To their way of thinking, a touch of rakishness
in a gentleman was considered a positive asset, while his
fortune combined with the sheer force of his personality
more than outweighed any trifling discrepancy of birth.
As for his amusing affectation—it merely served to
enhance his singularity. Young gentlemen of the *ton*
who aspired to emulate this unwitting paragon of
fashion, took to dressing their own servants up in outrageous costumes, but there was only one Hassan, and
they succeeded only in making themselves objects of
ridicule.

Soon, no guest list was complete without the name of

St. Clair placed close to the top in the order of precedence. The Marriage Mart had not seen so rich a prize in years, and, as predicted, malicious rumor was widely ignored by the more ambitious matchmaking mamas. Mrs. Thornton, though not in this category, had no doubt but that he must be invited to Elizabeth's coming-out ball, something which Olivia could not but notice as she and Jane sat in the drawing room of the Thornton's Grosvenor Street house, penning the invitations. When more than half of the three hundred had been completed, they abandoned their task for a while and fell to gossiping.

Elizabeth, who had done little to help except get in the way, declared herself very much in awe of Mr. St. Clair, and vowed that she would sink if he did but look at her.

"Well, I shouldn't lose any sleep," said her sister with good-natured raillery. "I doubt Mr. St. Clair's taste runs to ingenues."

"Beast," retorted Elizabeth with a well-rehearsed pout. "I have already received two proposals, and my come-out ball is still a week away."

Olivia sighed and endeavored to look lovesick. "One of which came from Mr. Peveral, if you please, whom I had grown used to considering as *my* beau until you arrived on the scene."

"Oh, no!" Elizabeth's skirl of dismay reduced her two companions to a state of unbridled mirth. She stared at them and then, realizing that Olivia was only funning, became indignant.

"And your other bleeding heart was Mr. Edding, who is scarcely out of short coats," gasped Jane, wiping her eyes.

"Well, you just wait," said her sister, flouncing out of her chair to admire her reflection in the mirror. She patted a golden curl complacently. "When I am really out, I'll have a whole string of beaux queuing up to marry me! . . . Oh!" She clapped a hand to her mouth and swung around to stare apprehensively at Jane. "Oh, I'm sorry!"

Jane smiled. "Don't be an idiot, Lizzie. Heavens, if you had to mind your tongue every time you wished to speak of beaux and marriage, life would become very tedious, I promise you. I want you to enjoy yourself."

With the ready tears starting in her eyes, the younger girl ran to fling her arms about her sister's neck. Olivia, much moved, glanced across at Jane, who was resolutely engaged in soothing away her sister's fears.

"Elizabeth," Olivia said casually, picking up a copy of *The Lady's Magazine* which she had been glancing through earlier, "do tell me what you think of this dress. I am sure it would be just the thing for you—it has the prettiest rosebuds embroidered on the bodice."

It was all the distraction that was needed. In a few moments Elizabeth was running from the room in search of her mama, the magazine excitedly clasped to her breast.

"Thank you," said Jane quietly. "It isn't easy for Lizzie. She is such a pretty innocent, and I don't want her pleasure to be spoiled."

"It can't be easy for you, either."

"No, but I am determined not to fall into a green and yellow melancholy over what cannot be mended, so we will say no more about it, if you please." Jane smiled to take any sting from the words. "Now tell me—I did not wish to speak of it in Lizzie's presence, but have you heard the latest rumor concerning your Mr. St. Clair?"

Olivia blushed. "He is not *my* Mr. St. Clair!" And then, as curiosity overcame prudence, "What is it that is being said?"

Jane came to sit beside her on the sofa. "It sounded quite exciting—though somehow one cannot visualize him being involved in anything of a humdrum nature. However, this, if it should be true, is beyond anything one might imagine. I overheard Papa telling Mama that he had met with an old friend of his who is but recently arrived home from India, and he—Mr. Garth, that is—reckoned that Mr. St. Clair left Lahore because his life was in danger—something to do with that diamond fob he wears. It was given to him by a grateful raja, in recognition of some great service rendered to him by Mr. St. Clair—only there are those who insist that it was not the raja's to bestow.''

"Heavens!'' Olivia quelled a sudden flutter of apprehension, to say lightly, "What a drama!''

Jane had a sudden thought. "Do you suppose that is why Hassan goes everywhere with him?''

"It's a fascinating idea. But surely there can be no danger here? In fact, if you really want to know what I think . . .''

"Yes?'' queried Jane.

"I think the whole thing is a Canterbury tale,'' she said lightly.

But that night, in the privacy of her own room, Jane's story about Damian St. Clair, which had lain all day in her subconscious, surfaced and would not go away.

She began to wonder whether it could possibly have any connection with an incident that had occurred recently when she and Pom were out riding. They had become accustomed to seeing St. Clair's closed carriage with its enchanting occupant in the park most mornings, but on this occasion he and Hassan were alone and on horseback, their mounts sleek-coated and pale with long tossing cream manes and tails like silk.

"Regular prime goers,'' Pom had exclaimed with some envy. "Arab, I shouldn't wonder.''

The two horsemen had obviously entered the park by a different gate, and were still some way off on a path which would eventually converge with theirs, so that she did not have a very clear view of the man who rode out to intercept them. Certainly he was not English, for both his dress and his skin proclaimed him a foreigner. Nor could she or Pom hear what was said, but the man seemed to be arguing and at one point raised his arm in a threatening gesture. Pom was all for leaving her and rushing to lend assistance, but quick as light, Hassan had interposed himself between his master and the stranger, and she had seen briefly a glint of steel reflected in the sunlight. Finally the man had ridden off at a gallop, his fist angrily punching the air.

"I say," Pom called out as they drew level. "Devilish smoky-looking cove, that one. Are you all right, St. Clair?"

The look Damian St. Clair turned on him held something of the fury she had seen in his eyes once before, but in a moment it was gone and he was thanking Pom for his kind inquiry and casually dismissing the stranger as a freakish creature, not quite right in his attic. "I shall naturally report the incident," he said. "We can't have bedlamites like that on the loose. Next time, he might accost someone less able to defend himself."

His glance had rested on Olivia, his expression inscrutable, and she had a curious feeling that his mind was elsewhere. At the time, she had been mildly affronted that he seemed not to notice her new riding habit. It was the first time she had worn it, and vanity had persuaded her that the soft green wool jacket, curving neatly into her waist and much ornamented with black frogging, was vastly becoming, as was the dashing black shako with a curling green feather that accompanied it.

But now, in the light of what Jane had told her, might there not conceivably be more to the incident? She certainly hadn't imagined that lingering glimpse of fury, but perhaps she had mistaken its cause. Never for one moment did she doubt that a man like St. Clair could make enemies—and if they had cause enough, did it not follow that those enemies might well have pursued him to England? Finally, confused by the endless possibilities, she told herself that St. Clair's affairs had nothing whatever to do with her, which did not explain why she tossed and turned for the greater part of the night, a prey to confused dreams, and awoke soon after dawn, hollow-eyed and drenched in perspiration, and feeling thoroughly out of sorts.

"My dear, I do hope you aren't sickening for something," exclaimed Mrs. Gilbey upon finding such a wan face next to her at the breakfast table. "It would be such a pity if we were obliged to call off our visit to Almack's this evening."

"Well, I am never ill, so you needn't fuss." Olivia spoke so sharply that her aunt looked quite taken aback and even Mr. Gilbey came out from under his newspaper to peer at her over his spectacles.

She stretched out a hand. "Forgive me, Aunt Constance. It was appallingly rag-mannered of me to take out my liverish ill-humor on you. But truly, there is nothing wrong with me that a good gallop in the fresh air won't cure."

"You are never going riding, child!" Mrs. Gilbey made it sound like a fate worse than death. "You had much better go back to bed and I will ask Polly to bring you up one of cook's soothing tisanes."

The expression on Olivia's face drew a chuckle from her uncle. "Let the girl be, Connie. If she's suffering from a attack of the blue devils, an invigorating ride is more like to shake 'em out of her than any amount of cook's insipid pap!"

"Mr. Gilbey!"

Her spouse suddenly bethought himself of an urgent matter which required his instant attention, but as he left the room he winked at his niece.

By evening, Olivia was wishing that some slight indisposition might for once have come to her aid—nothing too unpleasant, of course, just enough to enable her to cry off.

Mama had talked incessantly for most of the day, plying her with all kinds of advice about how she should go on at Almack's, and late in the afternoon was filled with sudden inspiration. "Do you know, Olivia—I believe I will come with you this evening. I have been feeling so much better of late, and an outing or two would be just the thing to set me up before I return to Bath and the children.''

Seemingly oblivious of the turmoil she had created in her daughter's breast, she sat back with a look of complacence to await her gratitude. Olivia swallowed and glanced wildly across at her aunt, who seemed to have been struck momentarily speechless.

''Why, Mama,'' she replied, striving for calmness, ''that is a splendid idea, but do you really think you should?''

The duchess stared. ''Dearest child, what an odd thing to say. I am sure I don't know what you can mean!''

''I think, Honoria,'' said Mrs. Gilbey, coming somewhat belatedly to the rescue, ''that Olivia fears the excitement may be too much for you. And I am bound to confess that I agree with her. Only consider how exhausted you were after attending Emily Cowper's musical afternoon?''

''Nonsense! That was entirely the fault of that tedious woman who sat next to me and prattled on without ceasing at every available opportunity! Small wonder that I suffered one of my migraines.'' The duchess smiled wanly, her air of languor concealing a stubborn determination. ''But a poor thing it would be, I am sure, if I could not make a push to attend at least one or two functions with my dearest child. And I well remember Charlotte's first visit to Almack's. 'Mama,' she later told me, so prettily and with such feeling, 'I do not believe I could have faced such an ordeal without you at my side!' Her words came back to me quite clearly as I lay awake last night waiting for you to come home from the Opera, and I knew then that I must make the supreme effort!''

The hurt expression on Mrs. Gilbey's face at this seeming ingratitude for all she had done galvanized Olivia into a spirited rebuttal. ''Oh, come, Mama, that is the greatest flummery, when we all know perfectly well that Charlotte never had a timid bone in her body. If she did say anything of the kind, it was out of a desire to please you!''

She might have added that she had, upon arriving home on the previous evening, quietly opened the door of her mama's bedchamber to be greeted by a gentle chorus of snoring—but that might be have been deemed a little too close to an outright accusation that the duchess had been telling the most shocking bouncers. It was her aunt, with a waspishness quite out of character with her amiable nature, who brought her grace to a belated recollection of how much she still depended upon her sister's generosity. "I am sure you are right about Charlotte, my love," Mrs. Gilbey said with a well-directed glare. "Just as I am sure your mama did not mean to imply any lack of appreciation of my poor efforts. You do realize, Honoria, that we have only two vouchers? Am I to take it that you wish to go in my place?''

But her grace clearly meant nothing of the kind. The thought of being obliged to assume full responsibility was more than she cared to contemplate. "Of course you must come, too, Constance. As for the vouchers—'' she smiled complacently— "I am quite certain there is not one of the patronesses would dream of turning me away!'' Mrs. Gilbey, only partially mollified, saw that her sister's mind was made up and could only hope that she might be proved right.

It would not have been so bad, Olivia reflected later, if Mama had been content simply to accompany them; instead, she made her own toilette in remarkably good time so that she might supervise her daughter's preparations. Polly exchanged a speaking look with the Lady Olivia and set a comfortable chair to one side for the duchess which she flitted in and out of constantly like a restless butterfly.

"Very becoming," she nodded approvingly as Polly fastened the tiny buttons down the back of Olivia's

gown of ivory *mousseline de soie*. "Exactly right, in
fact. Not too *jeune fille*, I am happy to see, for you are
not precisely in the first flush of girlhood."

Olivia accepted the comment with a wry smile, but
Polly's shoulders stiffened with indignation and was
hard put to it not to protest as the duchess continued to
interfere, her black gauze shawl floating around her
daughter with every move of her restless hands as they
twitched a fold here and there and plumped up the tiny
puffed sleeves.

". . . though I am not altogether certain that the
neckline is not a trifle too décolleté for Almack's.
Perhaps, a gauze kerchief, although that might hide the
pretty pearl edging . . ."

"Mama, there is nothing wrong with the neckline,"
Olivia said with a trace of exasperation as she sat at the
dressing table to allow Polly to put the finishing touches
to her rich brown hair, which Mrs. Gilbey's own hair-
dresser had fashioned *á la Greque* and had intricately
threaded with a rope of pearls. "Aunt Constance was
quite definite about it!"

"Yes, of course, dear, your aunt would know. Oh,
yes—quite charming! Almost regal, in fact!" she exclaimed, misty-eyed, as Olivia stood up at last and
pulled on a pair of long gloves. Mother and daughter
stood side by side for a last critical appraisal of their
mirror images.

Olivia was a little alarmed to see how her mama had
shrunk—something which must have happened so
gradually as to pass unnoticed. Or perhaps it was she
who had grown, thus making Mama seem more small
and faded than she might otherwise have done in her
black draperies, though there was still a certain grace of
carriage, a pride in the way she wore her black toque
with its lush purple ostrich plumes. Olivia felt a sudden
rush of affection which moved her to say with spontaneous warmth, "Dear Mama, how good it is to see
you looking as fine as you were used to do!"

She was rewarded by a becoming blush, and a laughing: "Oh, I am past the age of worrying about such things! But I confess, I had almost forgotten how pleasant it is to don one's finery and pamper oneself a little. If only . . ." She bit her lip, patted her daughter's cheek, and said with a sigh, "But there, we must not be wanting the moon. I am sure you will not fail us!"

Which brought her daughter back to the recollection of what was required of her with unwelcome suddenness.

By the time Mrs. Gilbey's party arrived in King Street, the assembly rooms known to the polite world quite simply as Almack's were already alive with the fashionable and the fortunate who had been granted vouchers for the Wednesday night subscription ball. The appearance of the duchess created something of a stir, but not even Mrs. Drummond-Burrell, the highest of high sticklers, had the courage to hint that she had no voucher—and dear, kind Lady Sefton had come forward at once to bid her welcome.

Olivia, remembering her sister's outspoken comments about Almack's, had been curious to see it for herself. "Such a very dull place," Charlotte had said. "Positively bristling with rules and regulations, and the refreshments frankly insipid. But its very exclusiveness, thanks to the patronesses, makes it the one place above all where one *must* be seen, especially if one wishes to find a husband!"

For once, Charlotte had not exaggerated. The ballroom was certainly a magnificent chamber, far bigger than those in any of the private houses she had so far attended, but the atmosphere was formal and somewhat constrained. It was all too easy to pick out the mamas who were seeking eligible husbands for their offspring, for the latter, clad in virginal white, fluttered like nervous doves and made Olivia feel very old as they giggled or peeped apprehensively over their fans at every

unknown gentleman who came through the door. The
gentlemen, as was decreed by the patronesses, were all
clad in formal evening dress with knee breeches—the
new-fangled trousers being absolutely forbidden.

Mr. Pommeroy had no difficulty in conforming as he
presented himself to Olivia in immaculate small clothes.
His coat of blue superfine fitted him to perfection
without the need for buckram—cut in a way that few
but Weston could achieve—his waistcoat was of silver-
striped brocade and, above shirt points that were higher
than usual so that they came to rest on his cheekbones,
his cravat blossomed as a veritable model of intricacy.
Olivia teased him, but admitted that he looked every
inch the beau.

"A pity you were not privileged to see Brummell," he
said in all seriousness. "Put all of us in the shade, don't
y'know. But the poor fellow got himself in bad odor
with Prinny, and before long it was all up with him.
Forced to leave the country . . . pile of debts. Last I
heard he was living in Calais."

"Is Mr. Peveral coming this evening?" she asked.

Mr. Pommeroy looked disgusted. "I doubt it. The
fair Elizabeth ain't out yet, d'you see, so he's more like
to be haunting the Thornton household."

"Elizabeth *is* very beautiful."

"Aye. A beautiful ninnyhammer," he said with a
decided sniff. "Dashed if I can see what is so wonderful
about that! I mean, take a look at all those simpering
young things in their insipid white dresses—no conversation, no style! Ain't a one of them can hold a candle
to you!"

Olivia smiled. "How good you are to me, Pom. You
always say just the right thing."

He grinned back at her. "Think nothing of it. It's no
more than the truth, anyhow." He put up his glass and
allowed his glance to drift around the room. "Tell you
who is here this evening—that unctuous oaf, Antrobus.
Ain't he the one who maunders on about worms?"

"Lizards," she corrected him mechanically. "Oh

Pom, he isn't here, is he? He is certain to ask me to dance, and will undoubtedly expect to be introduced to Mama.''

"Whatever for? Not interested in worms or whatever, is she?''

"No.'' Olivia laughed. "Perhaps if I left him to bore on about them for long enough, she would take him in aversion?''

"Bound to, I'd say, though I fail to see why you should want to do anything so drastic—could give her a nasty turn.''

"Perhaps, but it would be worth the risk if only he might fail to impress her as a potential son-in-law.''

Mr. Pommeroy looked shocked. "Livvy, you ain't serious about him dangling after you? I thought you and Jane were only funning. The duchess wouldn't favor his suit, surely? It don't bear thinking of!''

"Mr. Antrobus is *very* wealthy,'' she said in a voice grown suddenly flat. She looked across the room and saw her mama enjoying a quite animated conversation with Lady Sefton. "However, it's early days and I am probably worrying unnecessarily.''

Olivia had no shortage of partners and it was some way into the evening before Mr. Antrobus was able to solicit her for a country dance. Mr. Antrobus was the only son of a successful manufacturer who had himself married out of his class, being fortunate enough to court and win a baronet's daughter who was plain and past the age of being choosy. Mr. Antrobus Senior's obsession with wealth and position, and his wife's over-weening pride, had eventually produced a son who combined the worst characteristics of both parents. He was neither as fat or as old as Jane would have him, being no more than forty summers and a trifle on the portly side, but his conceit was enormous. And conceit dictated that the Antrobus line must continue onward and upward. Even so, it was doubtful whether he would have dared to look as high as a duke's daughter, and a beautiful one at that, had fate not, as it were, set her

within his reach. This being so, however, he could fore-
see no possible bar to their union, and seemed quite
oblivious of the fact that his chosen one did not share
his view.

"I am told that your mama has graced this evening
with her presence, Lady Olivia," he observed as they
went down the line. "May I say how very happy I am to
know that she is in better health. So unfortunate that I
have missed her each time I called in Mount Street.
Perhaps I might have the pleasure of meeting her a little
later." Here he was obliged to break off, as the dance
separated them. When they were reunited, Olivia made
no allusion to his request, and he hesitated to repeat it as
she was wearing what he termed her haughty look,
which because she was rather taller than he was, still
tended to unnerve him slightly.

At the conclusion of the dance, however, he made to
escort her to where her mama and aunt were seated, but
they had not taken more than a few steps when she
suddenly exclaimed, "Oh, do forgive me, Mr.
Antrobus. I have just seen a friend for whom I have a
most particular message. Thank you so much for—for
the dance."

Before he·could say a word, she was gone, disappearing into the crowd as fleet and graceful as a bird.
He stood, peevishly disconsolate for a moment, and
then, brightening, he strutted off toward the place
where he had seen the duchess sitting with Lady Sefton
on one side and Mrs. Gilbey on the other.

"Ladies," he said, braving the surprised stares of the
duchess and Lady Sefton as his ingratiating bow
incorporated them all. And then, in a low confiding
murmur directed at Mrs. Gilbey, "I am delighted to
find her gace here this evening—and your good self, of
course. I wonder, would you be so kind as to introduce
me to Lady Olivia's mama? She was about to do so herself when she was—er, unavoidably involved
elsewhere."

Mrs. Gilbey looked in dismay at the faintly ridiculous

figure before her, and unable to think of an excuse for refusing, turned reluctantly toward her sister, who had turned away again and was nodding at some confidence of Lady Sefton's.

Olivia, meanwhile, in endeavoring to put as much distance as possible between herself and Mr. Antrobus, was heedless of where she went. She was finally brought up short by a familiar sardonic voice saying, ''Running away again, my lady?''

Six

"MR. ST. CLAIR!"

He was the last person she had expected to see, yet here he was, attired with perfect propriety, while still managing to exude a distinct air of decadence.

"Well, Lady Olivia?" he persisted with teasing emphasis.

She was tempted to ignore him and turn on her heel, but knew that he was not that easy to rebuff. "Well indeed, sir," she said, evading the question by going on to the offensive. "I had not thought to find you entering this temple of rectitude."

His laughter was for once quite genuine. "Touché! Not quite my style, is it? I confess I haven't worn knee smalls in a long time, but—" the irony was minimal— "let us say it was something of a point of honor with me to conquer this, the last bastion of respectability. And as I happened to be acquainted with the Countess Lieven . . ."

"Really?" Olivia's surprise was hardly flattering, but he acknowledged it by no more than a brief quirk of the eyebrow.

"Really. We met in Russia a year or so back when I was a guest of the Czar, who wished me to advise him on his projected purchase of certain Chinese artifacts." He saw her eyes widen in surprise. "I have spent some considerable time in China, you see," he concluded gently, "so that it is a subject on which I can claim to be more than usually knowledgeable."

She bit her lip, vexed by the implied reproof. "The Prince Regent has a passion for all things Chinese. His pavilion at Brighton is purported to contain many such treasures. Perhaps he too would be glad to consult you."

"He already has," St. Clair said calmly, and this time it was her turn to laugh.

"I'm sorry. That will teach me to get on my high ropes! Is there anywhere you *haven't* been?"

He appeared to consider the point. "Any number of places, I daresay, if I could but bring them to mind." His gentle teasing disarmed her, and enabled her to hold her own with ease as they conversed.

Countess Lieven, coming upon them presently, found them in an unusually amicable mood, and it pleased the haughty wife of the Russian ambassador, well known for her love of intrigue, to foster this curious acquaintance. "Ah, here you are, Monsieur St. Clair. I was told you had arrived. And Lady Olivia, also." Her sharp eyes flicked over the slim graceful figure. "How very charming you look, my dear. As for you, sir—" she tapped St. Clair's arm playfully with her fan— "the waltz is about to commence. No doubt you would like to dance it with this enchanting young lady? So—you have our permission." She waved a dismissive hand and strolled away, leaving Olivia in a state of wild uncertainty.

St. Clair watched her too-expressive face in some amusement. "You are no doubt aware that Madame's permission amounts to a royal command?" he said softly. "It would hardly be politic to affront so powerful a lady."

"As if you cared for anyone's opinion!" she exclaimed. And then, annoyed that he had the ability to make her feel gauche, "Forgive me. That was extremely impolite."

"But true, I fear."

Olivia bit her lip. "Even so, it is not my place to comment. I do so despise people who make assumptions about others based purely on gossip."

"Then you must allow me to tell you that you are a most extraordinary young lady." He smiled as color flooded her face, making her dark eyes sparkle. "And that opinion is based wholly on observation, not assumption."

The conversation was becoming dangerously personal. Olivia strove to redress the balance. "We are straying from the point, sir, which is that Madame de Lieven will never notice whether or not you dance with me, and I am sure you would much rather waltz with Lady Bryony."

"I am sorry to seem carping, but that is another popular misconception. Lady Bryony does have a life of her own—as do I. She is elsewhere this evening. But even if she were not, I would still very much like to waltz with you."

"Oh." Olivia caught her breath. "Well, I am not sure. You see, Mama is here."

"Ah. And you fear she may react badly, seeing us together?"

"Almost certainly." Her voice held an unconscious wistfulness.

He smiled, and as the music began, he held out his arms. "Well," he said coaxingly, "we could always blame the countess."

And because a traitorous part of her wanted very much to waltz with this man, who would be accomplished in the dance as in all else, she allowed him to lead her onto the floor. They had not gone halfway around the room when she realized the enormity of her mistake. She had danced with many gentlemen over the past weeks, but never once had her body reacted in such a treacherous fashion! The music seemed to pulse in her veins, awakening in her a totally unexpected sensual awareness which delighted in the possessive warmth of his hand as it drew her ever closer until she could feel his breath stirring the hair that fell in soft curls across her brow. Shamelessly carried away, she reveled in his closeness—the tautness of his thigh touching hers as he whirled her around until the lights above them became dizzying fragments of brilliance.

"And I thought you were such a proper young lady!" he mocked, his voice little more than a soft breath against her ear, but bringing with it some belated measure of sanity.

How could she have so far forgotten herself? Had anyone noticed? Her step faltered, but St. Clair's firm hold steadied her. "There is nothing to fear," he assured her, as though reading her thoughts. "It doesn't show—except to me!"

He watched with interest as the betraying color stole into her cheeks. "Who *were* you running away from earlier?"

The question—the need to think, to answer—helped to steady her racing pulse, bringing some small measure of composure. "Mr. Antrobus," she told him, and was moderately pleased that only the faintest tremor remained to betray her agitation. "He wishes to marry me."

"The devil he does!" The suddenly increased pressure of St. Clair's hand was momentarily disconcerting, but she strove to ignore it. "And you?"

Olivia shook her head. "I—it isn't that simple."

"Such things seldom are," he said enigmatically. "Do I know this Antrobus?"

The thought made her smile. "I shouldn't think so. He is tedious in the extreme."

"He doesn't sound the kind of person usually admitted to Almack's."

"He isn't. In fact, he is the most dreadful mushroom. No one really likes him, but his mother's family, though dull, have an impeccable pedigree and have friends in high places, as well as being distantly connected to Lady Bessborough . . ." She heard herself saying the words and wondered in some dismay how often he had been spoken of in just such a contemptuous fashion. Instinctively, her glance flew to St. Clair's face and the grimness she read in his eyes was clear enough. She said helplessly, "I didn't mean . . ."

Her very genuine distress made him speak more harshly than he had intended. "My dear Lady Olivia, do stop apologizing. I have no sensitivity, no delusions of grandeur. Anything of that nature was knocked out of me a long time ago. Now, the world must take me for what I am, or not at all."

Most people would have looked away, but she continued to meet his eyes, her own dark and brilliant with some deep-held passion that moved him strangely.

"Do you still gamble?" she asked.

St. Clair was taken aback, and then found himself warming once more to this girl whose mood could change like quicksilver. A moment ago she had been disturbingly, enticingly aware of him as a man. And yet now, while her contemporaries dreamed romantic dreams as they dipped and swayed and made social small talk, she seemed quite oblivious of any incongruity in wishing to discuss his penchant for gambling.

"But of course. Not perhaps in the way you mean, not now—or hardly ever." There was a touch of the pirate in his sudden grin. "But I am reckless by nature—ambitious people usually are. Except that with the years I have learned to harness it to my advantage, so that nowadays I temper speculation with judgment."

"I probably shouldn't say so, but I do admire you for what you have achieved! You could so easily have slunk away in despair and bitterness after what happened, and spent the rest of your life bemoaning your fate. But you met adversity head-on and made your own destiny. In these past few years I often used to wish that I had been born a man!"

This was said with so much feeling that instinctively his arms tightened about her, though he answered with the ghost of a laugh, "Never say so! That would have been a terrible waste, my dear!"

Olivia blinked, uncertain whether to take him seriously or not. And then the music came to an end. It had been but a few moments in time, a few turns of the ballroom, and yet it seemed as though they had traveled a very long way together and she didn't want it to end. She felt more alive than she had ever done, and there were suddenly so many more things she wanted to know—to ask him.

Mr. Antrobus, meanwhile, upon the departure of Lady Sefton, had proceeded to outline his credentials to the bewildered duchess, and had thereafter kept up, virtually unaided, an unceasing flow of small talk until she had finally disconcerted him by falling asleep. Had it been anyone else, he would have thought himself insulted, but he consoled himself with the thought that her grace's constitution was delicate and must occasionally subject her to excusable quirks of behavior.

He looked uncertainly at Mrs. Gilbey, who might have felt more sorry for him had she not several times been obliged to waft her fan in front of her face, ostensibly as an antidote to the heat, but in reality to hide her own yawns. "I rather think that my sister has outrun her strength," she offered as he seemed to require some explanation.

"Quite so. But, do you feel I should remain?" he asked anxiously. "I would not for the world have her grace think me impolite!"

"I am sure such a thought would never enter my sister's head," she told him with perfect truth. "Do, pray, feel free to leave. You must have a great many other things you will wish to be doing, I daresay."

"Well . . . I . . ." He rose and bowed, a faint creaking betraying the presence of a corset beneath his immaculate waistcoat as he did so. "I had hoped that Lady Olivia . . ." He cleared his throat, "but it seems she is otherwise engaged."

As he departed, Mrs. Gilbey sighed her relief and

turned her attention once more to the dancers. A waltz
had just begun. She thought the music very pretty—so
gay and lilting—though she was still not quite certain
whether she entirely approved of the dance itself—there
was a certain want of delicacy—but then, now that
Almack's had accepted it, there could be no real
objection, and it was rather splendid to watch the
couples whirling around the floor.

And then she saw them—and for a moment felt quite
faint.

It was unfortunate that Honoria should choose this
precise moment to wake up. She did so like a child,
blinking at the light and staring about her.

"Ah, he has gone," she said. "Such a tedious man! I
never knew anybody to take so long to say so little,
which I suppose is neither here nor there. He is certainly
much enamored of Olivia, though I am sure she can do
much better for herself. By the way, where *is* Olivia?"

"I believe," Mrs. Gilbey began, desperately casting
about her for some convincing tale, but before she could
contrive one, Honoria exclaimed, "Ah, I believe I can
see her, dancing with a most handsome-looking gentleman. How well they look together! Who is he, Constance, do you know?"

Mrs. Gilbey suddenly felt very hard done by; not only
had she been obliged to endure Mr. Antrobus, but now
her dearest niece had put her in the most dreadful
quandary. Quite suddenly she was tired of shielding
Honoria from every ill wind that blew; she did not know
how Olivia had managed it for so long.

"As a matter of fact I do know," she said defiantly.
"The gentleman is Mr. Damian St. Clair."

There—the words were out. She waited for the worst
to happen. There was a shocked gasp followed by
silence. She chanced a sideways glance and saw that
Honoria was sitting forward, her figure tense as she
watched the couple's progress.

"So that is Mr. St. Clair. Well, I'm bound to say that
I would never have recognized him. Of course, it was all

a very long time ago, and he was no more than a youth. Nevertheless, I confess I am astonished to see him here. He must possess a great deal of address to have persuaded the patronesses to accept him, for unless matters have changed, gentlemen in particular are selected with the greatest care.''

''Oh, he has address right enough,'' agreed Mrs. Gilbey dryly. ''He also has all the power that comes with success on a grand scale, and such gentlemen, I find, usually get what they want!''

The duchess made no immediate answer; in fact, she was silent for so long that Mrs. Gilbey became apprehensive again. She was already preparing in her mind to deal with one of her sister's attacks when she surprised her yet again by saying with unaccustomed firmness: ''I have made up my mind. I shall meet him.''

Mrs. Gilbey stared. ''But, would that be wise? Might it not upset you dreadfully to meet the person who—''

''My dear Constance, I hope I may be magnanimous enough to extend the olive branch! Surely you must see that it foolish beyond measure to prolong a feud that was none of my making? Do see if you can catch Olivia's eye when the dance ends and indicate to her that she may bring Mr. St. Clair to me.''

I must see! Mrs. Gilbey fumed inwardly. And this from the woman who until today had referred to Mr. St. Clair disparagingly and with infinite bitterness as ''*that man*!'' What Mrs. Gilbey *did* see, and what disturbed her greatly, was that Honoria had suddenly discovered that her erstwhile *bête noir* was not only an exceedingly attractive gentleman—he was, which was much more to the point, an exceedingly rich gentleman. And it became an object with her from that moment to ensure that, insofar as she could prevent it, Olivia should not be coerced by her mother into the invidious position of attempting to ensnare Mr. St. Clair.

Olivia could scarcely believe her eyes when she saw her aunt's signal to her. Surely she could not mean—could not intend her to bring Mr. St. Clair across? Mama would have a fit on the spot! But no, for there was Mama nodding graciously. Olivia's mind, already in a state of confusion, seemed to function on two separate levels as she presented her partner. A swift glance at her aunt produced only an enigmatic lift of the eyebrows so that she could have no idea what had precipitated such a dramatic change of heart.

As a result, she scarcely heard a word of the exchange between St. Clair and her mama until the moment came for him to take his leave, when Mama said almost benignly, that should he care to call in Mount Street, Mrs. Gilbey would, she was sure, be pleased to receive him. But his look as he passed Olivia was such that she could scarcely fail to understand it—she had seen that faint curl of the lip too often, usually when people sought to ingratiate themselves with him.

"Honestly, Pom, I could have curled up and died on the spot!" she cried later. "How could she do such a complete about-face when everyone knew how bitter she was about what happened? I shouldn't wonder if it doesn't give him a general disgust of us!"

"Oh, that's coming it a bit strong, Livvy," Mr. Pommeroy protested. "Best thing all around, I'd say. Clears the air. No reason to fly up in the boughs that I can see."

Except, thought Olivia, sunk in irrational despair, that St. Clair will now be wondering how far my views have influenced Mama! It ought not to matter what he thought, but in view of her shameless behavior during the dance, pride if nothing else dictated that it did.

She did not see him again that evening, nor did he attempt to avail himself of her mama's invitation, which only served to convince her that she had been right.

"Are you sure you have done nothing to dissuade Mr. St. Clair?" the duchess demanded when several days had passed without his putting in an appearance.

"No, Mama, I have not. I have not even seen him. And I wish you will not refine upon it so much! Goodness! One waltz hardly constitutes a declaration of undying passion, and in any case—'' She stopped abruptly, remembering the gossip she had overheard at Lady Bryony's on that very first evening. When her aunt looked curiously at her, she concluded lamely, ''he has a very pretty little Indian mistress to satisfy his needs!''

''My dear, there is no need to be coarse,'' the duchess reproved faintly. ''Such . . . arrangements are common, I believe, in hot countries. And not only there. Gentlemen sometimes have . . . well, certain needs which marriage alone cannot satisfy.'' She was looking distinctly ill at ease. ''If one is sensible, one learns to ignore such little weaknesses.''

Olivia guessed with sudden bitterness that her papa had been unfaithful as well as improvident. ''Well, I am sure I could never do so!'' she said hotly. ''Not that the argument is relevant in this case, for even if St. Clair *were* hanging out for a wife, which I am sure he is not, I have no intention of entering the lists as a possible contender!''

Her mama pokered up. ''I am sure such an expectation never crossed by mind.''

Mrs. Gilbey put in quickly, ''Well, I am very glad to hear it, Honoria, for I don't think it would do at all.''

''No more do I,'' said Olivia, with rather more decision than was called for—or so her aunt thought.

Lady Crockforth's decision to invite the ladies of Mount Street to take tea with her was a conciliatory gesture on her part. Relations between herself and the duchess had been cool ever since the, in her opinion, trifling incident of the water jug. However, since she herself was not a woman to bear grudges and could not understand people who did, and since the duchess was due to return to Bath almost immediately following Elizabeth Thorton's come-out, she was quite prepared to ''do the right thing.'' As an extra inducement, Lady Crockforth had invited several other guests with whom

the duchess stood on good terms, including Mrs.
Thornton and her elder girl, who would be company for
Olivia.

Olivia had not been sure how her mama would react;
to be visiting so close to the house that she had once
called home might well overset her nerves. But to
everyone's surprise she exhibited a remarkable
resilience, even to the extent of being curious to see
what, if any, changes Mr. St. Clair might have effected,
and noticing with approval the shadowy figure of a
porter beyond the glass of the vestibule, which suggested that, whatever else he might be, St. Clair was not
penny-pinching.

"Truth to tell, I never cared for Egan House above
half," she maintained dismissively. "The fires in many
of the rooms smoked quite abominably, so that the
children were forever coughing their hearts up whenever
one brought them to town. I cannot tell you how many
times I begged Meriton to have something done about
it, but the chimney in his library behaved admirably,
and as he spent much of his time at one or other of his
clubs when we were in residence, he could never be convinced of the need." The duchess moved with a swift-
ness surprising in one so frail to claim one of the few
comfortable chairs among the spartan furnishings
which her ladyship had doubtless inherited from her
equally spartan mama. "I dare swear," she concluded,
"that a gentleman as fastidious as Mr. St. Clair will not
tolerate such discomforts, and will have already made
many improvements!"

Lady Crockforth was intrigued by the hint of
indulgence with which that once-hated name tripped off
the duchess's tongue. She directed an inquiring glance at
Constance Gilbey, who endeavored to seem unaware.
"Never had any trouble with the chimneys m'self," she
said, vowing to discover what had brought about such a
change in Honoria. "Imelda, do come away from that
window."

"Yes dear, of course, I wast just . . . that is . . ."

She lowered her voice to a confiding whisper. "One of *those* men—you know the ones I mean, Gertrude—is there again!"

Both Olivia and Jane pricked up their ears as Mrs. Thornton obliged them by saying in an amused way, "Why, what is this, ma'am? Is there some mystery afoot?"

"Only in Imelda's fertile imagination," said Lady Crockforth dismissively as two footmen entered bearing trays, one of which was set before her so that she might infuse the tea. "She has this cork-brained notion that St. Clair is being watched. A complete farrago of nonsense, of course. Comes from reading too many gothic novels. Mrs. Radcliffe and her like have much to answer for, in my opinion!"

"It is not nonsense, Gertrude!" Her sister's voice quivered with the force of her emotions. "I have taken the most careful note of their comings and goings—four of them, and they walk past the house at the same times each day and—and look up at the windows!"

Olivia and Jane exchanged glances, the same thought going through both their minds as they strolled casually across to stand beside Miss Imelda. "How exciting!" Jane exclaimed. "I do so love a mystery! Do tell us, ma'am, what do these men look like?"

Sadly, the question found Miss Imelda less than helpful. "You see, it is so difficult to—to describe them precisely. I mean, they are not in themselves remarkable, though I am quite certain that it is one of the same four men each time. In fact—" she had glanced down as she was speaking and now pointed excitedly—"yes, there is one of them now! Do you not see how furtively he pauses just for a moment to look up at the windows of the house?"

Both girls craned their necks eagerly. There was indeed a man walking slowly along the opposite pavement, but as to whether his movements could be termed suspicious?

"Did you ever hear such a tarradiddle?" Lady Crockforth was fast losing patience. "Young ladies, pray do not encourage my sister's fantasies. Come now and take your tea." Her voice sharpened. "Imelda, sit down."

With a half-defiant whimper, the timid Miss Imelda allowed the kindly Jane to lead her to her chair.

"Well, if it is burglary these people are contemplating," said the duchess, "I am sure that a gentleman with Mr. St. Clair's resources will have ample staff to repel them. That servant who goes everywhere with him must be enough to terrify all but the most persistent villain."

This new conciliating attitude of Honoria's was so out of character as to demand Lady Crockforth's attention; quick-witted as she was, it scarcely needed the embarrassment on Constance Gilbey's face to illuminate matters. So that was it. Honoria had decided that St. Clair's past misdeeds could, with justifiable prudence, be overlooked in consideration of his present fortune! Well, she might cast out all the lures she pleased, but she would find him a slippery fish to land—and even more slippery to hold!

Mrs. Gilbey, in an attempt to deflect Gertrude's train of thought, said lightly, "I was asking Arabella Bryony about Hassan only the other day. A fascinating story! As a child he was stolen from his father's fishing boat by pirates, who presented him to the Bey of Algiers, who in turn sold him to a rich Persian merchant who treated him with unspeakable cruelty. St. Clair was visiting the merchant one day when he found the boy trying to take his own life. He immediately offered a price for him that the merchant could not refuse, and Hassan has been his shadow ever since."

Olivia thought it was exactly the sort of thing St. Clair would do, though the opinions of the rest varied considerably, which led to a lively discussion. This enabled her to linger near the window unnoticed for a few precious moments. She wanted more time to study the man pointed out to them by Miss Imelda. But it was not easy to distinguish his features for he wore a greatcoat with several capes, the collar turned up, and the brim of his hat obscured the greater part of his face. However, she was almost certain that he was not the man who had accosted Damian St. Clair in the park. That being so, she might have dismissed the whole thing as the fiction Lady Crockforth declared it to be, had she not become aware that beyond the muslin curtains opposite, several figures were just discernible—watching the watcher, perhaps?

Seven

AT ELIZABETH THORNTON'S coming-out ball, Olivia acquired a new suitor. Sir Greville Barton was an acquaintance of Mr. Thornton's as well as being one of the gentlemen suggested by Mr. Gilbey as a possible husband.

"I don't understand what Papa can possibly find to like in him," Jane confided to Olivia when the formal reception was at an end. "He—" she shuddered— "he put a clammy finger beneath my chin and murmured that I was a fine figure of a woman, and I tell you, Livvy, I felt unclean!"

Olivia knew exactly what she meant, but as her uncle also appeared to find him tolerably acceptable, she was obliged to conclude that in the company of gentlemen, his behavior was unexceptional. Sir Greville was nearer fifty than forty, and indeed, there was nothing immediately repellant about him; in fact, she supposed he was not ill-looking if one discounted a rather unhealthy pallor and a pair of slightly protuberant eyes. He was fastidious in his dress, took snuff, and wafted a handkerchief in a fashion which might in other circumstances have been amusing, but unlike the tenacious Mr. Antrobus, there was nothing in the least comical about him.

"Y'r servant, Lady Olivia," he said upon being intro-

duced to her. "It has long been my wish to make y'r
acquaintance." He had raised her hand to his lips, and
his touch and the familiar way those eyes roved over
her, made her long to slap his face.

She managed to curtail the impulse, and had murmured all the right things before making her escape,
firmly resolved to tell her aunt at the first opportunity
that she could not, if it meant going barefoot for the rest
of her days, entertain the idea of Sir Greville as a
husband. Fortunately, the opening country dance of the
evening was already bespoken by Pom, as were several
later ones by different partners, so that she managed to
evade his pleas for the honor of dancing with her by
giving the impression that her card was filled.

"Don't know much about the fellow m'self." Pom
was vague. "Except that I've seen him frequenting some
pretty rum places."

"Oh, well—I don't intend to let him spoil my
evening."

Someone else had reason to feel less than content with
the way the evening had begun. Jane found Mr.
Perveral looking disconsolate, unable to tear his gaze
from where Elizabeth held court, beseiged by a host of
admirers.

"She does look lovely this evening, does she not?" he
said, catching a brief glimpse of the vivacious figure as
she laughed and chattered unceasingly.

"Very lovely," agreed Jane without a trace of envy.
"It is her night, after all. But why are you not wor-
shipping with the rest?"

He sighed. "Your sister had already promised me a
cotillion—or so I thought. But it seems that she also
promised it to Lord Brixham, so I agreed to waive my
claim."

"That was very naughty of Elizabeth—and you are
more generous than she deserves. But she *is* very
young."

"Yes, she is, isn't she?" he said.

Jane felt so sorry for him. On an impulse she said, "I

am not promised for the cotillion. If you would not find me too impossible a substitute, I am more than willing to take her place.''

Harry Peveral looked at Jane as if seeing her for the first time. He knew about her past grief, of course, but he had been so obsessed with her sister that he had taken her presence very much for granted. Now he looked into her pleasant, smiling eyes and thought what a waste it was that Fate should have treated her so unkindly.

''My dear ma'am,'' he said gallantly, ''I should consider it a very great honor.''

Olivia had managed to get through to suppertime without encountering Sir Greville again. She had seen him at one time in earnest conversation with her mama, but had kept her distance until he left.

''He is very much taken with you,'' the duchess said, bemoaning the fact that her daughter had just missed seeing him. ''However, I have assured him that you will be pleased to partner him before the evening is out.''

''Mama, you had no right to make promises on my behalf!'' she insisted, with so much vehemence that several ladies sitting nearby looked across.

''Nonsense, child. A mother has every right to secure her daughter's interest. And I may say I do not care for your tone!''

Mrs. Gilbey looked at her niece's face and said placatingly, ''Well, you know, Honoria—it is entirely possible that dear Olivia has not a free dance to bestow.''

This was not entirely true, but Olivia threw her a grateful glance, nonetheless.

''Always found Barton an oily individual m'self,'' she heard Lady Crockforth say in what her ladyship blithely assumed to be a murmured aside.

''*Some people*,'' declared the duchess, without acknowledging that she had heard, ''are quite unable to appreciate qualities that are obvious to others. I hope, Olivia, that you will not be swayed by superficial judgments.''

Fortunately for all concerned, Mr. Thornton at that moment arrived with Prinny, who had been prevailed upon to grace his daughter's come-out with a brief visit. The Regent, his mammoth figure richly garbed in tight white breeches and a coat of cerise satin liberally adorned with Orders, was in an expansive mood. He made much of Elizabeth, who was for once shy and incoherent, before passing on, nodding graciously to all, stopping now and again to speak to Lady Jersey and Lady Cowper and many other people he knew. When he came to the duchess, a word from Mr. Thornton brought Prinny to a halt. He greeted her effusively, his plump, raddled face sympathetic as he recalled his old friend Meriton.

"And this is your beautiful daughter, what?" he exclaimed, lifting Olivia from her deep curtsy. "Yes, of course. The very image of y'r grandmother, God rest her. A much loved lady!"

"Your highness is very kind," she murmured.

"Not kind at all. We were all in love with her, as I recall!" He tapped Olivia's cheek before passing on.

"Well!" said the duchess, much moved. "Only fancy his remembering me after all this time! And as for his addressing you so particularly, my love—I shouldn't wonder if your consequence goes up by leaps and bounds as a result of this evening's accolade!"

Olivia was not unmindful of the honor done to her; she only hoped that it did not impress the wrong people—or to be more specific, the wrong person. But as Pom had promised to take her in to supper, Sir Greville did not have an opportunity to accost her.

"I must join the family party," Jane said with good-humored resignation. "The prince is pleased to take supper with us, especially as Papa has invited Lady Bryony and Mr. St. Clair to join us."

"Well, Arabella was ever a royal favorite," Mr. Pommeroy said obliquely.

"And Mr. St. Clair is also on excellent terms with the Prince," added Olivia.

Pom stared at her. "Now, how would you know a thing like that?" he demanded.

"Never you mind. I don't tell you everything." She put up her chin at him, but grew a trifle pink nonetheless. To cover her embarrassment, she said teasingly to Jane, "Supper with the Prince Regent! That quite eclipses my little encounter. You will scarcely condescend to speak to us afterward, I daresay!"

"We shall see. At all events, I shan't be like Elizabeth, who declares that she won't be able to eat a thing. Whatever else, I certainly don't intend to let all this high living spoil my appetite!"

Harry Peveral, listening to all this good-natured banter, found himself smiling. Jane, he was fast discovering, might not have her sister's beauty, but she was the greatest fun to be with—a fact that he communicated to the others as they addressed themselves to the long tables laid out with all manner of delicacies, displayed in dishes of silver and gold latticework.

"Yes indeed, I am devoted to Jane," Olivia exclaimed as she tried to decide between lobster or crab patties. "A friend who combines the qualities of honesty, truthfulness, and good humor must be rare, and Jane is all of those things. Oh, Pom, those glazed pigeons look quite delicious, but I am sure I shouldn't succumb! Perhaps, as you are having one, I might steal just one tiny leg?"

Pom, his plate already piled high, said loftily that most ladies of his acquaintance never gave a thought to food and were content to nibble at the merest morsel, never mind stealing the most succulent *bonne-bouche* from their partner's mouth. And so the amicable argument continued throughout supper.

Some time after supper, Olivia was standing alone and a little apart, watching the sets beginning to form for a quadrille and listening with a half-smile to her unusually animated mama regaling all who would listen with a verbatim account of everything the Prince had said to her and she to him, including his kind words concerning her daughter.

"Ah, Lady Olivia! At last I find y' without a partner! Now, perhaps I may crave the pleasure of leading you out in the dance?"

There was no escape. She looked about her desperately as Sir Greville advanced. "I—that is, I was just looking for . . ." Heavens, what was she to do—to say? He was smiling, showing discolored teeth, extending a hand.

"For me, perchance?" His fingers were already closing on her wrist when another voice said smoothly, "My dear Lady Olivia, forgive me for keeping you waiting. This is our quadrille, I believe?"

She turned very slowly to find Mr. St. Clair regarding her in that bright, piercing way she was coming to know so well. In her relief, she scarcely stopped to question why, when he had made no attempt to come near her since the night at Almack's, he was here now and claiming a dance. Instead, she seized on the opportunity he was offering her to rid herself of Sir Greville.

Contriving an arch smile, she peeped up at him through fluttering eyelashes. "Why, yes, of course. Wicked man! I had almost given you up for lost." His eyebrow quirked, while Sir Greville turned an angry red and showed some reluctance to release her. There followed an uneasy moment when nothing happened, except that the air between the two men seemed to crackle with something more than a mere dispute over a dance partner.

"You heard the Lady Olivia," St. Clair said softly. "The quadrille is mine."

Sir Greville's fingers bit deeper into her flesh. "And the lady, too, mayhap?" he sneered, and then, seeing the expression in St. Clair's eyes, beads of perspiration began to stand out on his forehead.

"Were it not for the distress it would cause the

Thorntons, I would ram those words down your throat, here and now."

The softly spoken threat sent a chill through Olivia. She knew she must intervene before something terrible happened. "Sir Greville, I find your insolence quite insupportable. Either you release me this instant or I shall be obliged to summon Mr. Thornton." She lifted her chin a fraction and glanced pointedly at her still-imprisoned wrist. "This instant, sir."

For a moment it seemed as if he would call her bluff. Then he glared at St. Clair, muttered "Servant, ma'am," and strode away.

"Majestically accomplished. I make you my compliments." St. Clair's voice was expressionless. He took her arm to lead her onto the floor, and the latent violence emanating from him sent waves of shock tingling through her.

She came to an abrupt halt, and he glanced down at her with simmering intolerance. "What now?"

"Sir," she said, with a courage she had not known she possessed, "I have no idea what is between you and Sir Greville, but I have a great dislike of being made to feel like a bone that has been tossed between two snarling dogs!"

There followed a frightening silence, which lasted only seconds but seemed like hours. Then, to her amazement, he uttered a short laugh and said with surprising mildness, "You dare much, proud ingrate. But, as usual, with good reason. It was not well done of me and I offer you my apologies."

This had the immediate effect of making Olivia glaringly aware of her own ungraciousness; he had, after all, done her no small service by his intervention. And what was said thereafter was in defense of her good name. Her attempts to thank him, however, were cut short. "I want no thanks. Now, may we proceed?"

"Mr. St. Clair, I *am* grateful, but there is no need to take this any further. Sir Greville is gone."

"Don't be a fool," he said, and swept her willy-nilly

toward the waiting sets. "Dammit, must you always be
so reluctant? I don't usually have this trouble, let me tell
you!"

His insistence, his masterly presence, filled her with a
heady excitement that drove caution to the winds. "No,
I daresay women fall over themselves in order to attain
the privilege of dancing with you," she teased him gaily.
"Which is very bad for you, and no doubt helps to give
you that impossible air of consequence!"

"The devil!" he retorted. "And who was so coming,
pray, as to play the conquette, beguiling me with soft
words? How did it go? *Wicked man! I had almost given
you up!*" His mimicry was so perfect that the laughter
came bubbling up in her. "And do not attempt to deny
it, for your words are engraved on my heart."

"Oh, how unfair! You know very well that it was just
a device to make it sound more convincing."

"It certainly convinced me," he murmured
equivocally as the music began.

While they performed the figure of the *chaine
Anglaise* a question burned unasked within Olivia, but it
wasn't until he took her hands in his to perform the *tour
de main* that she found the courage to voice it.

"Why *did* you come to my aid?"

As he swung her around she saw the skin tighten
round his mouth. "Why?" he repeated the word softly,
as if speaking to himself. "Because your eyes had something of the look of a hunted animal."

"Oh!" It was little more than a whisper.

"And also because in my opinion that particular man
should not be allowed near anyone as lovely and un-
spoiled as you."

It was as well that the dance once more divided them,
for Olivia was by now deprived of speech. She had
thought she was coming to understand the rules of
flirtation, but here suddenly was no flowery commonplace, no hint of teasing or flummery, no Spanish coin.
In fact, there was a kind of suppressed anger in his
declaration, but whether it had been roused by Sir

Greville, or by the qualities with which he had—quite
mistakenly, in her opinion—endowed her, was far from
clear. If only his moods did not change like the wind—it
was very unsettling.

Little else passed between them, and when the dance
came to an end he returned her immediately to her
mama and aunt, and stayed only for the barest
courtesies before making his bow and leaving them.

"Such an odd man," mused the duchess. "There is a
distinguished air about him that is quite marked. One
had only to watch him in conversation with the Prince.
They seemed to be on the most intimate terms and there
was no the slightest hint of subservience in his manner."
She continued to prattle away, heedless of the effect her
words were having on her daughter. "And then, of
course, there was the masterful way he cut in on Sir
Greville! I do hope he will not take offense," she said,
suddenly bethinking herself that several irons in the fire
were better than one. "But then, I daresay you will find a
way to explain matters to him, my love. As for St. Clair, it
is my opinion that too much living in hot countries among
savages cannot be good for any man. One hopes that he
does not mean to return to India."

Olivia, feeling that no answer was called for, made
none. For her part, the sooner Mr. St. Clair returned from
whence he came, the sooner would her life return to
normal—for good or ill.

Hassan silently entered the breakfast room and
presented to his master the silver salver upon which lay a
single letter. Receiving no order to withdraw, he stood
impassively behind St. Clair Sahib's chair to await events.
His life and his master's were as one. It had been so since
the day St. Clair Sahib had found him, a small despairing
boy, trying to sever his wrists, and had given him back his
pride and self-respect.

St. Clair took his time, reading the letter through several
times. And when he had done so, he continued to sit
sprawled in the big chair, staring into space, his long,

muscular legs hidden beneath wide white cotton trousers stretched out beneath the table, and over them a tunic of raw silk edged with gold braid open at the neck, while a long, loose robe of the same silk, handsomely embroidered with gold dragons, carelessly trailed the floor. Suddenly, he flung the letter down, scraped back his chair, and strode across to the window where he stood staring down into the garden, his expression as inscrutable as that of his servant.

"Who delivered it, Hassan? Do you know?"

"The porter was taking breakfast, lord. There was a loud knocking at the door, but by the time the miserable servant who was set to keep guard had opened it, there was only the letter lying on the step."

St. Clair pushed his hands deep into the pockets of his robe and cursed softly. "No matter. We both know who sent it."

Hassan bowed his head in assent.

"The devil of it is, knowing isn't much help." He half-turned and met his servant's eyes. "The letter, however, takes a new tack. It threatens the life of Aysha if the Golden Eye of Adjamir is not returned."

A shiver of anger ran through the huge figure. "They shall not harm the little one while I live, lord."

Just for a moment something approaching a wry smile touched St. Clair's mouth. "That much I believe, oh terrible one, though you can hardly guard both our backs single-handed! No, I must think. Rashid's powers are limited here, but the hand in the letter is Kendall's and I have no doubt he and Rashid will have been given leave by the rani and the yuvaraj to recruit as many men as they need to do what they have to do."

"Then I shall kill Kendall Sahib—and Rashid also."

St. Clair shook his head. "This is London, Hassan, not Adjamir. You cannot go around killing people at will."

"If you say so, lord." Hassan bowed, deceptively servile.

"That is an order." St. Clair's voice immediately crackled with authority. "Go now, and let me think. And see to it that the door is not left unattended in future."

When alone, he took the jewel from the small leather pouch which hung on a long chain about his neck and never left his person. In the morning sunlight, its many facets glowed with fire, and in its limitless amber-tinted depths he sometimes fancied that it held all the magic and beauty of his adopted land.

Many times he had wondered what chemistry had drawn them together—the powerful Maharaja of Adjamir and the proud but resourceful young outcast from his own land. Their paths had crossed soon after his arrival in India—he little more than a boy and the maharaja already rich in years as in all else, and a great ruler. They had been so far apart in race and rank, and yet kindred spirits from the very first. To the young Damian, the maharaja was the father figure his own father had never been—and to the ruler, he was more precious than the yuvaraj, his heir.

So it was that although Damian traveled and prospered, growing in stature as his merchant fleet expanded to sail the world, it was to Adjamir, that precious jewel set in the northernmost mountains, that he always returned. Everything and everyone that he loved was to be found there, not least the young princess, daughter of the maharaja, whose delicate beauty had enslaved him from the first.

There had been periods of unrest over the years; princes of smaller states within the great ruler's domain who thought to overthrow the old man and claim the kingdom for themselves, but always they had been put down. Only recently, however, had the situation become truly dangerous, and at the heart of the conspiracy this time had been the yuvaraj, Prince Kassim, and his mother, the maharaja's third wife and the only one to give him a son. The rani had long since grown tired of waiting for the old man to die. But Kassim was clever. He had secretly paid others, among them an Englishman named Kendall who had left the East India Company under a cloud, to sow seeds of unrest and to arrange for the assassination of the maharaja while they appeared to remain loyal. It was the purest chance that St. Clair had gotten word of the plot on his return from Europe, and had been in time to warn the ruler, who had put on a great show of strength to crush the rebellion. The yuvaraj and the rani had been under suspicion, but nothing could be proved against them.

But the old man was failing and he knew it, just as he knew that before long they would try again. "It is the will of Allah," he had told Damian, and for the first time there had been a tremor in his voice. "But you must go now, oh son of my heart, and take the little princess with you, for they will never permit her to live."

It was then that he had given Damian the most prized jewel in his possession—the Golden Eye of Adjamir—a near-flawless tinted diamond the size of a pigeon's egg. "It was my bride gift to my first wife, my only love, and I do not wish it to fall into the hands of that scheming woman who now sits in her place. I charge you to hold it in trust for Aysha!"

No doubt it was this gift that had so enraged the rani and her son, and the presence in London now of Kendall and Rashid filled him with apprehension concerning the fate of his old friend, for if he still lived, they would not have left Adjamir. It would take time to discover their whereabouts—and their strength. And he was not sure how much time he had.

It was some while later when, having completed his toilette, he made his way up a short pair of stairs leading to a door. He knocked softly and it was opened by a wizened Indian woman who salaamed several times and bade him enter. The room was large and filled with diffused sunlight which filtered through white muslin curtains to glow upon rich furnishings augmented by many jewel-bright cushions scattered in great heaps.

A slight figure swathed in folds of jade-colored silk rose gracefully from one such pile and hurried toward him, her hands outstretched. "You have come at last, dearest one," she exclaimed in her charming, lilting English. "I have been so restless waiting for you! We shall now go driving in the Park, yes?"

St. Clair caught her to him, his anger melting as

always at the sight of her. "Not this morning, Jewel of my Heart. There are matters of business needing my attention."

He felt her disappointment as keenly as she did herself, for it grieved him to deny her anything. Already she was pining for her homeland, feeling the cold, growing thin and restive—a virtual prisoner in this great house with only the old woman, Muna, for company. Soon she would begin to wilt like any exotic flower plucked from its roots. Too late, he realized how selfish he had been.

He had planned to take Aysha to the country where at least she would have some element of freedom. But personal pride and ambition had overtaken him, and he had vowed not to leave London until he was accepted by all—until every club that had blackballed him opened its doors, until every family of note received him, and until men like Sir Greville Barton, who had so willingly aided and abetted Meriton to discredit him, had been brought low. He had even, God help him, contemplated seducing Meriton's daughter, though that at least he had abandoned. But the rest had accomplished with an ease that astonished him, and much of his success he owed to Arabella, who had dared to defy convention in his behalf.

But in the doing, Aysha's position had become impossible. He had known from the first what was being said of her, and he had made no attempt to quell the gossip. He had even reveled in shocking the sensibilities of the righteous—the more so as he knew that what society so sanctimoniously condemned in him, it conveniently turned a blind eye to among its own.

So he had told himself that Aysha was shy; that she was content with her morning drive and needed no one but himself. A convenient fiction. But he had grown hard in a hard world. It had taken Lady Olivia Egan, with her deceptive fragility and unvanquishable spirit in the face of all that life had thrown at her, to begin to make him see himself as he really was, and he wasn't at all sure whether he liked what he saw.

Eight

THE THORNTONS' drawing room was crowded on the morning following Elizabeth's ball, with people constantly coming and going—a sure sign that the affair had been a resounding success.

"My dear Damian," Arabella Bryony had murmured with a droll laugh as they arrived quite late in the proceedings, "are you perfectly certain that this is what you wish?"

"Certainly. It would have been the height of ill manners not to call, if only to compliment the Thorntons upon the successful launching into society of their beautiful widgeon of a daughter."

She glanced archly at him from beneath the brim of a charming straw villager hat. "Oh, what a quiz! When did you ever play propriety? That bland air of yours doesn't fool me! You are up to something, Damian. I can always tell." Her gaze strayed to take in the company. "Oh, good God! Almost half of Almack's ubiquitous 'seven' are here! Sally Jersey is being charming to the Countess Lieven! You know, of course, that they dislike each other most cordially! And dear Emily Cowper is over there talking to Lady Crockforth and her dab of a sister. And who else do we have? A-ha! Now I begin to understand why we have come! I have just spied Mrs. Gilbey and the duchess, and yes, over there, by the window . . ." Arabella's sparkling eyes challenged him. "Did you know Lady Olivia would be here, I wonder, or was it simply divine inspiration?"

"If you have a failing, my dear Arabella, it is that you are possessed of an overlively imagination," he drawled as Mrs. Thornton came forward to welcome them. "It would be surprising if she were not here, as she and the Thornton girls are such good friends."

Olivia had seen them arrive. Her heart began to thud and it took a determined effort on her part not to follow St. Clair's progress around the room but to concentrate instead upon Harry Peveral, who was asking if it were true that her mama was returning to Bath.

"Yes, tomorrow, if nothing untoward happens in the meantime."

"But you do not go with her?"

"Good gracious, no! Oh, dear," she added ruefully, "that did not sound at all as it ought!"

"Nonsense," said Jane, who had just joined them. "Who, after all, would wish to return to a drab existence in Bath when there are any number of giddy excitements promised here—midsummer masquerades and routs, and picnics in the country. . . . Olivia, did you know that your erstwhile usurper, St. Clair, is here?"

"He is not *my* anything!" Olivia protested, while all her senses were finely attuned to his presence, to the deep, distinctive tones of his voice. He was talking to Mama—she could hear the tinkling sound of her mother's laugh.

"My word, he is even going across to congratulate Elizabeth!" Jane said with a chuckle. "I only hope she may not fall into a quake!"

"Oh, I doubt she will succumb, with so many admirers to uphold her spirits," Harry observed dryly. Jane looked at him quickly, but there was no evidence of his being distressed to see her sister surrounded by so many would-be beaux.

Olivia heard every word, but deliberately focused her

attention on Lady Cowper, who was just leaving, and so she did not see the sudden look exchanged between Harry and Jane, nor was she aware of their moving discreetly out of earshot, though not so far away as to occasion comment.

"Lady Olivia?" St. Clair's voice made her jump. "I wondered if I might find you here this morning."

He has come especially to see me, said a small triumphant voice inside her head, while she made the usual polite reply. He brushed it aside with that half-impatient gesture, his strong-boned features looking more than usually hawkish.

"There is something I wished to ask of you."

Lord's sake! she thought in sudden panic. He can't—he surely wouldn't attempt to propose here in a room full of people. The blood came and went in her face, and then common sense returned. How absurd. She was sure that nothing was further from his mind. If Mama had not put the idea into her head, she would never have considered it a possibility.

"Shall you go riding as usual in the morning?"

The abrupt nature of the question, breaking into her thoughts, flustered Olivia. "No. Mama is leaving for home, and I must be there to see her safely on her way." She was painfully aware of a tenseness in him, as though a strong sensation of emotion were being rigorously suppressed. But before she could continue, he again made the dismissive gesture.

"No matter. Forget it."

"Gladly," she said, braving a snub. "I quite understand. After all, my domestic affairs can be of no possible interest to you."

A gleam came into his eyes. "I make you my compliments. I am well aware that my manners frequently leave much to be desired. It comes of having been too long out of genteel company, in a world where I have only to say 'do this' and it is done."

"What a feeling of power that must give you! I wonder this aimless, indolent life does not pall. It must

seem very trivial by comparison." Her chin lifted
fractionally. "Even I occasionally find its triviality
tedious, and I cannot claim to have accomplished
anything of note."

"Don't belittle yourself," he said roughly. "What
you call nothing—holding your family together at no
small cost to your own prospects, without recrimination, and under circumstances which would have
sunk most young women of your upbringing—is something of which you should be proud. Would that I could
claim to have achieved as much."

Olivia blinked at his vehemence. "You seem to know
a great deal about me."

"I hear things. But that is not important now.
Dammit, there is so much I want you to know, but I
can't tell you here, not with all the gossiping biddies
watching, putting two and two together and making
anything but four! It was ever thus, and some things, it
seems, never change." He looked into her beautiful
sloe-black eyes, bright now with interest, though still
with a hint of wariness in their depths. Would they
shadow and turn from him if he attempted to involve
her? Suddenly impatient to know, he broke into speech.
"When you do next ride," he said with none of his
usual *élan*, "would you do me the kindness of coming
across to my carriage to meet my little Aysha?"

It was outrageous! Also, it was not what she had
expected to hear, what in the deepest recesses of her
heart she had wanted to hear. And in her
disappointment she considered every possible objection.
What would Pom think if she did as he asked? What,
indeed, would anyone think? Lord, it was so outrageous
that had circumstances been otherwise, it would be
comic!

St. Clair watched the myriad expressions flit across
her face, and despair, an emotion quite foreign to him,
caused him to press his case with a low urgency. "Don't
refuse outright, I beg of you. For Aysha's sake, if not
for mine. She is very lonely!"

Olivia quashed the sympathy that flooded momentarily to the surface, and her answer came equally low and quite as urgent. "Mr. St. Clair, you may think me impossibly naive, and perhaps I am in Society's terms. But pray do not insult my intelligence! I do actually understand how cruelly I should be ridiculed if I did as you ask, and I dare swear you have not invited Lady Bryony to console your Indian mistress! So why me? Am I *so* different?"

For a moment his eyes flared with some powerful emotion—not simply anger; if it were not so fanciful she would have said it was nearer to being a kind of raw agony. It grated in his voice. "No, madam, I only thought you were."

He bowed curtly and turned away. A moment later he was at Lady Bryony's side again, and not long afterward they left.

Olivia, her throat thick with unshed tears, regretted her outburst almost at once. She had behaved with the worst kind of condescension and overweening pride—something that she deeply despised in others! Too late, her thoughts turned to the exquisite creature she had so often glimpsed and wondered about. How dreadful her life must be—to be so completely ostracized, alone day after day, a virtual prisoner in Egan House. How deeply she must love St. Clair to endure so much for his sake. And how cruel he must be to subject her to such a life!

The moment after St. Clair left, she was pounced upon by Jane, who was impatient to learn what they had talked about. "My dear, there was such a strangeness about you both that I was sorely tempted to eavesdrop! I am sure you must have quarreled, for he was looking quite fierce when he left!"

Olivia made some vague reply which went no way at all to meet Jane's curiosity, but something in her manner must have warned her friend not to proceed, for quite suddenly Jane said lightly, "Oh, very well. I shan't tease you further."

Her sharp-eyed mother had also marked the time St.

Clair had spent with her, though she saw it quite differently, the brusqueness of his departure having mercifully escaped her attention. "Most encouraging. Longer by far than he accorded anyone else," she observed complacently as they drove home. "It did not go unnoticed, you may be sure!"

Olivia wondered what she would say if she knew what St. Clair had asked of her. Feeling that she could not bear to listen to any more about him, she endeavored to turn the conversation into safer channels by saying what a pleasure it always was to visit the Thorntons, and how happy Mama must be feeling at the thought of seeing the younger members of her own family again.

"Well, of course," she said a trifle plaintively. "I hope I am not so unnatural as to feel otherwise! Although I am sure no one but a mother could know how painful it is to be torn by the ties and duties of parenthood! How one half of me is longing to see my little ones again, while the other half feels an overwhelming sense of duty to remain here where I can advise and guide you, my dear Olivia, at this, the most important moment of your life!"

"Mama!" Olivia looked helplessly at her aunt, sitting opposite her in the carriage. "Mama, you cannot possibly disappoint the children again. They have been expecting you home so many times during these past weeks, and I really don't . . ." She had been about to say "I don't need you," but a placating gesture from Mrs. Gilbey stopped her just in time. "I really don't feel that I can keep you from them any longer. I am sure you can trust Aunt Constance to look to my best interests."

It had been a close-run thing, as she told Jane when the post chaise, with Mr. Gilbey, who had nobly volunteered to see her safely home, riding beside it, had carried Mama from sight amid much waving of handkerchiefs, and to the accompaniment of tears and much last-minute advice. "Aunt Constance and I were utterly drained, for we both knew that it needed but a

word on our parts and Mama would have been out of
the carriage in an instant, which made me feel doubtly
ashamed to be wishing quite so desperately for her to
go!"

"My dear Olivia, you expect too much of yourself!
For heaven's sake, you aren't a saint! You're fallable
like everyone else. The plain fact is that part of your
pleasure in coming to London was to escape from your
mama, if only for a while. It's a perfectly natural
reaction which doesn't in any way make you a monster,
so pray let us have no more of these guilty maunderings,
or I shall begin to think you a tiresome bore!"

It was true, of course. It needed only a glance at her
aunt's face to see how already lines of worry were
fading. In fact, the whole household seemed to give a
great sigh of relief, and with the general lightening in the
atmosphere, Olivia, unable to remain out of spirits for
long, was soon enjoying life once more.

It would be idle to pretend that she did not
occasionally suffer from a vague feeling of depression,
but this was due to quite another cause, and one it
seemed that she was not to be given any opportunity to
remedy. Time and again she heard the scorn in his "*No,
madam, I only thought you were*," when she had asked
if she was so different. That she had deserved his scorn
made it doubly hurtful. In the days that followed she
attended many functions, and everywhere St. Clair was
conspicuous by his absence. Nor did she and Pom
encounter his coach in the Park, from which she could
only assume that he had left town, or had grown tired of
the constant round of pleasure, and had elected to take
his paramour elsewhere for her daily outing.

But life went on, the weather grew warmer, and the
number and variety of delights increased. Venetian
breakfasts were held out of doors, and many a *bal
masque* was planned with talk of gardens being trans-
formed into extravagant worlds of make-believe illu-
minated by colored lanterns. The east side of Berkeley
Square saw a steadily increasing influx of open

carriages, following upon a discreet advertisement in *The Times* by Messrs. Gunther, respectfully informing their honored clients that they had that day received a fresh cargo of ice and were able to offer a plentiful supply of their delectable cream and fruit ices. Also, they would be happy to supply picnic hampers at very competitive prices.

Picnics indeed became the order of the day, and small groups of open landaus could regularly be seen setting off in the direction of Richmond Park, or driving out of town to the home of someone fortunate enough to live adjacent to the river.

Mrs. Gilbey's friend Miss Titherton had just such a house—not by the river, precisely, but in pleasantly wooded countryside near Laleham. She extended an open invitation to Mrs. Gilbey to bring a party down whenever she so pleased, and as a delightful bluebell wood adjoined the garden, it proved an idyllic spot for picnics. Many an afternoon found Miss Titherton, a pale wisp of a woman, sitting on her veranda enjoying a comfortable coze with the older members of the party and watching the playful shimmer of muslin skirts disappearing into the trees, hotly pursued by handsome young gentlemen in their biscuit-colored pantaloons and elegant tailcoats, to the accompanying joyous echoes of much youthful laughter.

"Such innocent fun," she sighed happily. "How it takes me back . . . we were a large family, and there were always friends to swell the numbers!"

Olivia and Jane were content for the most part to let Elizabeth and her friends do all the running about, while they lay back in the shade of the trees reading poetry or being entertained by such of the gentlemen who considered themselves beyond the age of kicking up larks.

"Dashed if I know where they get their energy," Mr. Pommeroy complained gently as some young buck shot past with an eager "Yoicks!" He lay back and covered his face with his hat.

"Oh, poor Pom!" Jane soothed him. "You just lie there and rest. Olivia has her book of John Donne poetry, and will gladly read to you—a love poem, perhaps, or would you prefer something of a more pious nature?"

He lifted the brim of his hat and regarded them both with a baleful eye. "That's a deuced paltry way to treat a friend, I must say. But I am saving myself for this evening, so I refuse to be driven away. You may do your worst." As the evening referred to entailed nothing more tiring than a visit to the theater, where he would undoubtedly doze throughout most of the performance, preceded by dinner at Grillons, this observation merely evoked derisive hoots of laughter.

Of all the pleasures London had to provide, the theater was the one most enjoyed by Olivia. She never tired of it, whether it was Edmund Kean at Drury Lane, or a visit to the Opera, or, as tonight, a special Royal Gala Performance at Covent Garden. Nor did she ever cease to be entertained by the spectacle of fashionable London in the early evening, upon pleasure bent—the clamor of the traffic, the servants rushing from carriages to bang on doors, the multitude of vehicles clattering over the cobbles in all directions so that it was a constant source of wonder to her that they did not all crash into one another.

But the theater itself was magical, the auditorium filled to overflowing for this special occasion by a truly dazzling assembly. Much interest was focused on the box hired by the most notorious Cyprians of the day, Harriet Wilson and her two sisters, widely known and acclaimed as "The Three Graces," who with their friends and admirers frequently provided better entertainment, especially in the eyes of those gentlemen, with or without wives, who frequently ogled them quite openly.

"Disgraceful," murmured Mrs. Gilbey, but was fortunately distracted by the Prince Regent and his party, who at that moment entered the Royal Box.

While the anthem was played, Olivia's glance strayed to the other members of the party. One tall figure, elegant in black and white, stood out from all the color and glitter and during the applause that followed, St. Clair turned to speak to Lady Bryony, and in so doing, became aware of being watched. He raised his head, saw Olivia—and inclined his head.

The gesture was formal, and said more evocatively than words that she was not forgiven. It was no more than she had expected, and she determined not to let the evening be spoiled. The first part of the program was given over to a performance of *The Grand Melodrama of the Broken Sword*, which moved and excited Elizabeth Thornton to such peaks of excitement that her newly acquired poise quite deserted her.

During the interval several visitors came to their box, among whom was Sir Greville Barton. He said everything that was proper to Mrs. Gilbey and Mrs. Thornton before making his way to Olivia's side. She had begged Jane not to leave her alone with him, but when her mama claimed her attention for a moment, Sir Greville seized his opportunity.

"Ma'am," he said unctuously, drawing her aside, "I could not stay away. Y'r beauty drew me like a lodestone. There ain't a woman here can match the grace of y'r ladyship's face and figure." His eyes roved lasciviously over the latter, simply gowned in pomona green silk, and their overfamiliarity brought the angry color flooding into her face.

"That is not only untrue, it is also a little insulting to the other ladies in our party, should they hear you," she said in a low voice.

Far from being taken aback, he applauded her modesty, and she was mightily thankful when Pom, who had left at the interval, returned and rescued her. "I hope your aunt don't mean to encourage that paltry fellow," he said severely.

"So do I. I'm sure she shares my feelings about him."

"Well, that's all right then. I don't care to see you

importuned. What with that pompous oaf, Antrobus, following you around like a lovesick swineherd . . .'' He shuddered.

"Oh, Mr. Antrobus has already offered for me. Did I not tell you?''

"No, you did not! I hope you gave him the rightabout?''

Olivia laughed. "I declined as kindly as possible, though I fear he will try again. He proposed on impulse, you see, in the Park yesterday afternoon, being much moved by the sight of me in my new white muslin—and is convinced that I refused him only because he had not observed the proprieties by formally applying for permission to address me.'' She chuckled. "I believe he did try to do so, but his sentences became so involved that Mama quite missed the point!''

"The dog! Just say the word and I'll see him off for you.''

"No, no, I can handle Mr. Antrobus.'' She sighed. "But I fear Sir Greville will be less easy to discourage.''

Nine

THE FOLLOWING DAY brought the pleasure of a surprise visitor to Mount Street. Olivia heard the sounds of an arrival early in the afternoon as she was crossing the upper landing. Mrs. Gilbey was taking a short rest, and she hoped it would not be necessary to disturb her.

As she leaned over the banister rail, Olivia heard Blore's sepulchral instructions to Edward as he moved to the door, followed almost at once by an eager, youthful voice asking for Lady Olivia Egan, which had her running down the stairs in a most *un*ladylike way.

"Justin! My dear boy—oh, what a splendid surprise!" She glanced at the portmanteau already being borne away by Edward. "But how . . . *why* are you here?"

His grace, the ninth Duke of Meriton, suffered his sister's embrace with the reluctant stoicism of a sixteen-year-old before finally wriggling free.

"If you'll let me breathe, I'll tell you. Cut line, Livvy, do!" he begged with an embarrassed grin. "I've no wish to be smothered to death!" He glanced hopefully at Blore. "I say, there wouldn't be anything to eat, would there? I traveled most of the way from Malborough on the outside of the stage and I'm absolutely 'gut-foundered'!"

"Justin!"

He grinned. "Well, it's what old Grimble used to say,

and it's a jolly fair description of how I feel!''

The butler said indulgently that if his grace would care to go on up with Lady Olivia, Cook would rustle up a bite of nuncheon in a brace of shakes.

"Thank you, Blore." He gave the butler his most engaging smile and, as Olivia threw an arm around his shoulder, added diffidently, "And if you wouldn't mind, I'd as lief answer to Master Justin. All that 'your grace' nonsense makes me feel about ninety!"

"Very good, sir."

Up in the drawing room Olivia stood back and looked her brother over, noticing with a pang that his face was fast losing the childish curves and fining down. "My dear, you have grown inches!" she said. "You are almost out of your clothes. I suppose that means you will have to have almost everything new."

Justin's eyes lit up. "Well, I wouldn't at all mind. And if we are still a trifle purse-pinched, Perry—Peregrine Saltash, that is—knows of a man who can turn one out in prime twig for a fraction of the real lions like Weston and Stultz."

"Not so fast, my lad," she said, keeping her countenance with difficulty. "We will talk first, if you please, of what brings you to London when you should be in school."

Justin had discovered Mrs. Gilbey's sugar plums, and having helped himself to one, reclined on the sofa with his ludicrously long legs sticking out. "Oh, as to that," he said airily, "there was an outbreak of scarlet fever in the lower school, so they sent us down early."

"You weren't in contact . . . ?" she began, and then catching his eye, grinned ruefully. "Sorry!"

"Still playing mother hen? Well, you needn't fuss. We lofty fellows don't mingle with the lower school, except for the fags, and mine had it when he was a babe."

"So why did you not go straight home to Bath?"

Justin looked shocked. "What? And risk carrying infection to our own precious brood? Livvy—how could you even suggest it! Wouldn't be at all the thing. Besides—'' He reached for another plum, but she was before him and removed the dish. He wrinkled his nose at her and lay back again, with his folded hands behind his head. "Perry Saltash was coming to London, so I was able to travel with him. He said I could stay with them—his father is something important in the Government, I believe—but as I knew you were here, and possibly Mama, too, I thought staying with you would probably be best."

Olivia tried to remain serious. "Always supposing your uncle and aunt are agreeable."

"Oh, I shan't be any trouble. All I want is a bed and a bite to eat now and then. A bang-up fellow is Perry! He's a year older than me and up to every rig and row in town." The awed admiration in Justin's voice caused her severe misgivings, the more so as he added eagerly, "He's offered to take me around, show me some of the sights."

"Well . . ."

Her arguments never found voice, for at that moment Edward entered bearing a tray on which reposed a handsome portion of pigeon pie, several thick slices of rare beef, a few assorted pastries, an apple, and a large glass of cordial. Olivia knew she would get nothing further out of her brother until his appetite was satisfied, so she left him and went in search of pen and paper so that she might let Mama know that Justin was with her. And because she was very fond of him, she laid rather more emphasis than was necessary upon the risk of infection to the younger children, while assuring her that Justin was safe and perfectly fit.

"Which is more than you deserve, you abominable shag-rag of a boy," she told her replete brother when she presently returned to find that he had cleared the plate to the last crumb. "Heavens! You have never eaten the lot?"

"Wasn't I meant to?" he inquired innocently. "Thought I might offend Cook if I only picked at it."

He expertly dodged a cuff aimed at his ear. "Glaringly abroad, sister dear! You know, I believe I am going to enjoy staying here!"

"Poor Aunt Constance! I only hope she may not feel that we are abusing her hospitality. It has been bad enough to foist Mama on her as well as myself—but if she is now to be faced with having you eating her out of house and home, she could well be wishing us all at Jericho."

But Mrs. Gilbey was delighted to see her nephew. Nothing could be guaranteed to delight her more, she said, than to hear the sound of young voices about the place. "And you will be very good for Olivia, I shouldn't wonder, after weeks of . . ." Mrs. Gilbey suddenly recollected that she ought not to criticize his mama in his hearing. ". . . of my company! But I do agree with Olivia that you cannot go about looking like that, dear boy. I shall consult your uncle this very evening."

As she left the room Justin cast a despairing glance at his sister. "Oh, Lord, Livvy! Whatever shall I do if Uncle George wishes to choose what I wear? He won't have the least idea what is all the crack! I have a small amount of my allowance left, but not enough. You don't suppose old Scrimshaw would advance my next month's allowance?"

"No, I don't. And that is no way to speak of someone who manages our affairs so meticulously."

But her tone softened as she saw his disappointment. After all, she had been free to choose so many beautiful dresses. Surely her brother ought to be given the chance to indulge his fancy just a little. If she could just find some way around the situation without offending Aunt Constance or resorting to Perry Saltash, in whose taste, even without meeting him, she could repose little confidence.

"I wonder," she said. "Justin, you remember Pom—Edwin Pommeroy, who was Charles's friend? Well, he is a regular Pink of the *ton*. If I were to ask him, I'm sure he would know exactly how to go about things. Would you like me to put the suggestion to Aunt Constance?''

Justin thought wistfully of the striped cossack trousers, yellow waistcoats, and red-spotted neckcloths about which Perry had enthused on the journey home. But he was by nature easy-going, and even he could see that his chances of indulging such tastes were minimal. So it was agreed.

It happened that Mr. Pommeroy was to call that night to take Olivia to a rout, so that Justin was able to see him for the first time in the full glory of his evening clothes. Until that moment, he had resigned himself to the fact that Livvy's idea of a Pink of the *ton* was probably not his. But one look at Mr. Pommeroy was enough to convince him that he was wrong.

He had been a little in awe as the quizzing glass was raised and he was subjected to a critical inspection. But it needed only the faint "Good God! Can't expect a fellow to go about looking like that! Glad to help," followed by an engaging sleepy grin, to make Justin aware that Charles's friend was not in the least top-lofty.

In no time, he was turned out in prime style—Pom having dropped the word in his ear that cossack trousers were not quite the thing and that a pair of pale yellow pantaloons could be guaranteed to set off a leg to much greater advantage. Aunt Constance was momentarily startled to see her young nephew in the said pantaloons, a close-fitting coat of blue superfine with large mother of pearl buttons and a pale yellow neckcloth with black spots, but she could see how proud he was, and said kindly that he looked very fine.

"You look like a park saunterer," Olivia teased him, but privately she was more than a little startled to see how much difference the clothes made. Suddenly the boy had vanished and a rather coltish young man stood in his place.

Upon learning that Justin was a keen horseman, Pom

off-handedly let it be known that he had a pair of
almost new riding breeches which he never wore, and
which, with a trifling alteration, would serve Justin's
needs well enough, worn with the one remaining coat
that fitted him. Olivia knew that it was Pom's way of
helping to ensure that they did not run their aunt and
uncle into too much expense. But when she tried to
thank him, he brushed it aside with a muttered, "Tell
the truth, I never cared for those breeches above half,
but don't tell the young cawker that."

An extra hack was hired so that Justin could ride with
them in the mornings, and the rest of his days seemed
destined to be spent with his friend, Perry Saltash.
Olivia, having met this young man, felt that Justin
would come to no real harm in his company, though as
Pom said, they would undoubtedly explore many of the
haunts frequented by young rips of their age.

"They spoke of the Royal Menagerie and the circus at
Astley's Ampitheatre," she said with more hope than
conviction. "And Madame Tussard's Waxworks, all of
which sounds innocent enough. But I suspect they will
have other less salubrious venues in mind."

"Bound to," Pom agreed cheerfully. "No use
thinking otherwise."

"Such as?"

"Well, I don't precisely know what takes the young
uns' fancy these days. With Charles and myself it was
the Cockpit Royal, the Fives Court in Martin
Street—we saw many a good mill there, I recall—"

"Enough, Pom!" she cried. "I would as lief not
know any more!"

"No need to get in a fret. Justin has a good sound
head on his shoulders. And I'll drop him the odd hint if
he goes off bounds."

With this Olivia had to be content; her abiding fear
that someone might discover who he was and seek to
exploit him would sound mawkishly overprotective put
into words. Nevertheless, she was profoundly grateful
that Pom had taken on the mantle of "older brother"

—a boy growing into manhood needed someone like that to turn to, and for all that Pom liked to play the dandy, he was at bottom sound.

It was about a week after Justin's arrival in town that St. Clair's carriage made its appearance in the Park once more. Olivia saw it first and her pulse quickened as it appeared in the distance, with Hassan for once riding beside the vehicle. A moment later Pom also commented on its presence, and Justin professed himself all eagerness to see St. Clair, of whom he had learned much during his short time in London.

As the carriage came within about fifty yards of them it passed behind some trees, which temporarily hid it from their view, and at almost the same moment they heard the unmistakable crack of a rifle shot echo across the silence of the Park.

"The devil!" exclaimed Pom, as with a swift telling glance at Olivia, he urged his mount to a gallop. "Stay there, both of you! It may be nothing, but . . ."

But nothing would have kept Olivia away at that moment. She shouted to her brother to wait and went racing after Pom, with a disgusted Justin, determined not to be left out of all the excitement, following closer on their heels. All three rounded the trees to find the carriage slewed across the grass with the team in a high state of nerves temporarily brought to a halt and the coachman slumped on his box. Hassan was nowhere to be seen, though there were sounds of horses galloping hard. Olivia, who had been fearing the worst, breathed again as she saw St. Clair already climbing down and going to control the restive horses before they panicked and kicked in the box.

Pom and Justin dismounted and hurried to help him, while Olivia rode on up to the carriage. Through the open door she saw the frightened girl crouched in the corner with a fold of her beautiful embroidered veil, clutched in fingers that trembled, pulled protectively across her face.

In that instant all else was forgotten. Olivia slid from

the saddle and climbed in to sit beside her. "Don't be afraid," she said with a reassuring smile. "You are quite safe."

Enormous eyes, made even larger by the thin black lines drawn around them, were sheening with tears that welled and hung precariously on thick, dark lashes. The girl stared at her over the lowered fold of the fine cotton veil, unblinking, terrified. Olivia, uncertain whether she understood, tried again. "Do you speak English?"

The girl nodded.

"Well then, please believe that I am your friend—and the friend of Mr. St. Clair." This was not entirely accurate, but now was not the time to quibble. "He is calming the horses."

"Yes, I know." Her voice had an enchanting, lilting quality. "He told me that a part of the harness had snapped, but I know that this is not so. I have heard rifle shots many times in Adjamir." She sighed. "And often there were bad men . . ."

Olivia's heart hollowed, but she only said, matter-of-factly, "There are bad men here, too, but they are seldom so bold as to venture into the Park, and I am certain even if there were any such men, they will already have fled." She sensed rather than saw the slight figure relax, and again she smiled. "You are Aysha, are you not? Such a pretty name. I am Olivia."

The girl blinked at last, sending the tears cascading down her cheeks, to reveal eyes that, unexpectedly, were not black, but the clear light gray of a mountain stream. She giggled suddenly and blotted the tears with her veil before letting it fall. Olivia caught her breath; Aysha was little more than a child, but quite the most exquisite creature she had ever seen, with honeyed skin and a wonderfully pure fine-boned face that betrayed her pride of race. Even as she watched, those beautiful eyes suddenly came alight with something approaching adoration, and Olivia knew before she turned that she would see Damian St. Clair's tall figure filling the doorway, the shoulders broad, the waist and hips slim and supple. Jealousy, an unfamiliar emotion, twisted cruelly within her as, irresistibly, her gaze lifted to see the answering light in his as they rested on Aysha. And again her breath caught sharply in her throat.

He was hatless, his thick dark hair tumbled; but it was his eyes, light gray and presently bright with concern, that held her. She looked back—and back again. "But of course. Aysha is . . . ?"

"Quite so," he completed for her, his voice deep with emotion. "Aysha is my daughter."

Ten

"WHY DID YOU not tell me?" she demanded of him.

Damian St. Clair stared down at her, his expression unreadable, and then, still without speaking, he took her arm in a bruising grip and led her away from the carriage.

Olivia had stepped down to see if there was anything she could do to help, leaving the reassured Aysha in Justin's care. "Just talk to her as if she were Sarah or Alice," she had whispered to her awed brother. "Aysha may look like a miniature goddess, but she is only thirteen."

It seemed, however, that Olivia's services were not required. Everything, St. Clair assured her, was under control. The injured coachman had been helped, grumbling, from the box, and although nursing a ball in his shoulder, had insisted upon being allowed to supervise the inspection of his horses, which Pom had engaged to undertake. Hassan, too, had returned. She was in time to hear him murmur, "It is accomplished, lord," before going to judge for himself whether the horses were in any condition to be driven home, leaving her alone with his master.

When they had gone a short way, St. Clair stopped as suddenly as he had begun, and looked keenly about him. There was no one else in sight but for a nursemaid with a gaggle of children over near the Riding House, and the occasional incurious horseman. Satisfied, he ducked beneath the spreading skirts of an enormous beech tree within sight of the carriage, and drew Olivia in after him. It was like being in a world apart, she thought, as he maneuvered her not ungently until her back rested against the tree. And having thus virtually imprisoned her, he continued to stand, quite suffocatingly close, so that it took all her courage to look up at him, indignation vying with her need to know as she repeated her question.

"Would you have believed me?" His words had a jaded ring. "Would anyone have believed me?"

"But I am not anyone!" she protested. And remembered even as she spoke how quick she had been to cut him short when he had attempted to secure her friendship for Aysha. She blushed. "You did try to tell me, did you not? And I behaved very badly. I'm sorry."

The look of disillusion faded, and he laughed softly. "You do have the devil's own way of taking the wind out of a fellow's sail, my dear." And as her mouth curved into an uncertain smile, "Also, you have the most delightful dimple, just there." The tip of his finger was a silken caress, straying on to trace the outline of her lower lip. "You can have no idea how often I have been tempted to explore it further."

His sudden change of mood was so unexpected, so utterly incongruous in the circumstances, that Olivia seemed powerless to move. He watched the wild color flood into her face as he carefully removed her hat and dropped it on the grass before bending his head until his lips were lightly touching the place where the dimple had been. His breath fluttered seductively against her skin; his mouth lingered a moment before moving on to claim her mouth, where it clung, sending exquisite sensations coursing through her. The kiss lasted but an instant in time, and to her shame, left her wanting more.

The protest that should have been uttered died in her throat; in any case it would have had a hollow ring, for her whole body was confirming what, in her heart, she had known for some time—that she was helplessly, hopelessly in love with this exciting, unpredictable, and often infuriating bucaneer of a man. It was a love untrammeled by illusion, by expectation. She recognized that it pleased him to flirt, to tease; that he had a way of looking into one's eyes, as he was looking at her now, as though no one else existed for him. But it was a device she had seen him use too freely to trust its message. It was even possible that the very nature of the situation which existed between them, the fact that she was the daughter of the man who had sought to ruin him, intrigued him and aroused his predatory instincts. But whatever the motivation, he was, indisputably, a man whose head would always rule his emotions. And marriage, she was almost certain, would not be in his scheme of things.

So, if heartbreak was not to be her undoing, she must be equally steadfast in resisting the sweet seduction of her senses. It was not easy at such a moment to act a part, but pride dictated that he should not have the satisfaction of knowing how close he had come to succeeding. Olivia drew a deep breath, prayed her voice would not tremble, and looked him in the eyes, almost weakening as she felt the impact of that tantalizingly quizzical regard. She managed a light laugh.

"How infamous of you to use me so! And most unfair, for I have never played this kind of game before, and am therefore unfamiliar with the rules. You will have to give me a hint as to what should happen next. Perhaps, since you seem to have a penchant for attracting danger, I ought to affect righteous indignation and slap your face?" Her words certainly induced a reaction, but not quite the one she had been seeking.

St. Clair drew a quick breath. Then his eyes blazed wickedly. "You could try," he murmured, accepting the challenge. "But your heart wouldn't be in it. I know, you see, for I have felt it beating just as mine is doing now.''

She was unable to tear her gaze from his as he took her slim, gloved hand inexorably in his own strong fingers and cradled it beneath the curve of her breast. Oh, it really wasn't fair, the way that traitorous tumult betrayed her! Just when she thought she could bear it no longer, he guided her hand, still firmly clasped in his, beneath his own coat where, through the fine cotton of his shirt, she felt the warmth of his skin and his own heart's strong, uneven thudding.

"There," he said with the oddest note in his voice, "now you have proof of the power you have over me."

"Stop, oh please stop!" Olivia cried in a low, suffocating voice, and snatched her hand away. "You do right to mock me, for I should never have tried to play your ridiculous games! But I don't understand you! How can you joke and flirt and behave as if nothing had happened, when only a short time ago you might have been killed!"

In the silence that followed, she knew, though she could not meet his eyes, that he was looking at her in a most penetrating way. Whatever he saw must have had some effect, for when he finally spoke, she could have sworn he was less in command of himself than usual.

"Hush," he gentled her. "I didn't mean to . . . Oh, dammit! I just didn't think!" He stopped and began again, forcing a lightness into his voice. "As for being killed, there was never any danger of that. Hassan would never permit it."

She uttered a choking, unsteady laugh. "Can you never be serious?"

"Oh, but I am. Hassan has a saying, *My life for yours, lord*. And he means it, quite literally. He takes very good care of me—and of Aysha." But for how long? nagged a small, cold voice in his head, for he had no doubt that on this occasion Hassan had been Rashid's target, not himself. Thanks to Hassan's swift action, it was Rashid who lay dead, and his accomplices had scattered, but how many more Rashids would there be waiting to take his place? And how many ruffians might Kendall have at his disposal?

"She is very lovely, your daughter." Olivia's voice barely penetrated his uneasy thoughts. "I wish I might have gotten to know her earlier, but if it isn't too late I would very much like to make up for my lapse." The sound of youthful laughter came floating from the carriage. "I believe you are wrong to keep her so close. There would be some talk, of course, but people would very quickly come to adore her. I think she has already made a conquest."

"I have my reasons," he said in a tone that suggested he would not lightly tolerate interference, his pre-occupied expression suggesting that what had passed between them was, for him, already a thing of the past. It pained her to know how little it had meant to him, but the sooner she, also, could put it from her mind, the better for her sanity.

It should not be too difficult. Already the events of the morning seemed too bizarre to have been anything more than the stuff of make-believe. Justin had thought it a capital go—the greatest sport ever. "Just wait till I tell Perry!" he had exclaimed when the excitement was at an end, which had drawn from St. Clair a pithily worded rejoinder that the last thing he wanted was to become an object of conjecture as a result of what was no more than a badly bungled attempt to rob him, and that no one was to be told of the incident. Justin had been momentarily cast down, but the air of mystery aroused by St. Clair's sanction very quickly superceded his initial disappointment.

But Olivia could not accept that this second incident was not connected to the earlier one. And now, watching the brooding face which so short a time ago had been recklessly teasing, she was convinced there was more to it.

"Just what is happening, Mr. St. Clair?"

She blurted the words out before they could be halted. He looked up, frowning, as though resenting her intrusion. The denial was already on his lips, but she preempted it by rushing on: "And please don't fob me off with platitudes. You may bamboozle Justin with your explanations, but I am neither blind nor deaf, and I cut my eye teeth a long time ago! And so did Pom. He may give the appearance of being a fashionable fribble, but he's a lot smarter than you think!"

St. Clair was taken aback by her vehemence. "Have you quite finished? Because, if so, I give you fair warning that I don't take kindly to being interrogated, especially by young ladies who glare down their charming aristocratic noses at me!"

But her chin only rose a fraction more, and when he saw that she did not intend to back down, he shook his head impatiently. "Oh, very well, I have no wish to come to cuffs with you. Besides, I have a feeling you'll give me no peace until you know the whole." He peered through the umbrella-like sweep of the branches and saw that the carriage was ready to move. "But not now. I must take Aysha home, and Hassan will be fretting to get that bullet out of Marman's shoulder."

Olivia stared. "But surely you will send for a doctor?"

"Not unless I wish to offend Hassan beyond all forgiveness, which I don't!" He picked up her hat, set it on her head, taking infinite care not to disarrange her hair, and lifted a branch so that they might step out into the heat of the sun once more. "Furthermore, I have complete confidence in Hassan, who is a man of many parts. This isn't the first time he has been called upon to use his skills and I doubt it will be the last. I would certainly back him against any doctor London can produce." He looked down, one quizzing eyebrow raised, "Satisfied?"

"If you say so, Mr. St. Clair," she said primly. "It is your business, after all."

"Quite," he agreed with extreme dryness. "I suppose

you couldn't bring yourself to call me Damian? I
occasionally find your manner of addressing me as *Mr.
St. Clair* somewhat daunting."

"Oh, what a hum," she scoffed, in total command of
herself once more. "As if you would ever be daunted by
anything so trivial! And in any case, I don't think what
you suggest is at all a good idea. It could well be seen as
familiarity on my part and give rise to all kinds of
conjecture."

"Well, we certainly can't have that," he agreed
gravely. "You could perhaps confine your familiarity to
the times when we are alone."

"I could—" she was determined to keep the tone
light— "if there were the least likelihood of there being
any such times."

"Not easy, I agree. But we shall contrive. A drive in
the Park in full view of the world at large is not precisely
what I had in mind, but I can hardly expect you to visit
Egan House, even were it possible."

"I don't in the least mind that it once belonged to us,
if that is what you mean," Olivia assured him. "It was
never home to me in the way that Kimberley was. But
you are right. It would be difficult, especially with Miss
Imelda on permanent guard duty at her window!"

"Is she?" His voice was expressionless, yet Olivia had
the feeling that he was not pleased. "Well then, a drive
it will have to be—for now, at any rate. Hopefully we
should be able to talk reasonably freely and without
interruption."

"And you *will* tell me what I want to know?" she
persisted, as they approached the carriage where everyone was waiting.

He sighed, and grinned wryly down at her. "Tenacious, aren't you? Very well, you have my word on it."

There was no time to say more as the horses were
being brought forward and there were good-byes to be
said.

"Lady?" Aysha clasped her hand eagerly as she took

her leave. "You will please to come and see me? I should like it so much if you would."

"Little one, you must not pester Lady Olivia," her father rebuked her gently. The girl veiled her disappointment, immediately submissive.

All the warmth and compassion in Olivia's nature cried out to console Aysha, but she scarcely knew how best to do so. And Justin, oblivious of the delicate nature of the situation, complicated matters still futher by saying airily that he would be delighted to accompany his sister.

"Well, we shall have to see," she said, her eyes challenging St. Clair as pity for the child overcame caution. "Perhaps we could arrange for your father to bring you to tea in Mount Street one afternoon." It was worth risking his displeasure to see the light return to Aysha's eyes.

But she was not to escape entirely unscathed, as St. Clair, preempting Pom's move to put her up on her horse, lifted her easily into the saddle. "One day, my dear, you will go too far," he murmured pleasantly, tucking her booted foot neatly into the stirrup and arranging the folds of her skirt with an easy expertise.

"Stuff," she replied from the relative safety of her great height, and wheeled the little mare away. As they were about to leave she saw him go across to have a word with Pom. They spoke for several moments before Pom finally touched his hat and moved off, but she was too far away to hear what was said. As they rode home, neither he nor Olivia spoke much, but Justin was full of what had happened, and said enough for the three of them, seeming hardly to notice how preoccupied they were.

When they reached Mount Street, Pom for once declined to come in. "Things to do," he muttered uncommunicatively, but over Justin's head his glance was troubled as it met Olivia's.

"Fine," she said. "We shall see you tonight,

though?" Pom looked vague. "Lady Sefton's reception," she reminded him, puzzled by his behavior which, even allowing for the events of the morning, seemed decidedly untypical of Pom.

"Oh, that." He grew suddenly hearty. "Yes, by George! Looking forward to it. I'll be here in good time."

She would have thought his behavior even odder if she had seen him, not above an hour later, turning in at Egan House.

Mrs. Gilbey would have given much to forgo the delight afforded by the obligatory visit to the Park at the fashionable hour. It had been a tiresome kind of day, with all manner of strange undercurrents. She had been aware of it from the moment she had asked Olivia and Justin if they had enjoyed their morning ride; an unmistakable "look" had passed between them, as though they were deliberately keeping something from her, which was absurd for although boys of Justin's age could be and frequently were forever cutting wheedles, she had supposed him to have rather more sense. And Olivia most certainly would not be a party to any kind of deception.

In the end, she put it all down to the weather. Mrs. Gilbey did not at the best of times enjoy hot weather, which invariably caused her to perspire in a most unladylike way, to say nothing of bringing her out in a rash. And everyone was agreed that this year June had been quite unconscionably hot. A sigh escaped her. Left to herself she would have been more than content to remain indoors with the curtains drawn until evening, but she was not one to shirk her duty. Olivia was looking to her for support, and if that meant being seen at the hour of five in Hyde Park, then so be it.

But her distress had not gone unnoticed.

"Aunt Constance, you really don't look at all the thing," Olivia said as Mrs. Gilbey struggled from her chair to go and make ready. Beads of perspiration stood out on her aunt's upper lip, her skin was pallid, and there was a definite lackluster look about her eyes. "Do, pray, come and lie down, and I will send Polly to you. No, really," she insisted, silencing the half-hearted protests, "I won't hear of your going out in the sun in your present condition. A monstrously selfish creature I should be an' I permitted you to exert yourself beyond your strength."

"But, my dear, what will you do?" Mrs. Gilbey, torn between duty and the irresistible call of a cool bedroom, a soft bed, and a cloth soaked in lavender water tenderly laid across her brow. "It will be prodigious dull for you, to be obliged to stay at home while everyone else is out enjoying themselves."

Olivia laughed. "A horrid prospect indeed!" She teased. "Dear ma'am, what nonsense you do talk. My life is one long round of pleasure! A poor thing it would be if I could not support a few hours of my own company! Now, do come along, and let us have no further argument. And if you are no better this evening, I will tell Lady Sefton you are indisposed."

Damian St. Clair's curricle entered the Park a few minutes before five. It was already more than usually crowded. His mouth curled sardonically. Of course, the Season was approaching its zenith, the weather was perfect and the gossip irresistible. Beneath the trees, cool muslins were the order of the day, and both there and in the passing carriages, prettily adorned parasols in every possible hue shaded delicate complexions from the injurious rays of the sun.

He curbed his impatience, holding back his team as high-perch phaetons vied with elegant open landaus for a place in the procession, his eyes covertly scanning the crowd for one tall, slender figure. On the verge a familiar carriage was drawn up, lined in pale blue satin and surrounded as always by a gaggle of hopeful gentlemen; and beyond, a glimpse of auburn curls; a merry laugh. As he approached, Harriette Wilson, the most fashionable of the Fashionable Impures, saw him and waved. He touched his hat, inclined his head, and drove on.

Two thirds of the way around the Park, and there was still no sign of her. He had met almost everyone else. Arabella, looking particularly beautiful in peach-bloom satin, raised an amused eyebrow when he declined to take her up. Watching how his restless eyes scanned the crowd, and knowing him so well, she said with gentle malice, "Poor Damian! Can you not find her? I would help you, an' I could, but I have not seen her either!"

He glowered at her. "There are times, Bella, when you are a sight too busy!"

She laughed and moved on.

At last, he saw Jane Thornton walking with Mr. Peveral, and drew alongside him.

Jane, surprised by this signal honor, nevertheless refused to be overawed, and greeted Mr. St. Clair with her usual good-humor. They talked about the weather in the time-honored way, and remarked on how many people were taking the air, until quite abruptly, he asked if she had seen Lady Olivia. Masking her curiosity, she said, "Why, no, sir. How odd that you should mention it, for I was saying only a moment since that she did not appear to be here. I do hope she is not unwell—though I am sure that is worrying unnecessarily," she added hastily, noting his sudden frown. "More likely, Mrs. Gilbey is finding the weather rather too much. I know that Mama has complained of it several times."

A short time later, Blore entered the drawing room where Lady Olivia was endeavoring to assuage the disappointment of being obliged to forgo her visit to the Park, and—she could not but admit it to herself—the possible opportunity of seeing Damian St. Clair, by doing some tatting. Blore coughed delicately and announced that there was a gentleman below asking for her.

"Really?" She looked up, surprised and not altogether displeased at the thought of some distraction.

"Well, if it's Mr. Pommeroy, you may tell him to come up at once."

"No, my lady, it is not Mr. Pommeroy." Blore handed her the card which the gentleman had requested him to deliver. He watched with some interest as Lady Olivia's hand strayed absently to her cheek, which had grown decidedly pink. "Am I to show Mr. St. Clair up, my lady?"

"No! That is . . . yes!" Heavens, this was absurd! She met Blore's impassive, yet kindly gaze. "Yes, of course, Blore. Please do so at once."

She picked up her tatting in an attempt to look perfectly relaxed, but her fingers were all thumbs and by the time he strode into the room and stopped amid the impatient swirl of his long drab driving coat, her shuttles were all to pieces.

"What the deuce is that?" he exclaimed.

Olivia stared down at the tangled skein. "Tatting," she said in a small rueful voice.

"Good God!" There was amusement in his voice. "Well, put it away, there's a good girl. Tell me, why weren't you in the Park this afternoon? You aren't unwell?"

He had missed her! He had actually worried enough to come looking for her! The knowledge acted upon her like a heady wine, obliterating reason. Belatedly she remembered her manners. "Do, please, be seated, and—" she glanced up at Blore who still hovered near the door— "and permit me to offer you a glass of Mr. Gilbey's Madeira."

St. Clair declined the Madeira, but sat down as the door closed behind Blore, choosing a chair directly opposite her and leaning forward, continuing to regard her with that degree of intensity which she found so unsettling. In an attempt to evade it, she reached for her sewing box and bundled the lace into it, cramming the lid down with scant respect for her work.

"Aunt Constance was feeling unwell—the heat, I think—so I persuaded her to lie down."

"I see." He sat back, apparently satisfied, and Olivia breathed more easily. "Well, we did want to be alone, did we not?"

"Yes, but . . . I hardly think that . . ."

"But not here," he mocked her gently. "It wouldn't be quite the thing, I suppose. Always a chance that one of your aunt's friends might call and catch us *in flagrante delicto*?"

She bit her lip, half-laughing. "I'm sure Blore is far too discreet to allow that to happen."

"Perhaps. But Hassan is presently walking the horses below, which could easily give rise to speculation, so I suggest you put on your best bonnet and come for a drive. Not the Park, I think," he added. "I have already paid one visit there this afternoon. To return with you would certainly set the tongues wagging. But there are several agreeable alternatives, all of them highly respectable!"

To argue further, Olivia reasoned, would be ungracious and probably futile, for she doubted very much whether Damian St. Clair could be persuaded to take no for an answer even if she persisted—and in truth, she had no real desire to persist. So it was that, in a very short time, Olivia was sitting beside him in the curricle, wearing her newest dress of fine sprigged muslin, a highly becoming villager straw hat tied under the chin with jonquil ribbons, and carrying a lacy parasol.

Damian was well aware that she had taken great pains to impress him, and wondered if she guessed from his laconic expression of appreciation just how completely she had succeeded. Indeed, the filmy dress emphasized that almost ethereal quality which frequently made him half-afraid to touch her—the novelty of which never ceased to surprise him.

Olivia had no idea where they went; she only knew that very soon they were driving down an avenue lined with trees where all was peace and quiet. And there he presently drew up, and while Hassan remained in charge of the horses, St. Clair lifted her down so that they might stroll in the dappled shade speared only occasionally by the brilliance of the sun. And as they walked, he told her about his friendship with the maharaja—and its repercussions; he told her of the general unrest in Adjamir, fostered by the cruelly ambitious yuvaraj and his mother; and he related the history of the Golden Eye of Adjamir and the fury caused by the ruler's decision to bestow the jewel upon his English friend, to be held in trust for his granddaughter, who was very dear to him.

"The old man was close to death even then, and we were both convinced that Kassim would take steps to hasten his end." His voice had grown husky with the recollection. "There was nothing I could do, but still I would not have left him had he not begged me to take Aysha to safety before she too was killed."

Olivia was horrified. "Surely they wouldn't kill a child?"

"My dear, you can have no conception of the barbarity to which men like Prince Kassim will resort in their appalling greed for power. Aysha was no threat, but she was the ruler's grandchild, and her father his dearest friend. That is reason enough. There must be no one left to remind people of the past."

Olivia shuddered. "And the jewel? Damian, is that what the men who are trying to kill you are seeking?" She used his name without thinking, and neither of them noticed.

"That—and my own little jewel, my Aysha." Tenderness thickened his voice suddenly, the agony in it bringing a lump to her own throat. "The first they could take from me, though in allowing it I would be betraying the maharaja's trust, but Aysha they will never have!"

Both were silent for a moment, unable to speak. Then Olivia said huskily, "Tell me about Aysha's mother?"

St. Clair was slow to answer. He was looking across the fields into the distance as though his thoughts were winging away. "I had not been in India more than a few

months when a business venture took me to Adjamir.
And it was there that I met Kalida. I fell in love with her
on sight. She was barely sixteen, a curious mixture of
shyness and precocity, and I was a very green nineteen,
but learning fast with a deal or two already under my
belt. Kalida was the second daughter of the ruler's first
wife—and his favorite child." He smiled faintly.
"Daughters are of little account in a country where male
power predominates. The elder daughter had been
betrothed from an early age to a cousin of some
importance, but Kalida was not spoken for, and the
maharaja, who already thought of me as a kind of
adopted son, saw how things were between Kalida and
myself, and so he gave her to me."

"You mean as a . . ." Olivia did not quite know how
to go on, but he helped her out. "No. There would have
been no shame in that, of course, but I wanted to marry
her." His voice grew harsh. "But I was ambitious, and
spent more time away making my fortune than I spent
with my bride, who remained at the palace. She never
complained when we were together, and I suppose I
failed to notice how frail, how withdrawn she had
become. One day, I returned from my travels to find
that she had borne me a daughter, but it was a difficult
birth and she was near to death." His shuddering sigh
made Olivia long to comfort him, but he was beyond
her reach. "I blamed myself, of course, though the rani,
who was still alive at the time, insisted that no one was
to blame—that Kalida was too small, not built for child-
bearing, and that it was the will of Allah."

In the silence, a pair of linnets came swooping
through the trees, trilling repetitively at one another and
flirting like lovers. It struck an ironical note, but
somehow broke the spell that had held St. Clair in
thrall. With another deep sigh, he turned to look at
Olivia. "But to everyone's surprise, the tiny Aysha
survived, and with Muna, who had been her mother's
servant, to tend her, she thrived, growing in strength
with every day that passed. In a strange way it was as

though I had been given another chance. My ventures continued to expand, but instead of trying to do everything myself, I appointed agents to handle much of the routine work. That way, I was never too long away from Aysha.''

He shrugged. "Perhaps I have, in consequence, become overprotective. But for now, the need to protect her is very real, and until it is resolved, I dare not expose her to danger. So,'' he concluded wryly, "that is the gist of my story. Forgive me if I have gone on too long. Other people's reminiscences can be tedious, I know.''

"As if I could ever think that!'' Olivia cried. "I am only very grateful that you have felt able to tell me. It explains so many things!''

For the first time something of his old self surfaced as, with the ghost of a smile, he said, "Maybe, but don't, I beg of you, go filling your lovely head with all kinds of wrong notions about me. What I have told you doesn't change anything, though it may go a little way to explaining why I am what I am. And why,'' he added with some force, "I am now cursing my own stupidity in allowing you to become involved.''

"Oh, I shall be all right.'' She touched the diamond at his waist. "But if you wish to retain the diamond, isn't it very dangerous to display it so blatantly?''

To her astonishment, he laughed aloud. "I'm sorry, my dear. I am not laughing at you. Well, only a little. You see, this bauble is no more than a trifling affectation. The Golden Eye is rather more than that. Hold out your hand.'' As she did so, he reached inside his shirt and drew out the leather pouch on its heavy chain. A moment more and the fastenings were released. "This,'' he said, tipping the amber-colored diamond onto her outstretched palm, where it lay glittering in a shaft of sunlight, "is the Golden Eye of Adjamir.''

Eleven

MR. POMMEROY was not sure what to make of St. Clair's story. Were it not for the odd things that had happened, he would have been inclined to dismiss the whole thing as a hum.

But a diamond as big as an egg! You couldn't dismiss that, for a start. St. Clair had shown it to him. And the child was clearly his. No hint of artifice there. It was the rest of it that took a bit of swallowing—all that talk of maharajs and killing and revenge. Like something out of a deuced gothic novel!

It was flattering, of course, that St. Clair had seen fit to take him into his confidence, asking him back to the house like that. But it was an extraordinary tale by any standards. To be sure, he had come across a Major Kendall in Watier's—a bit of a boastful character, hadn't taken to him at all. He had been in India, right enough—bored on about it at considerable length, in fact. But as for his being involved in recruiting a band of ruffians for the purpose of stealing that Golden Jewel thing, and most likely killing St. Clair and the girl into the bargain—well, that was a horse of another color. If it were true—and St. Clair didn't strike one as the sort to weave fictions of that kind—it needed some thinking about.

"You will appreciate that although Lady Olivia knows the gist of the story, I have not seen fit to burden her with my fears about Kendall?"

"Quite so. Not for a lady's ears, though Olivia ain't your usual kind of flighty-minded miss," Mr. Pommeroy had ventured, sitting in the Red Saloon at Egan House, much changed from his admittedly vague remembrance of it, and sampling a port he'd damn near sell his soul for. "Any idea how you mean to deal with this Kendall? I mean, no sense in waiting around for the fellow to take another pot shot at you—which, if he means business, he will do soon enough."

"I couldn't agree more." St. Clair's voice was harsh. "The time has come for the stalker to become the prey."

"Eh? Ah, yes, I see what you mean." Pom settled more comfortably into his chair. "Play him at his own game, what? But, even if you have men enough, y'can't very well resort to open warfare. People wouldn't like it above half—sensibilities offended and all that! Don't suppose Bow Street'd care for it much, either."

"Quite. But you mistake my meaning. We shall have to be much more subtle than that." St. Clair's use of the collective *we* troubled Mr. Pommeroy more than somewhat, but, mellowed by the port, he was disinclined to comment until his host concluded ambiguously, "Infiltration—that is what's needed. I have just the man for the job, but I shall need someone to introduce him to Kendall—someone not obviously connected to me."

Mr. Pommeroy, feeling that there was something ominous about the silence, looked up, and saw that St. Clair was regarding him in a way that set all kinds of alarms ringing in his head. He fended off the unspoken question with one slim pale hand. "No, I beg of you! Happy to be of service, of course, but no heroics, I beg of you. It simply ain't my strong suit!"

"My dear sir," St. Clair's voice was softly persuasive, "no heroics would be involved, I give you my word. All

I ask is that you take my man along to your club and arrange for him to meet Kendall—the rest will be up to him. It is that simple.''

Mr. Pommeroy took a restoring sip of port, and eyed him warily. "It may sound simple—I daresay such havey-cavey tricks are the breath of life to you, but some of us are not built to withstand the assault upon our senses.''

"There is,'' and here his host came up with an absolute clincher, "a pipe of this port in my cellar which I would happily part with as a mark of my gratitude.''

His resistance crumbled in the face of such temptation; no man of discerning palate could do otherwise. He could not but be troubled, however, about Olivia's increasing involvement. Anyone but an absolute blockhead must recognize that she was halfway in love with the fellow—and when women were in love, they took some mighty odd notions into their heads.

Mr. Pommeroy was not alone in his concern for Olivia. Mrs. Gilbey had also read the signs. It was unfortunate in the extreme that she had succumbed to the heat, leaving her niece unprotected just when she most needed her. Not that Olivia would ever go beyond the bounds of what was proper, but she had lived so sheltered that she might well read too much into the carelessly uttered words of flattery employed by gentlemen of the world like Mr. St. Clair.

"Stuff and nonsense!'' declared Lady Crockforth, who just happened to have seen Olivia and St. Clair driving out in the direction of Marylebone. "It's plain as y'r nose those two have been circling one another for weeks!''

"Gertrude! I wish you will not be so indelicate as to speak of my niece in terms which—''

"Outraged y'r sensibilities, have I?'' Lady Crockforth sniffed. "Trouble with you, Constance, you're too niffy-naffy, by half, but then delicacy never was an object with me. The thing is, you can't stand in the way of human nature—at least, not if you've got an ounce of sense.''

As if Gertrude knew everything! There was absolutely nothing wrong in taking a drive in public with a gentleman. Olivia had made no attempt to conceal what she had done, but there could be little doubt that she was intrigued by Damian St. Clair, and who could blame her. He had a swashbuckling air about him, an aura of wealth and power that must always attract a young, impressionable woman. Except that Olivia was usually so sensible.

And now there was the vexing question of his daughter, if indeed the child *was* his daughter! Olivia seemed in no doubt of it, and was all eagerness to invite her to tea. But only suppose the girl should be what the gossips had originally dubbed her, and Mr. St. Clair had chosen to foist her upon Society in this guise as his ultimate revenge upon those who had once humiliated him? What a scandal broth there would be then! And Olivia at the heart of it. To be sure, he did not seem that vindictive, but hot countries had been known to do strange things to people!

Never, in her worst dreams, had Mrs. Gilbey visualized so many pitfalls when she had so willingly agreed to give Olivia a Season. She almost (but only almost) wished that Honoria were still here to shoulder the responsibility. Only she wouldn't, of course. She would simply succumb to one of her turns and leave the awkward decisions to someone else. Which did not prevent her from sending frequent letters of plaintive inquiry as to why Olivia had not yet secured an offer, so promising as things had been when she had left London. A great fear filled Mrs. Gilbey's breast that Honoria might, if matters did not resolve themselves very soon, return to plague them.

But common sense at last prevailed, and because Mrs. Gilbey was at heart a kindly soul, she found herself agreeing that St. Clair's "daughter" might take tea with them and an invitation was duly extended.

"You won't regret it, Aunt Constance, truly you won't," Olivia had said, giving her a hug. "In fact, I will engage to eat my best bonnet if you are not totally bewitched within an hour of meeting her."

"Fine words, my girl," returned Mrs. Gilbey, straightening her cap. "But I shall not hold you to them, for it is a very pretty bonnet."

So it was that two days later, at a little after four in the afternoon, Aysha arrived with her father and was shown up to the drawing room. It would have been difficult to decide who was the most nervous—Olivia, for fear that the experiment did not work; Mrs. Gilbey, who had not the slightest idea what to expect and feared that she might let her niece down; or Aysha, for whom the visit was a whole new experience which both excited and terrified her.

Only St. Clair appeared totally at ease as he introduced his daughter to Mrs. Gilbey, but Olivia thought she glimpsed a tenseness behind his eyes. He certainly had every reason to be proud of his daughter. Her tiny figure was draped in a robe of the finest deep blue silk, liberally embroidered with gold and caught into many folds. The same silk veiled her hair, and her eyes shone like stars—eyes, Mrs. Gilbey was quick to note, so like her father's that there could be no doubting her parentage. Her relief showed itself in the effusiveness of her greeting.

She watched, enchanted, as Aysha put her tiny slender hands together in greeting and made a little bow. "Lady, I am most honored to be invited into your home." Here the musical voice trembled into excitement. "It is the very first time I make a visit here in England!" She glanced at St. Clair. "Did I do it well, my father?"

"Very well, little one," he said, unable to hide his pride in her.

"Indeed, you are very welcome, child," exclaimed Mrs. Gilbey. "And you are even more beautiful than my niece had led me to believe. Now, do come along and sit down. Perhaps you would like to be with Olivia. And Mr. St. Clair, pray do be seated.''

As he did so, Olivia patted the sofa beside her for Aysha to join her. "I must tell you that I am quite overcome with envy for your lovely gown."

"You like it?" Aysha preened with childish pleasure. "It is a sari. I have many more at home. I will give you one. It will become you exceedingly well." Her eyes sought St. Clair's. "Am I not right, my father?"

"Undoubtedly," he agreed, grave-faced.

"And I may give her one of mine?"

"Certainly, if the Lady Olivia wishes it."

"Good. Then you must come to my house and choose one for yourself, and I will show you how to wear it." Olivia could almost feel the shock waves emanating from her aunt, if not from St. Clair. "Oh, but you will also need a *choli*!" Aysha indicated the short-sleeved bodice beneath the folds, and giggled. "Mine will not fit you, I think, but Muna will make you one very quickly. Her fingers are most nimble!" She gave an animated demonstration, which made everyone laugh, and the moment passed.

Later, when Aysha was busy talking to Mrs. Gilbey, St. Clair drew Olivia to one side. "I suppose you are feeling mighty pleased with yourself, oh, meddlesome one. I know your motives are of the best, and quite clearly my daughter is enjoying every moment of her visit. Ergo, there is now no going back, even were it possible—and seeing how she blossoms, I could not wish it so. Which means that her true identity will need to be established as quickly as possible, for you know—who better?—what the gabblegrinders of this infernal town will make of it.''

Olivia laid a hand on his arm. "You must not worry so. It will be a nine days' wonder, I daresay, but Aysha will quickly win the hearts of all who meet her! And we will all rally around—Aunt Constance, the Thorntons,

Pom, Justin . . . oh, lots of people." Diffidently, for she had to know, she asked, "Does Lady Bryony know her true identity?"

"Oh, yes. Arabella has always known. It may come as a surprise to some people that she is eminently capable of being discreet if necessary."

Olivia swallowed back feelings which she did not care to analyze. Did Lady Bryony know about the Golden Eye of Adjamir, the whereabouts of which he was so anxious to keep concealed? With a jealousy she hadn't known she could feel, Olivia hoped not, and immediately felt ashamed, so that she said a little too effusively, "Then she also will be able to play her part. She has always been very kind to me."

"Oh, there isn't an ounce of harm in Arabella," he agreed. "What concerns me most at present, however, is how best to ensure Aysha's safety. If she is to move about openly, protecting her is going to become tha much more difficult." He spoke quietly and calmly, yet she sensed the real agony of uncertainty behind his words.

"Surely the more Aysha is surrounded by people, the less likelihood there is of her being harmed? Better a crowded place any day than a deserted park."

His smile had a resigned quality. "Your reasoning makes a strange kind of sense. Please God, it will prove to be sound."

Certainly, Aysha's appearance upon the social scene did much to enliven the jaded appetites of those who loved nothing so much as a scandal broth; recent rumors had lost their savor, and no one had recenty run off with anyone else's wife, so the revelation of her true identity proved a godsend. Naturally, the more cattish among them cast doubts upon her legitimacy—like father, like daughter, was a frequently overheard observation. But as Aysha was blithely unaware of any disapprobation, she regarded all with the unfeigned pleasure of a child.

"Quite charming," Jane said, watching her proud progress around the Park with her father, who was driving a spanking new barouche purchased for that very purpose, with Hassan as ever in close attendance. "She exhibits the most wonderful mixture of regality and ingenuousness—like a child playing at being queen. Only fancy Mr. St. Clair having kept her close for all this time!"

"He had good reason," Olivia said defensively. "Aysha has led a very sheltered life until recently, and I think he was reluctant to expose her to the intense interest and speculation of Society." She did not reveal his other reasons for wishing to protect her, and indeed at that moment her attention was distracted as the barouche stopped to take up Lady Bryony.

Even from a distance, it was plain to see how eagerly Aysha chattered to her, or, she thought with a pang of jealousy, how like a family the three appeared. Indeed, from somewhere just behind her, a female voice drawled, "How diverting to behold St. Clair, the family man! One wonders now how long it will be before he sheds his disreputable image forever and persuades Lady Bryony to formalize their relationship!"

"Cat," murmured Jane, but Olivia only agreed with determined brightness that it would be an excellent idea, and just the kind of stability that Aysha needed. Then she excused herself, saying that her aunt was signaling her.

"Oh dear," Jane's kind face was troubled as she turned to Harry Peveral. "I very much fear that Olivia is heading for heartbreak. And that child, adorable as she is, will be an added complication. She is already more fond of her than is wise."

"Love seldom takes account of wisdom," said Harry diffidently. "If it did, I would not for one moment entertain the notion that you could ever see me as anything but the very dull dog I am." He turned impulsively to her, his eyes warily hopeful. "Whereas, in my foolishness, I am tempted to—to hope that you might not be wholly averse to the idea of granting me the privilege of devoting my life to making you happy.''

Jane's heart fluttered, although there was a twinkle in her eyes. "Harry Peveral, am I to understand that you are making me an offer, here in front of practically the whole of the *beau monde*?"

He grinned sheepishly. "Hadn't intended to. Should have approached your father first, of course, but it kind of slipped out.''

"Highly romantic! It would serve you right if I refused you point blank!''

"But you won't, I can tell!'' he said exultantly. "Lord, you can have no idea what this means to me! The devil of it is, I can't very well take you in my arms and kiss you here and now, with everyone looking on!''

"Then I suggest we find somewhere more private as soon as possible. Even in the Park there must be a few hidden corners!''

On the following day Mr. and Mrs. Gilbey received a dinner invitation which filled Olivia with dismay.

"But Aunt Constance, I can't possibly go! You know how I feel about Sir Greville!''

Mrs. Gilbey concealed her own unease behind a persuasively matter-of-fact approach. "Perhaps so, my dear, but he is a friend of Mr. Gilbey's, which does make the matter one of some delicacy. Also, your uncle feels, and I cannot wholly disagree with his reasoning, that you may be a trifle biased in your dislike, that you may not have seen him at his best—''

"It would make little difference, Aunt.''

"So you say, my love. But . . .'' The set of Olivia's chin caused her aunt severe misgivings and made her unsure how best to phrase her uncertainties with regard to the direction in which Olivia's aspirations might—and, she feared, possibly did already lead. "I am sure I have always regarded your ability to grasp the practicalities of your situation with the greatest admiration. And while I am deeply conscious of the attractions presented by . . . certain gentlemen as opposed to others, it would be absurd to suppose that your strong sense of duty would admit any notions of a romantic nature to hold sway in your eventual choice of a husband.''

She snatched a glimpse at her niece's face and hastily looked away, dismayed by the raw agony she saw there. "Oh, my dear, God knows, I want your happiness above all things, and if there were any real hope in that direction, I would be the first to wish you well. But for all that your mama nurtured such expectations of late, quite mistakenly in my opinion, the fact of the matter is that time is going on and little has happened to encourage one to believe . . .''

Nothing but a trifling dalliance, and the sharing of a few confidences which it transpired Lady Bryony had been privy to from the start, Olivia thought wretchedly.

"We must therefore be practical. You continue to rebuff Mr. Antrobus, and while in principle I cannot blame you—Mr. Antrobus is and always will be a *small* man, for all his money and connections—it is unlikely that anyone new will come upon the scene at this stage. Which leaves Sir Greville Barton. No, do pray hear me out,'' Mrs. Gilbey put up a hand as her niece looked set to argue. "Sir Greville has confided to Mr. Gilbey that he has already written to your mama asking for formal permission to approach you. He has not received any reply as yet, but meanwhile, he has arranged this dinner party—not above a dozen people, in order that you might meet away from all the bustle and publicity of the larger social functions—and all that we ask is that you accommodate him in this without in any way committing yourself to making a decision. There, is that not fair?''

Olivia realized how difficult this interview had been for her aunt. That she had little choice in the matter was less important for the moment than the need to remove the look of strain from the older woman's face.

"I'm sorry, dear aunt," she said, stooping to kiss her cheek. "I have been behaving very badly, have I not? A poor thing it would be, after all you have done for me, if I can not oblige you and Uncle George in this. Pray accept my apologies."

"And you will go to Sir Greville's on Tuesday?"

There was the briefest of pauses. "I will go."

Olivia resolved that she would not think about Tuesday until it arrived, which should not prove too difficult as there were many other invitations to engage the mind. That very afternoon Justin was to accompany her on the promised visit to Aysha. The child had given her no peace until she had agreed upon a day, and although seeing Damian St. Clair in Egan House would be something akin to rubbing salt in a wound, it would hopefully prove less painful.

"I remember very little about the place," Justin said as they walked down Mount Street together in the direction of Berkeley Square, having scorned a carriage for such a short distance in spite of their aunt's protests that a carriage would be more seemly. "I don't suppose I was ever in it above twice. What is happening at Kimberley, do you know?"

"No. I did give him a hint some while ago," Olivia admitted. "But I haven't liked to ask recently for fear of seeming presumptuous."

Justin gave her a sideways grin. "It ain't like you to be so reticent where your precious Kimberley's concerned."

"It isn't *my* Kimberley any more, brother dear, and I doubt Mr. St. Clair would take very kindly to being cross-questioned about what is clearly his own business."

"Well, I daresay you're right."

Olivia hadn't known quite what to expect of the inside of Egan House. Her memories were clearer than Justin's, but even so, the place had left no vivid imprint on her mind. As Hassan conducted them to the Red Saloon, it was immediately evident that the interior owed nothing to the past as she had known it, for the influence of the Orient was present wherever one looked—in the beautiful wall hangings and ornaments, in the musky indefinable perfumes that lingered on the air.

Damian St. Clair and Aysha awaited them in the Red Saloon, Aysha standing very close to her father, her very stillness accentuating the excitement in her huge, darkly ringed eyes. She looked up at St. Clair, who nodded. At once she ran forward, stopped, performed her quaint formal bow, and then held out a hand to each. "You are most welcome to our home. My father tells me it was once your home. You are happy to be here again?"

Olivia half-smiled at St. Clair, feeling unexpectedly at ease with him, and said, "Yes, indeed. But I hardly recognize it. You have so many beautiful things . . . so much color!"

St. Clair watched her face with interest as she looked about her, trying to take it all in—the lush carpet with its rich velvet sheen, the curtains and cushions fashioned of heavy silk, and as for the furnishings, her fingers itched to go around touching them; sandalwood chests and carved tables with ivory inlay and trellised edges; cabinets of great delicacy, with latticework doors; ornaments of infinite variety. She trailed a finger with the utmost care over one enormous procelain ornament.

"A Chinese water filter," he said, and Justin immediately asked to have its function explained to him.

Aysha seized the opportunity to take Olivia to choose her sari. An even greater surprise awaited her as she was admitted to the young girl's private apartments by a wizened old woman who salaamed many times. The apartment was comprised of the bedchambers and dressing rooms once used by her mama and papa. But how different they now appeared, for here the use of brilliant colors had been allowed full reign. There was almost no formal furniture, but silken cushions were indiscriminately heaped in piles, and exotic hangings in every texture from filmy muslin to rich silk lent an air of make-believe to the whole room.

"Oh, but this is all quite magical!" she exclaimed.

"My father has tried to make it like my own rooms in the *bibighar* at the Palace," Aysha said, and just for an instant Olivia detected a note of wistfulness in her voice.

"What is a *bibighar*?" she asked.

"It is the place where all the women live."

"And you miss it?"

Aysha sighed. "Yes. But only sometimes. And now that I have you for my friend and am getting to know so many other peoples, I am hardly sad at all!" She brightened at once and clapped her hands. "Muna!" The old woman came forward. "Muna, this is the Lady Olivia, who is to choose one of my saris."

The old woman bowed. "I have laid many out for the Sahiba to choose, as you will see, little highness."

But in the next room, furnished much as the first, a large bed was spread with so many exquisite lengths of material that Olivia could not begin to choose. In the end, it was Aysha who selected for her a sari of deep golden yellow silk that glowed as though with some inner life. It was liberally embroidered with gold thread, and Olivia protested that it was by far too fine for her.

"This is not so. The color is most becoming to you, and Muna will soon have your *choli* made for you." Aysha swept up the silk. "Now I will show you how to wear it." Her fingers were quick and nimble as she pleated and folded and stretched on tiptoe to throw the end over Olivia's shoulder. "And this can go over your hair, so! Now, see for yourself."

Olivia turned to the mirror and it was as if she beheld a stranger. The silk clung in soft glowing folds, making her seem taller and slimmer than ever; the color next to her face warmed her skin and made her eyes sparkle. "Oh, it is lovely," she said softly.

"We should go down and show it to my father. He will be most pleased."

"Oh, no. I couldn't!" In a panic, Olivia began to unwind the sari.

Aysha put her head on one side. "You do not wish him to see?"

"Not . . . just now."

Surprisingly, Aysha did not argue. Instead, she patiently showed Olivia how to cope with the great length of material. They laughed a great deal, and finally folded it up and returned to the others for tea, to find Justin talking away quite happily to St. Clair, who was listening with every appearance of interest.

"My father tells me that you are a duke," Aysha said, looking at Justin with fresh interest. "It is something important? Like a maharaja, perhaps?"

Justin and Olivia looked at one another and went off into peals of laughter. Aysha looked at her father in astonishment bordering on dismay.

"What have I said?"

"Nothing wrong, I promise you, Jewel of my Heart," he answered, his own eyes twinkling. "A duke is an important person, but perhaps not quite like a maharaja."

"Oh, I am sorry! We are being most impolite!" Olivia exclaimed, dabbing at her eyes. "It was just the thought of Justin . . ." Here words failed her again.

Justin tried to look offended. He said gravely, "One would expect one's sister to have more respect for the head of the family, but there—we all have our crosses to bear!"

But Aysha had seen through him. "You are teasing!" Her pretty laugh trilled out. "Father teases me sometimes too!"

"He does?" Olivia looked at him and colored faintly. "Yes, I can believe that."

"Thank you, Mr. St. Clair," she said as she was leaving, and while the two young ones were still talking together.

"Damian," he said. "Remember, we agreed?"

"Very well. Damian." She clasped the parceled sari

to her. "This is most generous. I feel I ought not to accept it."

"Nonsense." He looked broodingly at her. "You should wear it to the Midsummer Night Masquerade."

Twelve

SIR GREVILLE BARTON lived in Portman Square in a large house that seemed to have every conceivable luxury. The butler showed the Gilbeys and Olivia into the drawing room where he awaited them. Several guests had already arrived, none of them known to Olivia, though her aunt was acquainted with some of them.

Sir Greville came forward at once, his manners for once above reproach. His wine colored velvet coat was not entirely becoming to his rather high complexion, but Olivia was obliged to admit that although he kissed her hand, which she could not like, he did indeed say everything that was proper. Even his compliments upon her appearance, though fulsome, were not excessive.

"Allow me to make you acquainted with m' sister, ma'am," he said, leading her toward a lady in puce, with blond hair that owed more to artifice than nature. "Lady Olivia—my sister, Mrs. Winchley."

"Do you reside in London, ma'am?" Olivia said, struggling to make conversation.

"Not as a rule," said Mrs. Winchley. "I spend much of my time in Bath. Less rackety, though we lead quite a social life there. I come up for a week or two in the Season—stay with Greville."

"We—that is, my family resides near Bath."

Mrs. Winchley smiled thinly. "So Greville tells me. Unfortunate time you've had. Still," she lowered her voice, "you'll find things looking up from now on, I daresay. Never seen m'brother so smitten!"

"Oh, but—"

"Ah, there you are, my dear." The sound of her aunt's voice was as music to Olivia's ears. "Mrs. Winchley, how very nice to see you. And how is Mr. Winchley?"

"Tolerable, ma'am. No more than tolerable," said that lady offhandedly. "But then, I see very little of him. Comes up to his club, more often than not for weeks on end."

Olivia looked around the table during dinner, from her place immediately to Sir Greville's left, which was in itself dispiriting, and saw that almost everyone was at least twenty years older than herself, and for the most part dull. Would this be her lot, she wondered wretchedly, if she consented to become his wife? At the end of dinner, when the ladies retired, her aunt managed to whisper to her, "Well, my love, that was not so bad, I think?"

She smiled with an effort and agreed.

However, the gentlemen were a good deal livelier when they presently emerged from the dining room to take tea in the drawing room with the ladies, and the whole tone of the evening became more roistering, particularly on the part of a Major Kendall who had, so he had told Olivia at great and tedious length during dinner, served with the East India Company for many years. When ventured to ask, out of a desperate desire to make conversation, whether he had come across Mr. St. Clair in his travels, he had spluttered something uncomplimentary over his veal in aspic and had turned an angry shade of red.

Now, although he laughed a lot and had become very sportive with the ladies, he studiously avoided the part of the room where Olivia sat with her aunt. Sir Greville, however, made straight for her and said in a hearty whisper, "Well now, madam, what do you think of us, eh? Think you might take to living so high on the tide, after all y'r scrimping and scraping, what?"

Olivia scarcely knew what to answer without becoming offensive, but very conscious of her aunt's worried look, she murmured something noncommittal.

"Well then, how about a song or two? Come, m'dear—I'm sure you can sing mighty prettily, as lovely a creature as you are. We have a splendid pianoforte there, as you can see."

"No, truly, sir. I have little voice." In her desire to get away from his brandy-laden breath, she added hastily, "but I can play a little."

"Splendid." To her dismay he followed her to the instrument and insisted upon finding some music for her, and then staying to turn the pages, and brushing her bare shoulder with an overwarm finger as he reached forward.

It seemed an endless evening, and although, when driving home, her aunt and uncle expressed the opinion that it had gone reasonably well, Olivia could scarcely wait to retire to her room. She got rid of Polly as soon as she reasonably could and, instead of going to bed, sat on the windowseat staring out at the black chimney pots outlined like sentinels against the sky and thought longingly of a room brilliant with color and filled with laughter, and of a pair of eyes, sometimes quizzical, often ironical. Oh, what would she not give to wake each morning to those eyes instead of knowing, blood-shot ones!

"My dear Olivia, you are looking decidedly peaky," declared Jane the following afternoon. "Do I take it the evening was not a success?"

"It was . . . bearable."

"Oh, lud!" exclaimed Jane. "As bad as that? Well, I promise not to mention it again. Tell me, would you care to come with us to watch Prinny sail down the river in the full panoply of his royal personage?"

Olivia tried to raise some enthusiasm. Jane was clearly in good spirits, and why should she be otherwise? Harry Peveral was a charming man and Olivia was truly delighted that they had become betrothed. If only it had not put Jane in such high alt! No, that was not fair! Jane was the dearest girl and deserved every ounce of happiness that came her way. She made an effort to rally her spirits.

"Whyever should the Prince Regent take to the water?"

"Where can your wits have been that you have not heard? Tomorrow is the second anniversary of Waterloo, and Prinny is to sail down river in his royal barge to open the new Strand bridge. It should be quite a sight, for there will be bunting and flags and all the fun of the fair! We could make up a small party. Pom is all for it, and Lizzie and her current beau will probably honor us with their presence, though I doubt they will look at anything but each other!"

Olivia felt anything but festive, but she agreed, suggesting that Justin and his friend Perry might care to join the fun.

Justin was very much in favor. "Mr. St. Clair was telling me all about it when he and I were talking the other afternoon while you were preening yourself in your saris! It seems he has been invited by the Prince to accompany him—how about that for moving in first circles?" he teased her. "*And* he is going on to Carlton House in the evening for a celebration."

"Well, our day out won't be anything like as grand," she said, smothering the sensations his words brought to the surface.

Olivia met Damian St. Clair that same evening at an assembly given by Lady Cowper. It was the first time they had met since her visit to Aysha, when they had parted on amiable terms, so she was somewhat taken aback upon coming face to face with him to find him regarding her with anything but friendliness—in fact, although he was suavely polite to her, meeting her in a group with Pom and her aunt, she caught a glimpse of cold fury, gone in an instant, but quite unmistakable. She could not think it was directed at her, for she could find no cause for it.

It was some time later, when she was talking to Pom, that he came up to her, and with a curt, "You won't mind if I borrow Lady Olivia for a few moments?" swept her off without even waiting for an answer.

She was at first confused and then furious. "Mr. St. Clair, what in the name of heaven do you suppose you are about? Kindly release me this instant! People will begin to stare!"

He made no answer, though he moderated his pace somewhat, and they continued on, passing among the colorful assembly of people, with the lusters of the chandeliers making her dizzy as they glittered above the main saloon, and on through several anterooms until they finally reached one that was all but empty.

Here a pair of long windows stood open to the warm night air, and it was beyond these, on a small terrace, that they finally came to a halt. He pulled her around to face him. A half moon was riding clear in the sky and its light silvered her face, etching each pure line to a stark beauty.

Olivia was almost too angry to speak, but he did not give her a chance.

"What the devil do you think you are playing at?" he demanded, fury vying with intolerance in his voice.

"What am I . . . ?" She gasped the words. "I think you must have taken leave of your senses! You drag me willy-nilly through all those people, who must by now be wondering . . ."

"Why?" he said, cutting across her defiance, "did you accept an invitation to dine at that man's house?" In his fury, he shook her. "In God's name, what possessed you? Barton, of all people! You can't stand him! Do you not see what you have done?"

"How dare you lecture me!" Olivia returned, by now quite as incensed as he. "What I choose to do is none of your business. But since I know by now that you will continue to harass me until you know all, I will tell you that I went because my aunt and uncle wished it, and because Sir Greville intends to offer for me!''

"*Offer for you?*" His fingers tightened cruelly on her arms. "God in heaven, has everyone gone mad? You can hardly bear the man near you. How can you stand there so calmly and talk about the possibility of delivering your life and your loveliness into the charge of a man who is—" Just in time he stopped himself from uttering the crude vilification that hovered on his lips.

". . . .who is acquainted with my uncle," she completed for him, her voice shaking. In fact, she was shaking all over, but whether from rage or some other powerful emotion, she could not be sure. She strove to speak more calmly. "And also with Mr. Thornton, so he cannot be wholly bad. I consider myself fortunate to be presented with two suitors, being, as I am, past the first flush of youth." She heard him mutter some angry expletive beneath his breath, but went on steadily. "So now it only remains for me to choose between Sir Greville and Mr. Antrobus. And although both are wealthy, it would seem that Sir Greville moves in rather better circles and will therefore be more able to help Justin to establish himself, and in due course, to bring my sisters out in style."

St. Clair's voice was clipped. "Have you quite finished talking balderdash?"

"I have finished explaining my situation to you, yes."

"And you would in conscience consider entrusting Justin and your sisters to this man?"

Olivia stared up at him, stony-faced. "Not lightly, no. But beggars can't be choosers, sir. For a short while I was in danger of losing sight of the fact that it was out of a need to secure their future that I came to London."

"Then, marry me, for pity's sake!"

The breath was being slowly squeezed out of her. She

had not realized until now just how much she had wanted to hear those words from him. But not like that. No impassioned declaration of love, no tenderness. His fingers bit once more; he even shook her slightly as though he would shake the answer out of her. She was suddenly quite calm.

"For *pity's sake*? And have it said that you had bought me along with the rest of the Meriton estate? I think not, Mr. St. Clair."

"Damn your infuriating Meriton pride!" Roughly he pulled her close, so close that his breath fanned her cheek and his eyes seemed enormous and brilliant with anger in the moonlight. It was nothing like before, no gentleness, no teasing. This time his kiss was hard, relentless, fiercely bruising in its intensity. To resist would have been useless, and indeed she did not try, for even as his mouth invaded hers with complete and utter ruthlessness, something deep inside her exulted at his quest for possession. Her hands, struggling to be free, encircled his neck, her fingers entwining themselves in his thick curling hair.

When at last he put her away, Olivia thought she would fall, and his voice, though deeply ironic, was not quite steady. "So much for pride, my dear! Now tell me you don't have a choice."

Not waiting for an answer, he left her there—and she remained for some time, unable to face anyone, sure that his mark must be upon her bruised lips. It was Pom who found her at last, still leaning against the balustrade where Damian had left her. He looked around.

"Livvy? What the deuce are you doing out here in the dark all by yourself? I've been looking for you everywhere! Then someone said they saw you and St. Clair coming this way as though pursued by the hounds of hell! Seemed a bit rum to me!" He peered closer. "I say, you are all right? Only you look a trifle odd, if you don't mind my saying so."

"I'm fine now," she said, coming out of her daze.

"But just for a moment I believe the earth trembled. Did you feel anything?"

Mr. Pommeroy looked at her as if he thought she was a trifle queer in the attic. "It's the heat, y'know," he said kindly. "I daresay you were out in the sun too long this afternoon. Does strange things to people."

Olivia laughed tremulously and took his arm. "You could be right, dearest Pom."

The morning of June 18th dawned fine and promised yet another glorious day as the party of young people set out as early as was practicable to enable them to obtain a good view of the royal water cavalcade.

Olivia had never felt less like participating in such a lighthearted venture, but it would be unfair of her to spoil the day for the others, so she stood beneath the flags on their enormous poles, quite close to the new bridge, and cheered with the rest of the multitude as the crimson and scarlet barge came into view bearing the Regent in all the panoply of his office, lifting a royal hand in greeting as the procession passed along, his chest weighed down with an immense collection of Orders. And behind him came a positive throng of boats stretching right across the river and decked out in bunting of every imaginable color.

"From this distance, Prinny looks almost slim," murmured Mr. Pommeroy irreverently.

"It is all so magnificent!" sighed Elizabeth, gazing soulfully up at the young man who hovered over her with proprietorial eagerness.

"Quite," he agreed, without ever taking his gaze from her face, and causing her to blush prettily. Jane looked across at Olivia, one eyebrow lifted in humorous unspoken comment.

"D'you know," said Justin's friend, Perry Saltash, tugging at his arm with sudden enthusiasm, "seeing all this reminds me—we could take a steamer trip down the river. Cracking good sport!"

"They have been known to blow up," Harry Peveral

offered by way of warning. Far from putting them off, however, this seemed to be a distinct mark in favor of the expedition.

"Great!" Justin craned forward so far that he seemed in imminent danger of falling into the water. "Oh, look, there is Mr. St. Clair, and he seems to have a lady with him!"

"How unusual," Harry said, and was immediately dug in the ribs by his beloved, who had seen the expression on Olivia's face. "What? Oh, yes. Bad form. Sorry."

But Olivia scarcely heard him, any more than she registered Pom's "I'd know that fair head anywhere. Looks as if Prinny's invited all his favorites to participate in his great moment!" For she had already seen Arabella Bryony clinging possessively to St. Clair's sleeve. It hadn't taken him long to console himself, she thought bitterly, if indeed he had even needed consolation, which she doubted.

In fact, the more she thought about it, and she had spent most of a long night doing so, the more convinced she had become that his dramatic declaration of last evening had arisen more out of a desire to thwart Sir Greville at all costs than from any real wish to marry her.

"Did I tell you I saw St. Clair coming out of Rundell and Bridge's yesterday?" Pom said, carried away once more. "Buying Lady Bryony a ring at last, mayhap?"

"Shouldn't think so." Harry shook his head, trying to make up for his previous breach. "Got enough jewels to adorn half a dozen ladies already, I shouldn't wonder."

Jane looked swiftly at Olivia, but she gave no indication of having heard. Unobtrusively, she left Harry's side and moved closer. "Have you heard any more from Sir Greville?"

"Only an extravagant bouquet of flowers sent after the dinner party." It had prompted insidious memories of another bouquet—of pink and cream roses. She shrugged the memory away, and said with deliberate lightness, "I have, however, received one of Mama's rambling letters, in which—if I have interpreted the gist of it between all the crossings out—she has given her blessing to the union, should I decide upon Sir Greville."

"And will you?"

Olivia stared down at the dun-colored waves driven by the cavalcade of boats to lap rhythmically below them, the sun, bouncing off them, lending their crests a gunmetal sheen. "It's him or Mr. Antrobus—that bumbling idiot, Mama calls him—and to be sure, I cannot decide whether it is better to be bored to death by him, or be . . ." Here, words failed her.

"Don't do it, Livvy!" Jane implored her. She wanted to add, "A man like Sir Greville could break you!" but prudence prevailed. Olivia was not a fool, but with so many pressures upon her to *do the right thing*, she might well plump for expediency. The decision, however, must be hers.

As if reading her friend's mind, Olivia looked up suddenly, a touch of recklessness in her manner. "I know I ought to make up my mind, but the Season has still a few weeks to run, and I mean to enjoy them to the full! Only then will I make up my mind."

"Bravo!"

That same evening, Olivia attended a musical soirée given by one of her aunt's friends. Her heart sank when she saw that Mr. Antrobus was present. He made his way to her side the moment good manners made it possible, his face grave.

"I have, dear Lady Olivia, heard a most disturbing rumor linking your name with Sir Greville Barton—in short," his earnest face shone with a faint beading of perspiration, "I received the distinct impression that you had received an offer from Sir Greville and had all but accepted it. You can, I am sure, conceive of the distress—the blow to all my hopes—if such a rumor . . . but I am confident that you would not . . ."

Olivia could stand no more. Sorry as she was for him, the bumbling peroration had to be cut short. "Mr. Antrobus, I am sorry if you have been upset. I cannot say how this rumor came to circulate so freely. Nor at present am I able to confirm or deny it, but, dear sir, honored as I am by your continuing interest, I must tell you again, quite plainly, that your expectations can never be fulfilled." His face, puckering like a child's, unnerved her, but she concluded as kindly as she could, "Please accept my good wishes for your future happiness. I am sure you will find someone worthy of your excellent qualities."

She did not linger for fear that he would begin to remonstrate, but went quickly in search of her aunt and found her with Lady Crockforth, who was for once without Miss Imelda.

"Sniffling and sneezin' around the place," said her ladyship when Olivia inquired for her. "Told her she'd best keep to her room and take some of Dr. Willman's paregoric."

"Oh, poor Miss Imelda!"

"Don't you believe it! She's had enough excitement to feed her fancy in the last day or so to last her for weeks!"

"Only fancy, my love, Gertrude has just been telling me that Mr. St. Clair's house was burgled last night!" exclaimed her aunt.

"I didn't say anything of the kind, Constance!" Lady Crockforth declared, sitting rather more rigidly than usual in her chiar. "An attempted burglary was what I said. However, it don't alter the fact that things are coming to a pretty pass, when one cannot feel safe in one's own home."

Olivia's thoughts had flown at once to Aysha. If her father was at a Carlton House reception, she could well have been exposed to danger. However, it would be stupid to panic unnecessarily. Aysha was alone most evenings, and he was bound to leave her very well guarded.

"An attempted burglary, you say, ma'am?" Olivia deliberately made the question seem natural. "They did not then succeed?"

Lady Crockforth gave one of her sniffs. "Not a chance, I should think. The place is crawling with servants of all shades and shapes! Still, it don't make for an easy mind. Try finding an officer of the Watch when y'need one! Impossible! Seems that for once, Imelda's air-dreaming had some foundation. Not that I've admitted as much to her—she's fanciful enough as it is! There'd be no living with her if one gave her an ounce of encouragement!"

The evening dragged abominably from that moment, and Olivia was relieved when her aunt began hiding her yawns behind her glove, and shortly after declared that she had the headache.

It was frustrating in the extreme to have to wait until morning before she could do anything. After a restless night, she was up betimes for breakfast, and found only her uncle at table. He lifted an inquiring eyebrow.

"I couldn't sleep," she said briefly.

"Ah. A lot of things on y'r mind, I daresay." He studied her in silence as she toyed with a piece of bread and butter. "M'dear girl, no one wishes you to be anything but happy. It might help if you'll just remember that."

Her glance flew to his face, and faint color tinted her cheeks. "Dear Uncle George—you don't say a lot, but not much escapes you, does it?"

He patted her hand. "You could be right, but don't let on to your aunt. She likes to rule the roost!" He made a great show of coughing as his spouse at that moment entered the room, expressing surprise that they were both there before her.

"Restless night. The heat." He grunted, and winked at Olivia.

Mrs. Gilbey agreed that it had been overwarm, and chattered on until Olivia, feeling that she decently could, excused herself and sped in a most unladylike way to her brother's room. He was slow to answer the door, but she eventually detected a faint grunt which she took for permission to enter. A large hump of bed-clothes moved sluggishly and she marched across and pulled them away.

"Livvy, for the love of God!" he groaned, screwing his eyes up as she crossed the room and remorselessly threw back the curtains. "It ain't decent, bursting into a fellow's room like this!"

"Especially when he's been out on the town for most of the night!" She sat down on the edge of the bed, regarding his disheveled person with sisterly affection. "Well, I'm sorry, brother dear, but I have desperate need of you, so you will just have to summon what wits are left to you and get dressed. You may have exactly ten minutes."

"Impossible!" He squinted at her, outraged. "I can't possibly dress in ten minutes!"

"Ten minutes," she repeated inexorably, getting up and moving toward the door. "And if you're good, I'll send Edward up with a cup of strong coffee." At the door, she looked back. "It is truly an emergency—concerning Aysha."

"Well, why the deuce couldn't you have said that in the first place."

Thirteen

WITHIN THE HOUR, they were hurrying toward Egan House and as they went, Olivia told Justin as much as she thought necessary to account for what Lady Crockforth had told them, and made him swear not to repeat it to a soul. "I knew there was something smoky about that business in the Park!" Justin viewed his sister with new respect. "Dashed if I know how you come to have such cracking adventures!"

Hassan's demeanor gave nothing away as the porter admitted them, though in answer to Olivia's query he admitted that there had been some small disturbance. "My lord is at breakfast, lady, but I will inform him that you are here."

Olivia was not looking forward to facing St. Clair, but that was unimportant beside the need to know what had happened. "I have no wish to disturb him . . ."

Hassan bowed. "He will not regard it as such. You will please to wait here." He opened the door to the small saloon beside the door and signed for them to enter.

It seemed only moments before a firm, impatient stride heralded the appearance of Damian himself. Olivia had been dreading the moment, but now she stared, diverted by his appearance.

"I say," Justin exclaimed, also much taken by the

loose trousers and embroidered tunic. "That's a rather splendid rig! Looks jolly comfortable, too."

St. Clair lifted an eyebrow, his expression not encouraging. "I find it so. But you did not, I presume, come to pass comment upon my morning attire?"

"We came," Olivia said quickly, before she lost her courage, "because I heard about your burglary, and I was worried . . . about Aysha."

"I see. That woman across the square, I suppose."

"Lady Crockforth, actually," she said.

He shrugged. "Well, it is kind of you to come, but nothing really happened. Aysha wasn't even aware of the attempt."

Olivia felt that they were being dismissed. She turned to go, a lump in her throat, when something—Justin's obvious interest, perhaps—made St. Clair say tersely, "Now that you are here, you had better come on up." His eyes, resting on Justin's hastily assembled clothes, were softened by a glint of humor. "Get you out of bed, did she? In that case, you probably haven't had breakfast."

Justin's reaction might have conveyed to anyone gullible enough to believe him that he hadn't eaten for at least a month and was on the point of expiring. Hassan was summoned. "Take his grace along to the breakfast room and feed him," he said.

"At once, lord."

As Justin was led away, Olivia hesitated, not knowing quite what to do. "Come with me," Damian said, and led the way toward the stairs. When he looked back and saw her still standing where he had left her, he came back and stood, regarding her somberly. "I won't bite. Please. Come." He held out a hand and after a moment, she put hers into it, feeling an undefinable tingle run up her arm at his touch.

In the Red Saloon, he stopped, indicated a sofa, and watched her as she sat down, looking younger and slighter than her years in a simple round muslin gown, high-waisted but unadorned, and wearing a plain straw bonnet. Clearly she was not dressed for visiting. And there was an unmistakable look of strain in her eyes that moved him in spite of himself.

"Don't look like that," he said tautly. "I would not hurt you for the world! I know you will wish to see Aysha, but before you do there are things that must be said. My behavior the other night—" she made a small sound of distress which he ignored— "was despicable and unforgivable. Will you try, if not to forgive, to at least put it out of your mind?"

Olivia knew that such an apology would not come easily to him. She longed to say so much, but instead murmured something appropriate, assuring him that the whole affair was already forgotten.

"All of it?" he asked softly.

She uttered a small gasp. It wasn't fair. He had no right, at this hour of the morning, to sit on the arm of the sofa as he was doing now, looking more than ever like a bucaneer in his Indian robes, and looking at her as though he wished to go on where he had left off the other evening.

"Please!" The note of pleading was unconscious, but he took pity on her, nonetheless.

"Very well, I won't tease you now—only promise me that you won't take any irrevocable decisions in the next few days?"

Olivia sighed. "I had already decided not to do so."

"Splendid." Damian felt as though a great weight had been lifted. If he could just get this business of Kendall over and done with . . . "About Aysha—she knows nothing of last night's bungled attempt. Fortunately, I had advance warning that it would happen and had made the necessary preparations." He put up a hand. "No, don't ask me how—the fewer people who know, the better for all. But there is no doubt that over the next few days Aysha's situation will become more vulnerable. If only there was somewhere that I could safely house her."

He sounded so worried that she forgot their differences. "Have you considered sending her to Kimberley?"

"I have. I even went down there to assess the possibilities." He shook his head. "But there she would be even more open to danger. It would take an army to guard the place. And in any case, I have a feeling I might be expected to take her there. So, it seems that we must sit it out here and hope to repulse any further attempt to gain entry."

The door opened to admit Justin, replete and singing the praises of St. Clair's cook. The response being disappointing, he glanced from one to the other. "Lord, you are looking glumpish! Not been brangling, have you?"

"Certainly not." St. Clair was bland. "We were discussing last night's disturbance—your sister has told you? Incidentally, Aysha is inevitably aware that all is not as it should be, but she knows nothing of what happened last night, and I am anxious to keep matters that way."

"Well, I won't blab," Justin assured him. "Close as a crab if need be!"

St. Clair smiled faintly. "Excellent. Since it seems impossible to find her a place of greater safety, we shall continue to protect her here even if it means curtailing her pleasures for a while. That, however, is my worry, not yours." He stood up. "Now, I daresay you would like to see her. No doubt you will be able to think of a plausible reason for coming?"

Olivia also rose. "Oh, that is easy. Muna was making me a *choli* to wear with my sari. I have come to see if it is ready." She lifted her eyes to his. "You see, I am taking up your suggestion and mean to wear it at the Midsummer Night Masquerade."

"That is a sight I can scarcely wait to see," he said softly.

As they walked toward the door, Justin suddenly stopped short. "But, of course, Livvy! I know just the place for Aysha!" Both pairs of eyes turned to him.

"Well, it's obvious, really. She can go to Bath!"

"Bath?" echoed St. Clair.

"To Mama and the girls!" Justin grinned at them, overcome by his own brilliance. "She'd enjoy herself no end there, and the girls would be delighted to have her."

But would Mama? Olivia wondered. And yet, the more she considered the idea, the more she could see the advantages. "Justin could well have hit on the very thing," she said with growing enthusiasm. "The house isn't actually in Bath—it stands about twelve miles south and though the grounds are not extensive, they do afford a fair degree of privacy. If you could get Aysha there without anyone's knowing, there is no reason at all why she should not be perfectly safe."

But St. Clair had not missed her initial troubled look. "And your mother? How would she take to the idea?"

Even as Olivia considered her reply, Justin said airily, "Oh, Mama won't cut up stiff. We'll spin her some yarn about . . . oh, I don't know . . . How about telling her that you want Aysha to mix more with girls nearer her own age, and there not being anyone suitable in London. Or, we *could* hint that you were sweet on Livvy and . . ."

"Thank you, my boy," St. Clair cut in swiftly, as Olivia's color mounted most betrayingly. "I make you my compliments. Your imagination clearly knows no bounds. But your first suggestion should, I think, suffice."

Justin looked from one to the other, and grinned. "Treading on delicate ground, am I?"

"Certainly not," retorted his sister, a shade too emphatically. "And Mr. St. Clair has far too much to worry about, without having to listen to your fanciful notions!"

Damian took pity on her. "I should certainly feel a lot happier to have Aysha safe and out of London, but it will have to be planned with much care—and first, we will need your mother's consent."

"Oh, don't bother about that," Justin said offhandedly. "Only consider the time you'll waste. Much better to present her with a *fait accompli*."

"My dear boy, I can't chance that! Suppose she refuses?"

"She won't. Tell you what, I'll go with her," the youth offered magnanimously. "All said and done, it was my idea."

Olivia looked at St. Clair in some helplessness. "It might not be a bad thing."

"No, indeed. But I shall also need the services of your Mr. Pommeroy."

"Pom?" Justin sounded aggrieved. "Whatever for?"

"Because, my stiff-rumped young friend, the house is being watched, so I can hardly go myself, or send any of my men, who will all be instantly recognized." St. Clair smiled a little wryly. "I am sorry to sound somewhat melodramatic, but this will all have to be planned with great secrecy."

Justin's eyes lit up, but Olivia only said quietly, "Pom is in your confidence, isn't he? I have wondered more than once since that day in the Park."

"We have—a kind of understanding. The less said, the better."

If the morning had been full of incident, the afternoon soon turned into something little short of a nightmare. It began innocently enough with her aunt's choosing to take a short nap while Olivia sat quietly in the drawing room, ostensibly looking through the latest *Lady's Magazine*, but in reality going over the events of the morning in her mind.

But at a little after three o'clock, her uncle arrived home, and he was not alone. "Now, m'dear, see who I've brought with me," Mr. Gilbey said gruffly. "I suppose you won't need three guesses to know why Sir Greville is come, eh?"

Sir Greville Barton, immaculately attired, bowed obsequiously and made as if to step forward, at which point Olivia threw aside the magazine and rose swiftly

to stand behind the sofa, as if to put as much room
between herself and Barton as possible.

"Why, what it this, ma'am?" he said, momentarily
disconcerted. "Not takin' a fit of shyness at this stage,
surely?" He turned smoothly to Mr. Gilbey. "Perhaps,
a few minutes alone, eh—in the circumstances?" And
with lowered voice, "Y' know what strange creatures
women are!"

Mr. Gilbey saw the naked pleading in his niece's eyes
and cursed Honoria for giving the fellow leave to
address Olivia. "Well . . ." he hedged unhappily.

"*Uncle!*"

"A moment only—while I fetch your aunt," he said,
and hurried from the room.

Olivia stayed where she was, with the relative safety
of the sofa between them. "Sir," she began nervously,
"I really don't think . . ."

"Come," he said, growing impatient. "You have
heard from y'r mama, I know, and so have I, so we both
know why I am come. Y' don't, I trust, expect me to
propose marriage to you with half a roomful of
furniture between us!"

"No, sir. That is," Olivia decided that nothing was to
be gained by skirting around the issue. "The plain fact
is, Sir Greville, that, although I am deeply honored by
your proposal, I find myself unable to—to feel for you
that degree of affection which must surely be the first
consideration in any such bond between two people. In
short, sir, I must decline your offer."

Olivia felt certain that he would go off into a
apoplexy at any moment; his color, already high, had
taken on a purple hue, suffusing his face and what little
she could see of his neck above the florid neckcloth, and
his eyes bulged alarmingly. She prayed that her aunt
would come very soon. If he touched her, she would
surely be sick.

"Do y'mean to tell me, madam, that you have led me
on with y'r mother's blessing, and allowed me to come
here on a fool's errand?" His voice was rising as he

strode toward the sofa, one hand raised. "The devil y'will! I don't take that treatment from a painted street trollop, and I'm damned if I'll take it from you! What are you, after all, but a penniless little aristocrat sellin' herself in much the same way!" The words rained down on Olivia in a torrent of abuse until all of a sudden they were halted by a voice so cold and authoritative that she did not immediately recognize it as Pom's.

"Be silent, you miserable cur! One more word and you'll choke on it, I promise you!"

"Pom!"

Olivia had not been expecting him, but she was never more pleased to see anyone in her whole life. Also, behind, she could see Mr. Gilbey, almost hopping with anger—and with him her aunt, who pushed past him to throw her arms about her niece, uttering incoherent words of comfort.

"Sir Greville, you will leave my house on the instant," said Mr. Gilbey, his plump figure imposingly sturdy as he faced the dandified baronet. "And if I get the slightest hint of my niece's name being bandied about by you, it will be the worse for you. I am only sorry that I could have been so mistaken in your character as to have exposed my niece to your vileness."

"Oh, I'll go, never fear. But don't think I can't see what's goin' on!" Sir Greville sneered at Olivia, turning back on his way to the door. "You think to snare a bigger fish, but it'll never happen, and then where will you be? I'll tell you where—living the rest of y'r life in genteel poverty, that's where, and y'r family with you!"

Fourteen

ST. CLAIR'S note had been delivered to Mr. Pommeroy just as he was on the point of setting out for Mount Street. It told him very little, but nonetheless there was a hint of urgency about it that filled him with apprehension.

He had performed the relatively simple task originally asked of him—managed it rather well, too, he thought. The fellow, Grant by name, had picked up on some casual mention of St. Clair and had made a caustic comment in Kendall's hearing which had the latter pricking up his ears. The introduction had then arranged itself quite naturally. And that, he had thought, was the end of the matter.

However, it wasn't the kind of summons one could easily ignore, and so he decided to call at Egan House first. St. Clair, as was his wont, came straight to the point; thanked him for his invaluable part in getting his spy into the enemy camp, and assured him that even in the short time Grant had been courting Kendall's friendship, he had been vilifying the name of St. Clair, and by listing the many wrongs suffered at his hands, had encouraged Kendall to make use of him.

"In this way, I became privy to Kendall's plan to break into Egan House two nights ago—you will have heard about that, I suppose? Lady Crockforth was bandying the news about at yesterday's musical soirée."

Mr. Pommeroy grimaced. "Don't care much for all that nonsense. Lot of scrapin' fiddles and catawaulin'. Leave it to the old ladies."

"Ah, then I must tell you that a determined effort was made to effect an entry at the rear of the house, which was repulsed by my servants with total success—largely because I had warned them to be particularly vigilant."

"Ah! Because Grant had tipped you the wink?"

"Exactly. However—" St. Clair's manner became more pensive— "it did call me to review my situation, or to be more exact, Aysha's situation. Until recently she has remained relatively free of danger, but my agent here has reported to me that one of my ships, which berthed yesterday in London docks, was carrying two Indian passengers. Their names mean nothing to me, but it would seem logical to assume that they have been sent by the yuvaraj to discover whether Kendall and Rashid have yet accomplished what they were sent here to do. If I am right, then an all-out attempt to steal back the Golden Eye, and eliminate both myself and Aysha, would seem to be imminent. Therefore, I must get my daughter to a place of safety."

Mr. Pommeroy was by now beginning to grow decidedly hot under his collar. "I follow y'r reasoning, St. Clair, but I don't quite see—"

"Be easy, Pommeroy." St. Clair's tone was dry. "Your apprehension is without foundation. I demand no supreme sacrifice of you." Mr. Pommeroy's grin was sheepish. "However, there is something you can do for me, if you will." He told him the gist of Justin's idea.

"Forgive me," Mr. Pommeroy shifted in his chair. "No offense intended, but do you think the duchess will accept y'r daughter?"

"Because of what has been said of her? My dear sir, your guess is as good as mine. All I know is that she would happily have swallowed the idea of Aysha as my paramour had I ventured to offer for Lady Olivia."

One eyebrow quirked sardonically. "If she still cherishes any such hopes, I doubt she will turn Aysha away in the infinitely more respectable guise of my daughter. If she can be persuaded to hold her tongue for the present, it might even titillate the *grande dame* in her to learn that she would be offering hospitality to the granddaughter of a maharaja!"

"Hadn't thought of that, I must say." Something, however, was troubling Mr. Pommeroy, and, embarrassing though it might be, he thought it better to clear the air. "No wish to pry into y'r private affairs, of course—your intentions toward Livvy are your own affair—but it occurred to me that you might not be aware that the duchess has given her blessing to a match between her and Barton."

"The devil!" For an instant, St. Clair looked furious. Then he said in a tone that brooked no argument, "She won't have him!"

"I hope you may be right—if only the duchess don't prove obdurate. Can't stand the fellow m'self—told him so in no uncertain terms a while ago when I found him trying to coerce Livvy . . ." He saw St. Clair's expression darken and said hastily, "Anyhow, that is neither here nor there at present. About y'r daughter, if young Justin thinks he can turn his mama up sweet, there shouldn't be any problem."

"Except for the delicate exercise of getting Aysha out of here and spiriting her out of London without Kendall's spies, or indeed anyone else, being privy to it." St. Clair grimaced. "You will know about Miss Imelda, of course, who doesn't?"

"The all-seeing eye," drawled Mr. Pommeroy.

"Exactly. So we must devise something to deceive that 'eye,' and any others that may be watching. Endeavor to persuade them that what they see is what they expect to see."

Mr. Pommeroy shook his head. "You've lost me, I'm afraid."

"Well, I do have an idea—slightly preposterous in

concept, but needs must, and I'm sure we could make it work."

It was there again—that ominous use of the world *we*! "Look here," he began tentatively, "I've no wish to spoil sport, but—"

"I'm sorry, Mr. Pommeroy. I haven't yet explained how you can help, if you would be so kind. All I want you to do is to hire a post chaise and take young Justin to Bath—to the duchess. He will, to all intents and purposes, be taking a rather special gift from me to his mother." St. Clair was bland. "Naturally, at his age, one cannot expect him to travel alone, so I would like you to accompany him. Only, the thing must be done quickly, so if you have no pressing engagements in the next day or so?"

Fifteen

ON THE FOLLOWING day a post chaise drew up outside Egan House, and Miss Imelda, being sufficiently recovered from her cold to resume her vigil, was able to report to her sister that its passengers were Mr. Pommeroy and the young Duke of Meriton.

"Well, that is hardly a surprise, Imelda," returned Lady Crockforth with her usual irritation. "If you had been listening to me earlier, you would know about the portrait."

"Portrait, dear?"

"God give me patience," muttered her ladyship. "Olivia was telling us last evening that Mr. St. Clair's servants had come across a large canvas in one of the unused upper rooms at Egan House, painted by Reynolds, or someone of his school, depicting Honoria with most of her children grouped about her. Mr. St. Clair, rather surprisingly in view of everything, decided that he would present it to Honoria, and as Justin was about to go home for a visit, it seemed an admirable opportunity to send it. Only the boy could hardly take such a bulky object by the stage, so Mr. Pommeroy gallantly offered to convey him and the portrait to Bath."

"Oh, what a kind thought!" Imelda said with a sigh. And then, "Yes, you must be right. The servants are bringing out a large rolled up object which could, I suppose, be a canvas. It is not quite what I had thought to see, but yes, they are putting it in the carriage!''

''Lud! What did you expect, for pity's sake? Something in a great gilded frame? Do use y'r senses, Imelda! I, for one, would not care to share a post chaise with some enormous unwieldy family portrait! But then, you wouldn't catch me giving such a thing house room.''

''Oh, but only consider the memories, Gertrude?''

''Humgudgeon!'' retorted Lady Crockforth.

Aysha, meanwhile, was enjoying her adventure. Her father had explained to her that he wanted her to go with Justin to his mama's until the bad men who had fired on them in the Park had been caught, and although she was sad to be leaving him, and all her new friends, he had promised that it would not be for long. He also explained that he did not wish anyone to see her leave, and told her how he meant to ensure this. She clapped her hands.

''It will be most exciting! Just like a story!'' Her lovely eyes clouded suddenly. ''Oh, but how is Muna to travel?''

''Muna will not be coming, little one,'' he said. ''Even if there were room for her in the coach, her presence would betray everything.'' He smiled encouragingly. ''It will seem very strange to you, I know, but you can surely manage without her for a very short while?''

It was not to be expected that Olivia's rejection of Sir Greville Barton would long remain secret. He had been in a wild mood at White's that same night, drinking and losing heavily at Faro, and generally making himself unpopular with his personal and extremely offensive references to the Gilbeys and their ''whey-faced'' niece, who thought herself too good for a mere baronet but would come to regret her high-handed ways.

It was perhaps fortunate that Mr. Gilbey was not

present, though Mr. Thornton was. He had coldly advised Sir Greville's companion, Major Kendall, to remove his friend before he said too much and found himself facing a writ for slander, if nothing worse.

"My dear," her aunt said, not unkindly, "I fear you may not hope to meet anyone else half so eligible. Oh, not that I blame you entirely—in fact, Sir Greville's reprehensible conduct at the time and later, leads one to the conclusion that he would not have been very comfortable to live with—" an understatement, if ever there was one, thought Olivia— "But, in view of your refusal of Mr. Antrobus also, I very much fear you may be in danger of gaining a reputation for being difficult to please. And while that is no bad thing in itself . . ."

"My circumstances do not allow of such nice distinctions!" Olivia tried hard to keep the bitterness from her voice, for her aunt's sake. She was all too aware that not everyone would be so forbearing with a recalcitrant young woman who, out of sheer stubbornness, was in serious danger of dwindling into spinsterhood. "I am truly sorry, Aunt Constance. You have been so good and understanding. I did infer at the beginning that I would not be easy to please, but, pray, bear with me a little longer." Her smile trembled a little. "If all else fails, I might yet throw myself upon Mr. Antrobus's mercy, though that would be grossly selfish in me and unfair to him."

"Oh, my dear child! I shall pray every night that you will find what your heart desires!"

Ah, Olivia sighed inwardly, if only I could have *that*, all cares would be at an end!

Inevitably, she was obliged to endure a certain amount of quizzing, and not everyone was kind, but with the Midsummer Night Masquerade only days away, the talk soon gave way to the much more important topic of what was likely to be worn—and by whom. For weeks, every modiste of note had been working night and day to accommodate the infinite variety of requests from her clients, all of whom wished to outshine their acquaintances. But through it all, Olivia smiled, and would not be drawn.

Mr. Pommeroy, meanwhile, returned from Bath with the reassuring news that Aysha, though a little shy at first, had settled in reasonably well and was enjoying the attentions of the younger members of the family, who were at first awed by her, and soon became her slaves.

"What of Mama?" had been Olivia's first question.

"You may well ask. It was, as Wellington would have said, the nearest run thing you ever saw! I quite expected her to go off in an apoplexy on the spot, but Justin, God bless him, knew exactly how to handle her and explain everything to her—and what with her being so pleased to see him, and the child herself so charming and appealing, we were all very soon as merry as grigs!" Pom grinned. "Justin is remaining at home, to protect Aysha, if you please!"

Olivia laughed. "Well, Aysha is bound to feel a little strange, and Justin will provide a link between her life there and here."

"The oddest thing," said Pom, remembering, "was that portrait. Demned thing *was* of the family group, just as St. Clair said it was! The duchess was quite moved by it—said it brought back all kinds of memories."

"Now, that I didn't know! I wonder how it came to be overlooked when the house was sold?"

"I asked St. Clair. Said it really had been found rolled up in an attic room. Simple carelessness on someone's part when the furnishings were being cleared, I suppose."

"Yes." Olivia was suddenly pensive. "I suppose Mama hadn't received any word from Sir Greville before you left?"

"I think not. I feel sure the whole house would have known of it an' she had!" His feeble attempt to raillery brought only the faintest reaction. "But I was vastly relieved that you gave the fellow his congé. Turned my stomach, the thought of you shackled to a man like that!''

Olivia gave a hiccuping little laugh. ''The thing is, Pom, I seem to be making a habit of turning down suitors, and I very much fear that Mama will not understand. She had accused me more than once of being too nice in my notions of what is acceptable in a husband, and Sir Greville did have her blessing.''

''That's because she don't know him!'' Pom said forcefully.

''Yes, well you see, I think she and Papa were never—that is, she was able to accept the absence of any closeness between them. Marriage to her was a simple matter of duty.'' Olivia looked a little bleakly at Pom. ''Does that sound dreadfully unfilial of me?'' He shook his head vigorously. ''But I cannot be like that! Oh, I hope I am sensible enough not to expect to have all my dreams fulfilled, but I must at least feel some warmth of regard, some ability to communicate, some measure of respect for the man I marry, or I should wither away like a plant deprived of water!'' She raised a wry smile. ''Which, circumstances being what they are, seems to become more improbable by the minute, and suggests that I am probably destined to dwindle into spinsterhood.''

''Never!'' Pom retorted. And then, diffidently, ''If it came to that, I'd offer for you myself like a shot. Deuced fond of you, as you know, though I ain't really a marrying man. Only my prospects would never be acceptable to her grace—a younger son with no hope of inheriting, and an allowance that would scarcely stretch to two.''

''Oh, Pom! You are a dear!'' Olivia hugged him. ''But I am far too fond of you to inflict marriage upon you!''

He was clearly touched, though he could not quite disguise the relief in his eyes. ''I had begun to wonder about you and St. Clair?'' he hazarded.

"Oh, no!" she said, a shade too vehemently, he thought. "St. Clair is the last man I would contemplate. I will concede that he has some good qualities, but he is still too ruthless and ambitious for my liking, except where his daughter is concerned. If he marries at all, Lady Bryony is the wife for him." She shrugged, suddenly finding the whole topic distasteful. "Enough, Pom, I am weary of talking husbands. As I told Jane, from now on I mean to enjoy myself."

Olivia had seen St. Clair only once since Aysha's departure, and that was in the Park at a moment when any kind of personal conversation was difficult. But Pom had obviously given him an account of how things had gone, and he was obviously both grateful and relieved. The answer to all who asked about the absence of Aysha was the same—that she had been suffering from a severe stomach upset and was slow to recover.

He had obviously heard about Olivia's unfortunate encounter with Sir Greville. He was quite short about it, but she found it hard to judge whether his anger was directed at her or Sir Greville, and in the end decided that it really didn't matter. From now on, she would simply take life as it came.

The masquerade was to be held at a mansion near Chiswick, loaned to Lady Bryony for the occasion by an elderly and extremely wealthy relation of her late husband, Sir Joshua. It had an enormous ballroom running the whole width of the building, a conservatory filled with exotic plants from all parts of the world, and—most appropriately of all for the occasion—a most beautiful garden which ran down to the river.

This, Lady Bryony had taken over and made her own. No expense had been spared in her determination to make it the most talked-of ball in the whole Season. Even the weather, it seemed, had conspired with her, for it remained perfect. The house was bedecked and garlanded with every conceivable flower and plant; in the ballroom the mirrors and the crystal drops of four exquisite Venetian chandeliers reflected a panoply of light and color wherever one looked.

But it was the garden that was to be her *pièce de résistance*. Here, every combination of art and artifice had been employed to create a grand illusion. Along one side ran a high wall, interspersed with alcoves from which a series of Grecian figures benevolently surveyed the scene, and as if to compliment them, the trees were hung with Greek lanterns, while colored lamps, concealed among the flowers, shone like brilliant jewels. The perfume of every conceivable kind of flower hung in heady profusion on the warm night air. And as if all this were not sufficient to sate the senses, there was one final touch—her grand illusion. The end of the garden was hung with a transparent backcloth depicting a moonlit torrent of water rushing down through a ravine which, as if by magic, became a real waterfall as it neared the ground, splashing down in gentle steps of rock between the flowers.

"Give Lady Bryony her due, she never does anything by halves! This must be the ball to end all balls—at least seven hundred people, so Mama was told," Jane murmured to Olivia as they were carried along by a fast-swelling crowd of masked guests, all laughing and talking excitedly. Some were in historical costume fashioned in every conceivable guise, others wore dominos, and some were content merely to be in elegant dress. The ballroom was vast, with flowers everywhere, and greenery surrounding the dais where the orchestra was already assembled.

There were eight pairs of long windows open to the warm night air, and between each was set a sparkling pier glass in a heavily gilded rococco frame. It was by one of these windows that Jane and Olivia finally stopped to draw breath and gaze out on the wonderland beyond, where already a few couples were to be seen wandering toward the screening shelter of the trees.

Nearby, Elizabeth Thornton stood, entranced, a pretty shepherdess in a flounced dress, her golden curls topped by a ridiculous froth of muslin and lace, and a mask, made of the same lace.

"Did you ever see anything so young as Lizzie?" Jane exclaimed ruefully. "I declare that at such times she makes me feel a positive antidote!"

Olivia's laugh pealed out. "Well, you certainly don't look it. And what is more, I'll vow Harry will agree with me."

It wasn't simply that her friend's Junoesque figure showed to excellent advantage in a simple Grecian robe—happiness had also given her an extra glow which even a mask could not hide.

But it was Olivia who had caused all heads to turn. In entering the crowded reception area she had become separated from her uncle and aunt, and as she moved forward in her exquisite golden yellow sari an audible gasp ran around the room like a flame, momentarily consuming all conversation. Olivia stood quite still, partly from sudden embarrassment, which made her thankful that her face was hidden, and partly from an odd feeling of . . . she wasn't sure what—apprehension? uncertainty? She shook it off and stepped forward, very conscious of the whispered comments on all sides—some thinking she was Aysha, others speculating wildly.

Aysha's choice of which sari she should have had been inspired; the vibrant color and gold embroidery alone would have set Olivia apart, but it was more than that; the silk folds seemed to flow over her, caressing her body, lending it a more than usually supple grace. Her hair was dressed high, and the matching gauze veil thrown over it in place of a mask, obscuring her face, thus adding a further tantalizing air of mystery.

But Arabella Bryony was not deceived. And just for an instant, jealousy consumed her. It was not simply that this girl was stealing St. Clair from under her nose, but rather the realization that Olivia had the advantage of years as well as beauty—and that was something with which she could not compete.

"My dear," she murmured so sweetly that those close by were almost willing to swear that they detected a faint note of asperity, "how delightfully ingenious of you! I vow you will put the rest of us quite in the shade!"

"Oh, but I cannot hope to surpass you, ma'am," Olivia replied with genuine admiration, while trying not to stare at the transparent layers of *eau de nil* gauze which revealed far more of her ladyship's voluptuous figure than many would think seemly, and which, from the wreaths of greenery entwined in her fair curls, she deduced must be meant to represent some kind of water naiad. "I have never seen such a beautiful costume. One might well imagine that you had risen up out of the river, so delightfully ethereal as you look!"

"Do you think so?" Arabella murmured, quite restored to spirits by the compliment which was so patently sincere. "I do so adore to shock people a little!"

Olivia mentioned the incident to Pom when she found him presently surveying the scene with a jaundiced eye, having steadfastly refused to be talked into wearing any form of fancy dress. "It's going a bit far, even for Arabella," he murmured, averting his gaze.

"Why, Pom, I do believe you're blushing!"

"Nothing of the kind," he said stoutly. "But it ain't decent, for all that. I vow she hadn't a stitch on underneath that rig! Give some of the old dowagers an apopletic fit, I shouldn't wonder!"

Mrs. Gilbey was saying much the same thing to Mrs. Thornton. "Such a pity Gertrude Crockforth has taken Imelda's cold and is prevented from coming this evening. She can be exceedingly tiresome on occasion, but I would give much to be privy to her comments."

"I have not seen Mr. St. Clair as yet," Mrs. Thornton said. "There can be no doubt of his being invited, so intimate as he is with Lady Bryony. He cannot be here, for of a certainty one could not mistake his figure. I do hope his daughter has not taken a turn for the worse. Is it not remarkable how nearly Olivia resembles her? Except that she is taller, of course. But that only makes the dress even more becoming."

The proceedings had become decidedly lively by the time St. Clair did arrive. Olivia was on the terrace when she saw him. He was standing at one of the open windows, looking out, and at once her heart leapt into her throat. Had he done it deliberately, she wondered, as she saw that he was wearing close-fitting white trousers and a long coat of rose-colored silk fastened high at the neck, and on his head he wore a turban of the same rose silk topped by a tuft of white feathers.

She moved toward him without conscious volition, and he, seeing her, stepped out onto the terrace and met her half way. She put out a hand to touch his coat. "How beautiful your coat is," she whispered.

Behind his mask, the gray eyes glittered as they beheld her in all her golden loveliness. "Ridiculously fanciful." His voice shook slightly. "It was a farewell present from my old friend, one that it would have been discourteous to refuse. I thought it might be particularly appropriate for this evening, though nothing could have prepared me for the way you look."

Suddenly all restraint between them seemed to vanish as though it had never existed. There was a dreamlike quality about everything as he took the hand she had extended, and neither seemed to notice when a party of revelers ran past them, the young women squealing in mock terror as their pursuers sought to preempt the hour of midnight by unmasking them there and then.

"I thought perhaps you were not coming."

"There were things I had to do."

The words spoken were almost banal, but they conveyed a whole wealth of meaning. Together they turned and walked down into the garden, Olivia's hand still firmly clasped in his. Here and there, in shaded alcoves, were couples oblivious of all that was going on around them, others were sitting on benches talking quietly, and everywhere, as indoors, servants hurried back and forth constantly with refreshments. And standing back in a sheltered corner of the terrace, Hassan, impassive as ever, kept watch.

At the far end of the garden, where a faint breeze came off the river and the sound of water mingled with the distant music from the ballroom, St. Clair stopped, drawing her into a patch of shadow. And there, where the gleam of a lantern just showed her face to him, he lifted back the veil and after looking long and intently into her eyes, he bent almost reverently to claim her mouth. Her surrender was sweet and total, until the passion mounting in them both sent them soaring into realms where reality ceased to have any meaning.

"So much time wasted, dearest girl," he murmured when at last they descended to relative sanity.

A tiny laugh caught in Olivia's throat. "Two months ago we hadn't even met!"

His fingers stroked back an errant strand of hair. "Two months, two weeks, two hours—how long does it take? I believe I wanted you within the first two minutes of meeting you. Do you remember?"

Shyly, she nodded. "I had never met anyone like you, and I was ashamed because I almost succumbed to your blandishments—and then I found out who you were—"

"And felt obliged to hate me."

"Oh, no! I don't think I ever hated you! Perhaps I didn't quite trust you—or perhaps it was my own feelings I mistrusted. I had never felt that way before, you see, and—"

He stopped her with a kiss, and said shakily, "You know, that is what I love about you—your shining candor! Oh, I want to give you so much, show you so many wonderful things! Soon, my dearest Olivia, when we are married . . ." Her small gasp of surprise at what was not so much a proposal as a statement of fact, made him laugh softly.

"I think I may die of happiness," Olivia said dreamily. She reached up and touched his mouth. "Is this St. Clair of the poetic soul the same man who rules whole mercantile empires?"

He caught her up and kissed her mouth once more. "You cannot love India without succumbing to its poetic heartbeat. As I was saying, soon I mean to take you there and you will feel it for yourself." Regretfully, he arranged her veil in place again. "But first I must rid myself of these tiresome men who plague my life."

Olivia was so lost in the magic of his love, in the joyful expectation of the life he planned for them, that she resented the intrusion of reality. "Must we think of that now? You never know—they might give up and go away."

He was silent for so long that were it not for the way his hands tightened their hold on her, she might have wondered if he had heard what she said. When he spoke there was a strange note in his voice.

"No, they won't give up, but it will be over soon now."

There was a hardness in his voice quite out of keeping with his mood of a few moments earlier. And it frightened her. "Please, Damian, please promise that you won't take any foolish risks?"

"My dear, I seldom, if ever, do foolish things."

Olivia was not wholly satisfied, but knew that to demand more of him would be futile. They began, reluctantly, to walk back along a side path, still close, still holding hands. A servant approached with a tray of drinks. "Champagne, m'lord?"

"Excellent timing." St. Clair took two glasses and presented her with one. "To us," he said, saluted her, and drank.

She had taken but a sip, disliking its dryness, when he gave a strangled shout and knocked the glass from her hand. "Poison," he gasped. To her horror, even as she saw him slowly falling to the ground, her own vision began to blur, and she, too, was falling, falling. . . .

Sixteen

OLIVIA COULD HEAR VOICES, excitable foreign voices. They penetrated her fluctuating consciousness through a nightmare miasma in which there was no way of separating fact from fantasy. She was awash on a sea of nausea, in some kind of boat . . . sometimes she could distinctly hear the repetitive grind of oars . . . and the next moment she was being lifted high in the air . . .

The voices grew more distinct, and full of vituperation. Now she could at least understand what they were saying, even if it didn't make sense.

"Fool! Dolt! Of what use is the St. Clair Sahib to us dead, when we do not have the Golden Eye and Hassan is even now on the loose? Also, this woman is not Aysha. You have bungled the whole thing!"

Next, an English voice. Major Kendall! "It is you who are fools, Mahomet—coming here, interfering. You should have left the whole thing to me instead of attempting to bring your barbaric customs to England. Rashid found that out to his cost."

As her senses returned, Olivia longed to move her cramped limbs. But the longer she could feign unconsciousness, the more she might learn. And yet, something lying dull and unbearable at the back of her mind must be faced—they had spoken as though Damian were dead, and if that were so, did she want to live? But there was still Aysha to be protected. It was what he would expect of her. She forced herself to remain inert.

"Kassim did not entirely trust you, Major Sahib—and with reason, perhaps, for it seems you have been in no hurry to carry out your instructions. However, we cannot wait here forever to see if St. Clair Sahib lives or dies. He must be searched."

The intensity of Olivia's relief betrayed her. The movement was only a tiny one, but it was enough to catch Major Kendall's sharp eye.

"So, you are awake, Lady Olivia. Good." His voice was brisk, cold, utterly unfeeling. "You can answer some questions."

She cleared her throat, which felt parched. "A drink," she gasped, to gain time.

Impatiently, he summoned one of his men to fetch a glass of wine, and while she waited, Olivia sat up a little and glanced around, fighting a lingering queasiness. She was in a small saloon, lying on a sofa. On the floor nearby Damian lay stretched out, very still. His beautiful turban had gone, and his hair was very disheveled, but otherwise he looked unharmed and she thought he still breathed. With them in the room, there were two Indian men, Major Kendall, and two others. It would not be easy to outwit so many, though she had heard them say that Hassan was free and he must even now be planning to help his master. Time therefore was all-important.

The wine was brought, and while she sipped it, one of the Indians began to go through Damian's pockets. Kendall watched him with an air of complacence which puzzled her, before turning his attention to her.

"Now, Lady Olivia, before we begin I should tell you that this house belongs to Sir Greville Barton." Her glance flew to his face, and she saw him smile as her hand trembled, spilling the wine onto her beautiful sari. "He uses it, I believe, as a 'love nest,' " His lips twisted disparagingly. "Sir Greville is not very pleased with you at present, but I am sure he will be only too happy to take his revenge, should you prove unhelpful to me."

His voice was cold and the threat very real, so that it took every ounce of Olivia's courage to appear unmoved. "I cannot imagine in what way you expect me to help you. If you have some idea of holding me for ransom, it will be a fruitless exercise."

"Enough, ma'am. We both know why you are here. I assume you attended that ball hoping to pass yourself off as Aysha. So," he barked the question at her, "where *is* Aysha?"

"Where else but at home in her bed," she answered, hoping that she sounded more confident than she felt. "It is no secret that she has been unwell."

"I know what is being said, ma'am, but to be frank, I don't believe a word of it."

Olivia set her wine glass down on the small elbow table beside her and gave him the full Egan look from head to toe, taking her time. "I do not have the slightest interest in what you believe, Major Kendall."

He took a step forward, his face red with fury. But at the same moment, the man who had been searching Damian stood up. "The Golden Eye is not on his person."

Kendall sneered. "Did you expect it to be? Only a fool would carry such a valuable object around with him."

Mahomet and the major glared at one another, but before the Indian could carry the argument forward, Damian stirred and opened his eyes. Olivia sprang to her feet with a cry of relief and would have gone to him, but was held back. He raised himself on one elbow, his eyes turning swiftly to where she stood, looking pale but unharmed.

"Are you all right?"

Olivia nodded, unable to speak. He let go a deep breath, his relief almost unbearable. Then he turned his mind to what he must do.

"When I set out this evening," he said, his voice

sounding remarkably strong for a man who had so
recently been poisoned, "the jewel was safe on a chain
around my neck. If it is not there now, someone has
removed it." He looked inquiringly at each of their
captors in turn, his glance coming to rest at the last on
Major Kendall. "Now who, I wonder, would be enter-
prising enough to take such a risk?"

Alarm, swiftly masked, flickered in the major's eyes.
"Don't listen to him. Can't you see what he is trying to
do?"

"But I find what St. Clair Sahib suggests most
interesting," said Mahomet in his precise, unhurried
English. "Prince Kassim himself was troubled, you see,
that greed might overcome you, which is why he decided
to send me to England. And what do I find? Firstly that
Rashid is dead—"

"That was Hassan's doing, not mine!"

"Perhaps, but with Rashid so conveniently out of the
way, what was there to prevent you from killing the St.
Clair Sahib and taking the Eye for yourself?"

"Precisely," murmured Damian, sitting up and
resting his arms on his knees. "Why don't you search
the good major? The outcome could be most
revealing."

"I don't advise it. Major Kendall had drawn his
pistol from his belt and cocked it. "We are three against
two, and I shoot the first man who moves."

The Indians stood, irresolute—and for a moment all
was still and silent. Then Damian spoke again. "Highly
dramatic, but inaccurate, I fear. Grant, my good fellow,
do relieve the major of his gun before someone gets
hurt."

Major Kendall, hearing one of his own men so
addressed, half swung around, discharging the pistol
harmlessly into the air just as Damian hurled himself at
his legs and brought him crashing to the ground. The
next few moments were pandemonium, as the fair
young man called Grant disabled the third man, and

tied him up with a cord from the curtains, while the Indians fell on Kendall, pulling his clothing apart in a feverish desire to find what they sought.

Mahomet rose at last, triumphant, brandishing the small leather pouch which contained the diamond. "Dog!" he snarled at the cowering major. "Defiler of honor!" And before anyone could move, a wickedly curved knife appeared in his hand and he had plunged it into the prone body.

A scream died in Olivia's throat as his companion turned to kill the others. But Damian's voice, whiplash hard, stopped him. He had Kendall's gun leveled at Mahomet. "This has two barrels, and only one has been fired. I would prefer not to use it, but if I have to, I will."

Uncertain what to do, the Indian looked to Mahomet, who in turn eyed Damian warily.

"You have the Golden Eye of Adjamir," Damian said harshly. "Go, and let that be the end of it."

"But it is not the end, St. Clair Sahib. Prince Kassim demands also that you and your daughter should die."

"God, but you people are stubborn! Can't you see? We are no threat to Kassim, and I have no particular desire to shed any more blood, so go while you still can."

For a moment it seemed that Mahomet would listen to reason. All attention was focused on him, and in that instant the second Indian, a fanatical light in his eyes, reached across and seized Olivia, pressing the point of his knife against the skin beneath her chin. She froze, terrified that the slightest movement would release the frenzy that exhibited itself in the nervous panting of his breath, which reeked in her nostrils. Her wide unblinking gaze was fixed on Damian, waiting to see what he would do.

Mahomet and his excitable companion exchanged a flurry of words. Then Mahomet said, "Put down the gun, St. Clair Sahib, or Achmed will drive his knife into the lady's beautiful white throat. As you can see, he is in a rather reckless state at present and I would not like anything to distress him.''

Damian dragged his glance away from the tiny spot of blood on Olivia's neck. Tight-lipped, he laid the gun on the table. "Right. Now tell that madman to let her go, damn you!''

"Presently. Move away from the table, if you please. Good. That is much better. Also, you will tie up the man Grant.'' When all was done to his satisfaction, Mahomet spoke again to his accomplice, who reluctantly lowered the knife, but only by a few inches.

Olivia realized she had been holding her breath. She let it go in a great sigh. Her case was not much better, but she was still alive, and so was Damian. It was at this moment that she became aware of a faint movement outside the window—something pale against the darkness, moving stealthily. Hassan! In all the furor, she had forgotten Hassan. She dared not move or in any way indicate to Damian what was happening for fear of upsetting the very delicate balance between life and death. She could only hope that Hassan would have been able to see for himself how matters stood.

Mahomet, meanwhile, was feeling pleased with himself. He was telling Damian exactly what they were about to do. "You will take me to Aysha—and Achmed will remain here. If all goes as I wish it, the lady may live. She is not a part of what is between us.''

"Oh, but I am!'' Olivia exclaimed, forgetting all else for the moment. But a quick prick of the knife reminded her.

Damian's mind was working furiously. Where the hell was Hassan? This wasn't at all how he had planned for things to go. There was no way that he was going to leave Olivia with that madman! But what alternative was there? He glanced at Grant, who managed to indicate that he had almost freed his hands, but unless they could get Achmed away from Olivia, his freedom would avail them little.

And then, out in the hall a floorboard creaked. They all heard it—and waited. Nothing happened.

"Kendall had two men outside," Mahomet said, sounding confident, but with apprehension in his eyes as he watched the door. "It could be one of them." He jerked his head toward the door. "Achmed, you will see." Achmed hesitated, and received a stream of abuse. Mahomet snatched up the gun and, trembling, pointed it at Olivia. "I will make very sure that everyone here behaves most sensibly while you do so." He stood well out of sight behind the door and urged Achmed forward.

But before he reached the door, it suddenly burst open. Hassan stood there, massive and invincible; before Achmed could use his own knife, Hassan's was whistling through the air to bury itself in the crumbling body. Mahomet was ineptly struggling to fire the gun and uttering wild curses when Hassan landed on top of him, and had half-strangled the life out of him by the time Damian's voice penetrated his concentration.

"Enough, Hassan. I want him alive." The massive figure shuddered and threw the Indian from him like a spent rag before climbing to his feet, shoulders drooping. "Well, you took your time, but thank God you came!"

The huge shoulders sank lower still. "Lord, I have failed you. My shame lays about my neck as a great boulder. Give me leave to go, Lord—I am no longer worthy to remain in your service."

"Certainly," retorted Damian curtly, in no mood for histrionics. "If you mean to maunder on like some whey-faced whelp!"

"Oh, no! Damian, how could you be so ungrateful?" Olivia ran across the room to the servant's side. "Hassan, you mustn't blame yourself! You came just when we needed you! Oh, my love, tell him!" she cried, seeing the servant turn away, his figure sagging as though he hadn't heard. It was as he put out a hand to grasp at a chair that she saw the blood beneath his arm, and spreading down his tunic. "You're hurt! Damian, come quickly—Hassan is hurt!"

St. Clair was across the room in no time, calling Grant to come and help. Together they eased him into the chair and St. Clair tore open the tunic to expose a long jagged wound running along the ribs, exposing the bone in places.

"Good God, man! However did you come by this? Grant, take a lamp and see if you can find some water and something to staunch the blood."

While Grant was gone, Olivia did what she could with part of the torn tunic, dabbing as gently as she could, distressed by the obvious pain it gave him to breathe. Now and again she was obliged to swallow down the nausea that still lingered from the poisoned drink. "Several men, lord. More than we expected. Most are now dead, and some of our men, also. And the fault must be mine, for they were upon us before I saw them."

St. Clair guessed that the servants had probably been overeager, and had precipitated the confrontation. But Hassan would never see it that way. "If you mean to talk such addle-pated nonsense, I shall assume that you are suffering from delirium and treat you accordingly," he said roughly. "Good God, man! You're not totally invincible, you know! And if it will salve your accursed pride somewhat, I shall tell you that your action of a few moments ago saved us from almost certain death."

"Indeed it did," Olivia assured him. "But I was not worried, for I always knew that you would come."

Hassan gave her a long, hard look, and some of the dull torment left his eyes. "The lady is generous," he said, and from the weakness of his voice it seemed likely that the loss of blood was sapping his strength.

"Grant," St. Clair said without looking up from what he was doing, "be a good fellow and see if you can find our carriage. It should be waiting where we arranged."

"Right." Grant glanced at Hassan and hurried out.

From the corner of his eye St. Clair saw Mahomet picking himself up and looking from the group around Hassan to the door, assessing his chances. "Don't be in such a hurry, Mahomet," he said calmly. He explained to Olivia how to keep the pressure on the wound, and stood up, a trifle ruffled, but still imposing in his regal robes. The two men faced each other, and a casual observer might well have thought they were of the same race.

"I could kill you, here and now, and take back the Golden Eye, but that would solve nothing. Prince Kassim would simply send more men and the whole wearisome business would be repeated." St. Clair eyed Mahomet thoughtfully. "I take you to be a man of sense—and honor. So I intend to let you go." He heard Olivia's little skirl of protest and made that curiously personal silencing gesture. "Take the Golden Eye of Adjamir to Prince Kassim and tell him that if he will leave us in peace, he need have nothing to fear from me or my daughter in the future. I shall, of course, return to India many times, but never to Adjamir as long as he lives."

Mahomet weighed the words in silence, and then bowed. "You also are a fair and honorable man, St. Clair Sahib. I will do as you say, and may Allah grant Prince Kassim the wisdom to accept your words."

As he reached the door, Damian asked abruptly, "The old ruler is dead, of course?"

The Indian bowed his head. "It was very quick, thanks be to Allah."

It was very quiet when he had gone; only the rasp of Hassan's breathing disturbed the silence. His eyes were closed, his face very still.

"Will he be all right?" Olivia murmured anxiously.

"He is as strong as a bull. Once we get him home and comfortable . . ."

She went and put her arms around him. "Oh, my love! He *will* live, I am sure." She laid her head against his shoulder. "It has been quite a night! Do you suppose we will have been missed? Poor Aunt Constance, I hope she won't be worried out of her mind!''

"By now, the rumor may be abroad that we have eloped," he suggested with a quiet, weary chuckle.

"Heavens! I didn't think of that!" She yawned and settled closer. "Oh, well, now you'll simply have to marry me."

His arms tightened around her. "I know." His voice was suddenly harsh. "Though I could think of pleasanter ways of compromising you."

Olivia lifted her head, voicing at last something that had been bothering her for some little while. "Do I take it that you knew all this was going to happen?"

He moved her away from him, looking down at her with a faint, ironic gleam. "There's no fooling you for long, is there? God help me, yes it was planned, but not quite like this." They heard Grant's quick footsteps in the hall. "Later," he said.

It was in fact much later, for there were a great many more important issues to resolve—Hassan to be got to his bed, her aunt and uncle to be found and pacified with as much of the truth as could be told without alarming Mrs. Gilbey beyond her present state of nerves. And after all that—sleep. The long, long sleep of total exhaustion.

Seventeen

THE NIGHT OF Lady Bryony's masquerade ball became a talking point for many a day after the event. Nobody would ever know the whole truth of it, but the disappearance of Lady Olivia and Mr. St. Clair at approximately the same time instigated a great deal of delightful speculation, the more so in the light of the announcement of their engagement that appeared in the *Gazette* two days later.

There was also considerable mystery surrounding Sir Greville Barton, at whose small "out-of-town retreat" the constabulary had discovered a number of dead bodies, of varying nationalities, including an acquaintance of Sir Greville's. He was unable to vouchsafe any convincing explanation for the findings, though for want of evidence no action was taken. Nevertheless, Sir Greville deemed it prudent to repair rather hurriedly to his Somerset acres.

"Such an odd, unpleasant occurrence," Mrs. Gilbey vouchsafed to Lady Crockforth when she came to inquire after Olivia's health. "Only consider the scandal which must have ensued had Olivia become involved with him!"

"Instead of which, everyone is talking about where she and St. Clair vanished to on Midsummer Eve," said her ladyship dryly. "And I doubt you would tell me the answer to that, even if you knew!"

"Certain matters, Gertrude, must retain their confidentiality within the confines of the family."

Lady Crockforth sniffed. "High-flown claptrap which probably means you don't know, either. Don't trouble to deny it, Connie—I can read you like a book."

Mrs. Gilbey bridled. "That is quite uncalled for. I am sure I don't know why you should expect to be privy to everything that goes on here. Mr. St. Clair has called, of course, though Olivia was sleeping at the time. But he had a long talk with Mr. Gilbey, who is more than satisfied with his explanation."

"I haven't a doubt of it," Lady Crockforth said dryly. "He is, after all, the catch of the Season."

"That has nothing to do with it. I have every reason to believe that Olivia and Mr. St. Clair are deeply in love!"

"Well, of course they are. Told you that m'self some time ago! By the bye, you wouldn't happen to know if that child of his has taken a turn for the worse? Only there's been a good deal of coming and going, according to Imelda—doctors and suchlike."

Mrs. Gilbey didn't know, and was much mortified to have to admit it. In fact, there was a great deal she didn't know. Olivia had told her very little since her arrival home, what with sleeping the clock around and showing a quite untypical tendency to go off into a state of dreaminess. Of one thing she was certain, however—Olivia was in love. It lit up her eyes whenever she spoke of Damian St. Clair. And as he was due to call again that afternoon, there was every expectation of being enlightened eventually.

It was quite late in the afternoon when he came. Olivia had been in fidgets, crossing to the window and back, for some considerable time. But the moment she heard his deep voice, followed by his step on the stair, she rushed to the door to meet him and was enfolded in an embrace that almost brought a tear to her aunt's eyes.

Over Olivia's head, his eyes met Mrs. Gilbey's. "Do I have your permission, ma'am, to take your niece for a drive?"

"I am sure I can have no objection, sir." She beamed upon him—upon them both. "It is perfectly natural in view of your betrothal, that you should wish to be together. Olivia dear, do run along and fetch your bonnet quickly." When the door had closed behind her niece, Mrs. Gilbey added with obvious sincerity, "Pray allow me to say, Mr. St. Clair, how delighted I am to see this day. It has always been my dearest wish to see the child, not simply established, but happy. God knows, no one deserves happiness more, and I was so afraid . . ."

Damian St. Clair took her hand in his strong, comforting grip. "Ma'am, I have not always behaved well in my life, but you may be very sure of one thing—I love your niece as I never hoped to love anyone again, and I will never knowingly do anything to harm her."

Mrs. Gilbey was much moved, and as she told Mr. Gilbey later, she had every confidence in Mr. St. Clair's ability to make Olivia happy.

"I don't know what you said to Aunt Constance while I was away," Olivia teased him when they were alone. "She was so pink-cheeked that if it had been anyone else I might have suspected you of flirting with her!"

He glanced at her. "Well, you would know, of course!"

She laughed, so full of happiness that she was almost frightened in case it should vanish, but when she voiced her fears, he took a hand from the rein briefly and rested it on hers. "It won't happen," he said quietly. "You will never lose me or my love. I swear it."

For once, there was no Hassan to accompany them as Damian drove out to the place where they had gone once before, although his very absence in a curious way made one aware of him.

"He will pull through," Damian said. "But, oh, what a time we've had! I had to get a doctor to him—in fact, more than one. But the moment he was conscious, he threw all their physic and ointments away and insisted upon treating himself."

"Oh, no!"

"So now, I am scarcely on speaking terms with any doctor of repute in London. Pray God we never have need of one! Mind you, since he has decided to forgive himself for what he considers his lapse, and live, we shouldn't have need of one."

"About the other night?" Olivia asked tentatively, when they had stopped the curricle much where they had done on that previous occasion.

"Before God, my love, I never meant you to become involved! I have lain awake every night since reliving the nightmare."

"But you knew—when we walked in the garden together—that they would come for you?"

"Grant told me," Damian admitted. "He has been with Kendall ever since Mr. Pommeroy introduced them to one another."

"Pom did?"

"At my request. Grant proceeded to make much of some slight I had inflicted on him and Kendall fell for the ruse—thought he'd have a foot in both camps, as it were." He smiled thinly. "And too full of himself to realize that I was doing exactly the same thing. The party by the river was an excellent opportunity to seize me—only, unfortunately, one of his less bright cronies took you for Aysha and thought to kill two birds, if you'll pardon the expression!" He held her close. "And for that, I will never forgive myself."

"But then, I would never have had such an adventure," she complained, making him laugh, albeit unwillingly. "Then the servant who brought the drinks . . . ?"

"Was one of their men. Easy enough to infiltrate the party with so many servants about." His voice grew hard. "I knew at once that the champagne was drugged, though with what, I wasn't sure."

"Which was why you knocked it out of my hand?"

"Not quite soon enough, but still . . . The rest, you know."

Olivia was silent for a moment. "Will it serve, do you suppose? Your suggestion to Mahomet, I mean?"

"I devoutly hope so. Not only am I growing too old for these rough games, but I would very much like to live in peace with my wife and daughter without having to look over my shoulder every five minutes." He glanced down at Olivia, his eyes intent. "You won't mind—about Aysha, I mean?"

"Oh, my dear! How can you even ask? I love Aysha dearly!" Olivia reached up and kissed him, which led from one thing to another, so that it was considerably later when she said breathlessly, "I suppose Aysha will be able to come back to town now?"

"We'll go down and fetch her soon." He smiled wryly. "I have written to your mama, but I suppose the sooner I allow her to weep dramatically all down my best shirt front, the better."

As they wandered back to the tree where the horses were tethered, Olivia said with a sigh, "It did seem such a pity that you had to relinquish her grandfather's parting gift—your Golden Eye of Adjamir. And to such an unworthy successor."

"Ah, well—as to that," Damian said in the oddest voice, so that she turned to look at him, "I'm afraid I did cheat a little." He reached inside his shirt and drew out a small leather pouch.

"But . . . ?" She was lost for words as she stared down at the beautiful jewel. "But Mahomet took it!"

"No, my trusting love," he said on the ghost of a laugh. "Mahomet took a very clever copy of the Eye, made for me by one of the city's most skillful jewelers from a very fine piece of uncut topaz I happened to have in my possession.''

"Damian! How . . ."

"Unscrupulous?" he suggested wickedly.

"Resourceful," she amended, and remembered Pom or someone talking about having seen him entering Rundle and Bridge's. At the time she had thought he might be buying a ring for Lady Bryony. "But won't Prince Kassim know that it isn't the genuine Eye?''

"I sincerely hope not. There is no reason why he should. It was a most excellent piece of workmanship, so like the real thing, in fact, that it would take an expert to tell them apart. And since hardly anyone has seen the jewel close to since it was in the rani's possession, there is no one who remembers it that intimately. Besides, the thought of anyone's making a copy would never enter Kassim's head." A wry note entered Damian's voice. "I just hope to Allah that no one ever drops it!''

The wedding was provisionally arranged for early July. St. Clair would have preferred it at once, but Olivia used her considerable persuasive powers to modify his demands, pointing out that it would be neither right nor fair to deprive her mama and Aunt Constance, to say nothing of the other members of the family, of the society wedding they craved and would indeed already be busy planning.

"If there were no one but ourselves to consider, I would fly away with you tomorrow," she coaxed. "But only conceive of their disappointment. Mama will be so full of it, don't you see? And we have all the rest of our lives to do as we please!''

He looked more than usually sanguine. "I hope you don't think to continue in this vein throughout our married life, for I give you fair warning that, much as I adore you, I have no intention of being led by the nose.''

Olivia's laugh pealed out. "Well, I should like to see that happen, I must say!" She sidled up to him. "Do you really? Adore me, I mean?" The next few moments became rather involved, and by the time she emerged, breathless, from his embrace, the initial argument had long been won.

There was much talk of bridals in the air; Jane's wedding was already fixed for September, and several of their friends were also looking to name the day.

"Mama is thanking heaven that Lizzie is still enjoying life far too much to think seriously about marriage," Jane said in some amusement. "One at a time is quite enough."

"But they must be delighted for you, just the same. Harry is a lucky man. And there is lots of time for you to be my chief bridesmaid, and still prepare for your own wedding."

"Thank you, dear girl." Jane's voice was droll, though nonetheless sincere. "If you are quite sure that your sister Emily will not mind?"

"Of course she won't! All the girls will be bridesmaids, and I mean to ask Justin to give me away, but I do want you for my very special maid of honor."

Pom said that all this talk of weddings filled him with *ennui*, for all that he was delighted to see Olivia so happy. But when Damian St. Clair asked him if he would do him the honor of standing up with him, Pom amazed everyone by agreeing.

On the day they set out for Bath, the weather was beginning to show signs of breaking and farmers were busy in the fields as they passed, checking the crops for any close to being ripe. It was years since Olivia had traveled in such elegance and comfort, and they made excellent time on the journey, arriving at Beauforth Lodge late in the afternoon.

The wheels had scarcely stopped turning when they were beseiged by an excitable onslaught of small children, who eagerly helped to let down the steps and generally clamored for attention, all talking at once. Olivia was a little apprehensive, fearing that Damian would not care for so much fuss. But he bore up surprisingly well.

As they approached the square, unpretentious manor house, however, there was a sudden cry of "Father!" and a single figure with silken robes flying hurled herself upon him and was caught up in his arms.

"Oh, Father, I am so pleased that you have come at last!"

"And I, too, Jewel of my Heart. I have missed you so much!"

"Truly?" She gazed eagerly up into his eyes, her own shining with happy tears.

"When have I ever lied to you, oh treasured one?"

Olivia watched the reunion with tears pricking her eyes.

"Touching, isn't it?" Justin was beside her, giving her his lop-sided grin. Together they walked across to join father and daughter. "You'd think that at the very least we had ill-treated her. In fact, she has been enjoying herself enormously."

Aysha was quick to penitence. "But yes, everyone has been most kind, but you see my father is . . ."

"I know." Justin's grin widened. "Your father is about half a step below Allah! I was only teasing!"

There was much to be told, the words tripping over themselves in the excitement. ". . . and Sarah has sometimes lent me one of her dresses, because I am so small . . . and it felt so strange to be wearing it . . . like a real English girl! You do not mind, Father?"

"Whatever pleases you, pleases me," St. Clair told her.

The duchess was waiting to receive them in her drawing room. She gave, as St. Clair later declared with wicked gravity, "a superlative performance."

"Oh dear." Olivia was laughing in spite of her embarrassment. "I honestly believe she does it out of habit, now, without realizing how overly dramatic she appears. I sometimes think she ought to have been an actress." Her eyes, though twinkling, were wry. "Does that sound dreadfully disloyal?"

"Dreadfully," he agreed, and pulled her to him. "My darling, don't trouble your head about it. The truth is, I find your mama vastly entertaining in small doses, and so, I'd guess, do most people."

They stayed at Beauforth Lodge for several days, talking bridals and settlements, the latter causing the duchess to wave a hand airily and say that she knew nothing of such matters and was more than happy to leave anything of that nature to her man of business. "For all the world," St. Clair chuckled later, "as if money was of no account and she hadn't been trying all Season to get you married off to the highest bidder!"

Olivia's indignation was only partially feigned. "Damian! You make me sound like a—"

"Not you, my love!" He kissed her soundly. "Never you. Quite otherwise, in fact. It was your reluctance to put yourself in that position that first drew my interest; from there it was but a step to falling desperately in love with you!"

On the morning they were due to leave for London, Olivia got up very early to walk as she was used to do, across fields where the heavy dew formed lacy patterns in the grass. She strayed farther than she had meant to in the hazy sunshine, looking back every so often in the hope that Damian too would have risen early and might have followed her.

It was very peaceful—only the birdsong, and in the distance a lone horse and rider cantering across her line of vision, also taking advantage of the morning air. Inevitably, it reminded her of Kimberley, which in a roundabout way had now come back to her. The thought gave her a deep sense of the rightness of things. It was a very English scene, she supposed, and wondered briefly how different India and all those other exotic places might seem by comparison.

She was about to turn for home when she saw that, while she had been air-dreaming, the horseman had come considerably nearer, and with a sickening jolt, she recognized him.

"Well now," he said, reining in within feet of her, "here's a flower I had thought no longer mine for the plucking!"

Sir Greville Barton's clothes were as impeccable as ever, but for all that there was a seediness about him that suggested a marked degree of overindulgence.

"I am waiting for my fiancé to meet me," she said with all the composure she could muster. "He will be here at any moment."

"Will he, now?" He lifted in his saddle. "I don't see him. Careless of him, leaving so comely a wench to her own devices. He thinks himself so clever—mayhap we should teach him a lesson!"

Olivia looked wildly back toward the house. There was a figure, but so distant that she could not make it out. She began to hurry toward it, but Sir Greville followed, walking his horse so close to her that its breath was hot and steamy in her nostrils. Each time she retreated, he moved closer.

Frightened, and angry too, she said, "This is very stupid, Sir Greville. I have no desire for your company!" It was the wrong thing to say. The moment the words were out she knew it, and cursed her want of judgment.

"Don't you, by God! Well, we'll have to see about that!"

Before she could move, his riding whip snaked out, its thong twice the normal length, and wrapped itself around her neck, almost choking her as she tried to tug it loose. He laughed, a terrible sound, and leaned down, hauling her with unceremonious ease across the horse's neck. Then he wheeled around with an exultant cry and rode back the way he had come.

Damian St. Clair had indeed been on his way to meet

Olivia, and was therefore in time to witness what happened, though too far away to stop its happening. His cry had all the wild rending impotence of an animal in pain, and it echoed and re-echoed across the fields as he turned and raced back toward the stables behind the house. There he found Justin tightening the girth on his saddle prior to riding out. His laconic greeting was cut short, as Damian explained what had happened in a few terse words.

"Take Bounder," Justin said, thrusting the rein in his hands, his face white. "I'll saddle Bess and follow you."

Damian mounted without a word and wheeled around. Justin could hardly bear to meet the expression in his eyes. "One thing—would you know if Sir Greville Barton has a house anywhere nearby?"

Justin stared—his jaw sagging. "Oh God! About three miles—" He flung a hand out. "That way!"

Eighteen

IN THE PARLOR of Sir Greville's house, Olivia sat in a chair near the fireplace nursing her throat, knowing that, painful as it was, it was at this moment the least of her problems. She had been manhandled into the house, and when the housekeeper appeared and began to remonstrate, she had been cursed and ordered back to the kitchen.

"Now, Lady High and Mighty! We'll see just how passionate you are under all that damned pride!" Sir Greville was in a mood of great excitation and clearly meant to waste no time. He brought two glasses to the table, poured brandy into them, and set a small bottle of intricate design beside one of them. "Major Kendall made me a present of this potion—for services rendered, you might say. He brought it from India. I have tried it but once on a young girl. The dosage was minute, but the results were quite unbelievable." He laughed, and uncorked the bottle. "So I think, for you, a few drops more—and you will be amazed how your inhibitions will melt away. You, my fastidious young lady, will do exactly what I ask of you, no matter how bizarre—" his voice sank into lustful anticipation— "*and you will enjoy every minute of it!*"

"Never!" She could manage no more than a croak, but her mind was working feverishly, trying to form some kind of escape. Oh, it isn't fair, she raged, when I am so close to my heart's desire!

"You can't stop me," he roared, pouring the liquid into one of the glasses. "And very soon you won't even want to try!" He picked up the glass and walked toward her. Olivia slid out of the chair, not taking her eyes off him for a moment, and edged behind it. He laughed the more. "So you want to make it more difficult, eh? I don't mind. It's all the same in the end. Console yourself—think how experienced you will be for your husband! If the stuff don't turn your brain!"

As he uttered the words, the door crashed back. St. Clair's figure filled the opening and there was murder in his eyes. For an instant no one moved; then Olivia croaked his name and ran across the room to him. His face was the face of a stranger, though his touch on her neck was gentle. "You are hurt."

She shook her head. "It doesn't matter! You have come!"

His glance had already returned to Sir Greville, who stood transfixed, the glass still in his hand. "Oblige me, my dear, by going outside. You will probably find your brother there."

"What are you going to do?" she faltered. He didn't reply, and she was filled with a great fear. "Damian—he isn't worth it!" She croaked the words, knowing they wouldn't move him one iota from his purpose. She looked at his face once more—and left.

Justin was dismounting as she stepped out into the misty sunshine and drew air painfully into her throat. The world looked so normal. There was a bench nearby and she sat down, leaning back with closed eyes.

"Livvy? Are you all right?" Justin was beside her, his voice shocked. "Livvy—your neck? What has that brute done to you? Is St. Clair here?"

She gestured toward the house, and as he moved, gasped urgently, "No! Don't go in! Please!"

Much later, back at Beauforth Lodge, with her neck

salved and loosely wrapped, and having sipped a
soothing tisane prepared by Cook, Olivia already felt
considerably better. Damian had been very gentle with
her, and they, Justin included, had agreed to invent
some excuse for her throat condition—a cold, anything
to satisfy her mama's inevitable questions. For this
reason also, they decided to return as planned to
London.

Olivia knew that she would never learn what had
happened between Sir Greville and Damian that day in
the parlor. She didn't want to know, recognizing that
there was a side to Damian's nature that was totally
ruthless. But she could guess at some of it.

Mrs. Gilbey was delighted to have her back, if a little
quiet due to having contracted a sore throat. "We must
have Dr. Grantley at once, my love," she exclaimed. "It
would not do at all for it to putrify so close to your
wedding!"

But Olivia, not wishing her aunt to see her bruises,
had laughed off the suggestion, and with a balm
provided from Hassan's infinite store of cures, the
bruising had faded to almost nothing. Damian was with
her almost constantly at first—it was as if he could not
bear to let her out of his sight. But as her spirits
returned, she was able to laugh away his fears and
gradually life returned to normal.

It was at a reception given by Lady Cowper that the
subject of Sir Greville Barton came up.

"Never liked the man," said Lady Crockforth. "But
one can't help thinking it would be better an' he had
died."

"But what happened exactly?" Mrs. Gilbey asked,
much shocked.

"No one seems to know the right of it. The doctors
seem to agree that he inadvertently swallowed something of a poisonous nature. Didn't kill him, but his
mind has become deranged, and they can hold out no
hope for a recovery. So, he'll spend the rest of his days
locked up where he can do no harm—to himself or

anyone else.'' Her ladyship sniffed. ''So, y'r niece had a lucky escape.''

"Quite! But how dreadful!" Mrs. Gilbey exclaimed.

Dreadful, indeed! Olivia shuddered. But it was, after all, no more than he would have done to her.

Nineteen

THE MARRIAGE IN July between Damian St. Clair, only son of Sir Patrick St. Clair of Ballacray, and Lady Olivia Egan, daughter of Honoria, Dowager Duchess of Meriton, and the late Eighth Duke of Meriton, was talked about for many a long day.

The bride, radiant in ivory silk, and given away by her younger brother, the ninth Duke, was one of the most beautiful of the Season. The groom, impressive both physically and by reputation, was one of the richest, if not *the* richest gentleman in the whole country. The dowager duchess looked frail, but bore up surprisingly well under the strain of the occasion, and much was made of the bridesmaids in palest pink—and of one in particular, who was the Indian daughter of the bridegroom and, so gossip had it, the granddaughter of a maharaja.

Aysha had been almost speechless with delight at the thought of walking down the aisle behind her beloved Lady Olivia, in a dress exactly like all the others. "I shall look quite splendid, I think," she said imperiously, and then giggled.

Olivia had a special word of thanks for her aunt and uncle. "Without you, dear Aunt Constance, none of this would have been possible," she whispered as she said her good-byes.

"Oh, my love!" Mrs. Gilbey's eyes were misty. "Who would ever have thought, but a few months ago, that everything would end so perfectly? And one does not even have to say 'be happy,' for it is writ large on your face for all to see!"

Damian would not tell Olivia where he was taking her for their honeymoon, but she didn't really mind, she told him blithely, heedless of the little bubbles of excitement that kept running along her veins. "Just as long as we are together."

Jane had already decided that it would be somewhere highly exotic. "India, perhaps—or even China." And then, hugging her suddenly, "Be happy."

"You too, dearest Jane—and Harry. And we will keep in touch, I promise."

All too soon, the celebrations were at an end and they were driving away, watched over by Hassan, who was fully recovered and had resumed his duties, determined that never again would he fail to protect his master. Aysha was to stay with Olivia's family until their return, and although she was sad to be so soon parted from her father again, she was already becoming philosophical about it—and was overjoyed that this time Muna would be able to accompany her.

Olivia, tired out by all the excitement, had fallen into a light sleep, from which something—she wasn't sure quite what—wakened her. They were bowling up a long straight drive lined on each side by huge elm trees. She sat up, peered out of the window for fear that she was mistaken—and then turned to Damian, who was watching her, a faint smile in his eyes.

"It is . . ." she began. "Tell me I'm not dreaming? It really is Kimberley?"

"Take another look, if you are in any doubt," he said smugly. "I thought perhaps we might begin our life together here, quietly." He was serious suddenly. "I was right, wasn't I? You wouldn't rather go somewhere very grand and exotic?"

She was about to fling her arms around him when the coach rounded a bend and she landed in a heap on top of him, her bronze green traveling dress awry, her beautiful hat resting incongruously over one eye. Amid laughter, Damian caught and held her tightly, thinking her flushed, excited face more beautiful than he had ever seen it.

"There isn't anywhere in the whole world that I would rather be!" She sighed.

"That's all right then. I'm glad you're pleased," he murmured.

The house came into view with the late afternoon sun warming its creepered walls, and Olivia thought she would die of happiness. Inside, very little was changed. "I had one drawing room and the master bedroom refurbished," he told her, "and thought that you would enjoy planning the rest for yourself. Most of the staff have been drawn from the estate, though I have taken the liberty of engaging a butler and chef, your original ones having moved with the family."

Olivia found them inside with all the other servants, some of whom she recognized. "Very grand," she whispered, as the butler, who answered to the name of Masterson, moved silently from the room and closed the door. "Now, can we explore my beloved Kimberley?"

"I can think of better things to do, but your wish is my command."

"Do you know," she said some time later, though still finding it impossible to remain quiet for more than a moment before coming back to him to twine her arms about his neck, "that you are the most generous, wonderful man in the whole world to think of bringing me here, of all places."

"Would that it were true, but I will take your word for it," he murmured, and bent to kiss her. One thing led to another, and somehow they ended up in the master bedroom. A long time later, over dinner, Damian said with unaccustomed diffidence, "I have done something, my love, which—in view of your ecstatic behavior today—may have been a mistake.''

Olivia looked up, surprised, and full of love and wine and silliness, and decided he must be joking. "But, darling, you never make mistakes!" she teased him. "You are . . . omnipotent!"

"Ah, but am I?" He rose and went across to a side table, and from a drawer took out some papers. He brought them back and laid them beside her plate. "This, you see, was to be my wedding gift to you."

Olivia picked it up, looked inquiringly at him, and began to read. After a few moments, she stopped and looked up at him again. He could read little from her rather dazed expression. "But this is . . ."

"A deed of gift, making Kimberley over to Justin on his twenty-first birthday," he finished for her. "I thought it would be what you wanted, but in view of your unbridled joy at coming home, perhaps it is not such a bright idea?"

To his dismay, he saw that she was crying, and went swiftly across to take her in his arms. "Darling girl, don't! It can be changed! I'm a fool—I should have asked you . . ."

"No! Oh no!" She looked up at him through her tears. "My dearest, dearest Damian, I thought it was impossible to love you more than I already do, but if you had asked me what I most wanted in all the world after your love, this would be it. I can never thank you enough!"

"Oh, I don't know," he said, enfolding her in his arms. "I'm sure we can think of something!"